Siren's Song

Witches of Rock Cove Book One

Elizabeth Salo

First edition 2025

EBOOK ISBN: 978-1-962460-06-4

PAPERBACK ISBN: 978-1-962460-07-1

HARDCOVER ISBN: 978-1-962460-08-8

Contents

To the North Atlantic right whale population.
I sincerely hope your numbers rebound.

The Prophecy

The day shall come when storms will rise,

Evil comes in friendship's guise.

Chaos reigns to ill effect,

Giving rise to an Architect.

While lives are lost and costs incurred,

He shall raise the Harbinger.

Yet hope remains while bonds stay strong,

Friendship rules and all belong.

Fire, Air, Earth, and Water,

Must stand against the endless slaughter.

Prologue

THE STONE CIRCLE THROBBED with power. The design carved into it—a series of interlocking circles known as a witch's knot—glowed dimly with the magic he was feeding it. The more magic he funneled into the stone beneath his feet, the brighter the light became, but the more his magical reserves were drained.

He dug deep. Failure was not an option. This was his destiny, his purpose in life.

"Harbinger, I summon thee,
and prostrate myself on bended knee.
Come to me and be my guide,
by your rules I shall abide.
The path is laid, your road unfurled,
the time has come to join this world."

A loud rumbling surged from somewhere deep within the earth. The stone circle vibrated and shook beneath him like an earthquake, but he clenched his muscles to stay upright. He would greet his master on his knees as promised, not sprawled on the ground like a weakling.

Sweat poured from his forehead, and he gritted his teeth as he fought to sustain the magical forces flowing through him. He was channeling more magic than he ever had in his entire life, but it was working. He could feel it in his bones. The Harbinger was coming, and *he* would be the one to bring it into this world.

He just needed to hold on a little bit longer.

He fell forward, catching himself with his hands. His power was failing him, and the light of the witch's knot started to blink out. He dug deeper, funneling even more of his energy into the stone. He could taste blood in his mouth as he forced himself to take labored breaths to focus through the pain.

If his sovereign demanded this payment from him, he would pay it. Gladly.

The glow sputtered again, then died. The earth stilled. "Noooooooooo!" His voice echoed in the suddenly quiet and still night.

The Architect collapsed onto the cold stone circle, barely stopping his head from slamming into the unforgiving surface. His muscles twitched involuntarily, and he couldn't have moved from that spot even if the hounds of hell were after him. Which they weren't. At least, not yet.

He'd failed. Again.

He'd gotten further this attempt than in any prior ones, but still, he'd fallen short. Performing the ritual in the stone circle—unlike any of his prior attempts—had clearly played an important part this time around, but something was still missing. Sweat beaded on his brow, and his hands and feet were numb. His magical stores were so empty, there was barely a flicker of power remaining in his veins. His strength alone clearly wasn't enough. Another attempt like this just might kill him. The time had come to take drastic measures.

"Architect?" a tentative voice called from across the grove.

He had forgotten about the girl. His shame was complete. The novice witch had witnessed the humiliation of his defeat while he was still trying to instruct her in his ways. He should not have brought her here.

The Architect heaved himself to a standing position, unwilling to show any more weakness in front of someone who was so far beneath him. "Danika, gather my things!" He barked the order at her and watched with glee as she jumped. "I need to regroup and try again. This is my destiny. The Harbinger shall rise." The mania flooded his veins once more. He might have failed today, but one day he would not. He would unlock the key to bringing his sovereign into this world, and they would rule together. Side by side.

The mousy-haired young woman scurried to grab his candles, crystals, and potions, hastily shoving them into his leather satchel. "But sir, doesn't the prophecy specifically mention the four elements? Don't we need them for this to succeed?"

He spat on the ground, making her jump back so she wouldn't get hit. Her eyes dropped immediately to the grass near his feet. "The elements, ugh. They're completely overrated. I am the Architect. The elements are nothing!" It was his destiny to raise the Harbinger, and he intended to do it alone.

But what if the little wretch was right? The prophecy talked about the elemental powers of water, earth, air, and fire. Witches with those powers could be his downfall and the very thing that could defeat the Harbinger. But if they alone could defeat it, could their powers also raise it? If that were the case, then it couldn't be just any elemental witches, it would have to be the strongest—the Elementa. Four witches born on the same day, at the same time, in the same location, each one having the gifts of one of the four elements. If the Architect could siphon enough of the witches' magical energy to raise the Harbinger, perhaps they would then be too weak to oppose it once it rose.

The Architect had been preparing for this moment for decades. He'd done his research, knew the playing field, and knew the location of each of the witches. Unfortunately, one of them wasn't where she was supposed to be. It was up to him to correct that.

He needed to do whatever it took to bring Jenna Hastings home to Rock Cove.

Chapter One

"RESEARCH ONE, THIS IS Research Two, do you copy?"

Jenna Hastings heard the tinny voice of the pilot, Carl Mattingly, through the headset clamped firmly around her ears. The headset was of decent quality, but not quite good enough to drown out the constant roar of the plane's engines. They'd been flying for hours, and the droning noise had settled in the back of Jenna's mind as a constant irritation, one she did her best to tune out.

Kind of like the fact that she desperately had to pee, but these tiny planes weren't exactly equipped with bathrooms. There would be no peeing in a bottle on this trip.

"Research Two, this is Research One. We copy loud and clear, Carl," the other pilot, Amanda Seale, responded. "Any signs yet on your end?"

"Nothing yet."

"Nothing on this side either." The two planes flew in parallel about five miles apart, trying to cover as much area as possible.

"Volunteers sighted a North Atlantic right whale in this general area several hours ago," Jenna said as she bounced her knee impatiently, "I hope we didn't miss her," Her eyes carefully scanned the unbelievable aqua blue of the coastal waters below, searching for the distinctive V-shaped waterspout—the unique sign of a right whale surfacing and exhaling twin streams of mist from its blowholes.

Flying in a plane showed the full scope and scale of the ocean-wide hide-and-seek game they were playing with the whales. Being in a boat might let you get up close and personal with the marine life, but only from the air could you see the entire outline of the enormous mammal beneath the waves—assuming you could even find it in the vast expanse of the Atlantic Ocean.

A burst of movement drew her attention, but it was just a small pod of dolphins jumping and playing in the waves. Beautiful in their own right, but not what they were out here to find.

It was February, which was birthing season for the right whale. Every winter, the whales made their way south and congregated off the coast of Florida and the Carolinas. And each year, a slowly decreasing number of those female whales—also known as cows—would give birth to their calves in the warm coastal waters before making the long journey back to the coasts of Massachusetts and Canada for the summer feeding season.

"So, what are we looking for?" Carl asked over the headset from his position in the front seat.

"Any right whale sightings are useful, but I'm hoping we have a cow and a newborn calf. Since the population is critically endangered—with only around 350 left in the world—every new calf that's born increases the chances of the population recovering."

A sudden plume of water drew her eye. "There!" Jenna yelled into her mic. Excitement permeated her body as she directed Carl to where she'd seen the whale. He guided the small plane until it was circling the area where she'd seen the blow, and there, directly below them, was the forty-foot body of a whale, skimming just below the surface. "It's Diamond. She looks healthy, but she's alone." While it was always exciting to see a whale and know that they were still alive, Jenna was disappointed that she hadn't stumbled on a mom and her baby.

Diamond, so named because of her distinctive patch of rough white skin on the top of her head in the shape of a diamond—markings that were unique to each right whale—was an older cow who, as far as they had been able to track, had never been a mother. Researchers weren't sure why she had never had a baby, so it was sad but not surprising that she didn't have a calf swimming next to her.

Jenna lifted her camera to her eye and snapped as many photos as she could of the whale. She and her team would use them back on the ground to help document the whale's life cycle and catalog any injuries. She was just about to lower her camera when a sudden dark stain spread in the water around Diamond.

Blood.

"There's a lot of blood in the water. It's possible Diamond is injured or entangled. Should we try to get a team out here to help?" Jenna relayed the information to Richard Fromm, the biologist from the other plane and Jenna's close friend.

"How much is a lot of blood? It would take hours for a rescue vessel to arrive."

There was so much blood in the water that Jenna's heart raced. Richard was right. They might not even have time to wait for a boat.

Jenna's fingers tingled, her protective instincts kicking in. A cool wash of water flowed beneath her skin, her elemental powers desperate to help in any way they could. Carl's back was to her, which meant he wouldn't see if she did a little hocus pocus to save this precious creature from dying, right? Was it really breaking the code that said she shouldn't do magic in front of ordinaries—people without magical powers—if he didn't see anything?

Just as she was about to direct a little of her healing magic in Diamond's direction, something else caught her eye. A small tail. Much smaller than Diamond's. Suddenly certain of what she was about to witness, Jenna reeled her gifts back in and hit record on her camera.

Jenna watched—tears in her eyes—as moments later, Diamond gave birth to a calf. The proud momma swam up next to her new baby, put her head underneath the calf, and lifted it out of the water to take its very first breath.

"Way to go, Momma," Jenna whispered. She sent all the love and care she could muster in the direction of the mother and the newborn. They were going to need all the luck and happy thoughts they could get to survive the dangers that humans unintentionally threw in their path.

They watched the new family for as long as they could, but the tiny plane could only hold so much fuel. Carl turned the plane back to the shore and landed on the small airstrip at the regional airport. Amanda and Richard had already returned and were waiting for Jenna as she extricated herself from the plane. She climbed down the short staircase onto the small tarmac and greeted them.

Jenna felt like she was floating on a cloud. It was incredibly rare to see a whale giving birth, and as far as she knew, it was only the second time a right whale birth had been captured on camera.

"Richard, can you believe it? Wait until you see the footage. It's incredible." Jenna was already rummaging through her bag to remove her camera and show him what she'd captured, her smile permanently affixed to her face. The high from today's adventure was going to carry her through weeks of paperwork.

She held up her camera and aimed the screen in Richard's direction, but he wasn't smiling. In fact, his tanned and stately face looked more sober than she'd ever seen him in the five years they'd been working together.

"Jenna, the footage might need to wait. Something has come up," Richard said.

"What's more important than enjoying the birth of a baby whale?" She scanned his face, looking for any clue of what he was talking about.

Jenna's cell phone rang loudly and made her jump. She'd been out of range for the last several hours, so the sudden noise was unexpected. Plus, who calls anyone these days? Wasn't it just easier to text?

"You're going to want to answer that," Richard said, gesturing to the still ringing phone.

She handed Richard her camera and bag and fished her phone out of her pocket. She didn't recognize the number on the screen, but it had a Massachusetts area code. Dread hit her stomach like a giant ball of ice. She was sure she wasn't going to like whatever she was about to hear.

"Hello?" She clutched the phone to her ear far harder than necessary. Her instincts were screaming at her, but she couldn't wade through them quickly enough to figure out what they were trying to tell her.

"Is this Jenna Hastings?" a deep male voice said on the other end of the line.

"Yes, who is this?"

"This is Holden Kay. I don't know if you remember me or not."

Holden Kay, now there was a name she hadn't heard in more than ten years. Ever since she'd left her hometown after high school graduation and hadn't looked back. "Yes, of course I remember you, Holden. What can I do for you?"

"I'm now a detective for the Rock Cove Police Department." He paused, and his breath hitched before he continued. The ice in Jenna's stomach turned to lead. "Jenna, there's no easy way to say this. There's been an accident. Your parents were driving home from a friend's house last night, and their car was struck by a drunk driver. They were both killed instantly. I'm so sorry."

Chapter Two

Denver watched as the mourners slowly trickled away from the graveside in twos and threes. Brooke and Russell Hastings had been extremely well known and well liked in the small town of Rock Cove, Massachusetts. Half of the town had turned up for their funeral. Around him, people his age mingled with those his parents' age as they paid their respects and headed home.

His feelings for the Hastings were strong and very close to the surface. Russ had been a father figure to him, at least after Denver had graduated from high school. His actual father had been a useless piece of garbage, but Russ had always made him feel valued and cared for. It might have been a stretch to say that Russ thought of him as a son, but it wasn't far off.

That feeling was even more complicated because of the woman standing near the open graves, her devastated blue eyes awash with tears—Jenna Hastings, Russ and Brooke's daughter. Denver and Jenna had gone to school together growing up, though he was a year ahead of her. She'd always been the shy, bookish type, wearing jeans and sweaters and hugging her textbooks to her chest like they were a life vest.

He can't say he'd known her all that well but enough to say hi if their friend groups had ever mingled in the school hallway. She was cute, in an understated way, but her timid nature meant that they'd never really gotten past basic formalities. Plus, she'd had her circle of friends—Sierra, Aura, and Brigit—whom she'd never been far away from, and they had cast long shadows. Shadows that were difficult for Jenna to escape.

She'd left Rock Cove right after graduation, and he hadn't seen hide nor hair of her since. Russ and Brooke talked about her, of course. He'd been around them enough over the past twelve years that it was natural for him to hear updates here and there on what Jenna was up to. She'd apparently gone to some fancy college on the West Coast for biology, and—much to Brooke's dismay—didn't seem inclined to move back home.

Yet here she was. Obviously, a funeral was a terrible reason for her to have to return. Rock Cove wouldn't be the same without the Hastings. *Denver* wouldn't be the same without them. He couldn't imagine how much pain Jenna was in. She didn't have any siblings, and since there hadn't been a lot of strangers at the funeral, he guessed she didn't have much in the way of out-of-town family.

He knew he should pay his respects to her. He was one of the only remaining people still lingering, and yet here he sat, frozen in place, unsure of what he could even say. The standard platitudes of "Sorry for your loss" and "They're with God now" just weren't going to cut it.

He drew a deep breath, doing his best to push his feelings down long enough for him to try to offer her what little comfort he could. He pushed to his feet, rising from one of the flimsy folding chairs the funeral home had set out for the guests. He crossed the twenty feet to her side, each step feeling like he was moving through quicksand.

"Jenna," he cleared his throat, "I can't begin to say how sorry I am for your loss. Your parents were remarkable people."

Jenna turned her elfin face toward him, her alabaster skin a stark contrast to her midnight black hair and icy blue eyes. "Thank you...Denver? Denver Wallace?" Her voice was laced with confusion and considerable grief.

He nodded and started to reach for her arm to offer her comfort but stopped himself before touching her. They weren't friends. He might have been close to her parents, but he hadn't talked to Jenna in more than a decade. "Yeah, it's me."

She tugged a tissue out of her pocket and wiped the moisture off her delicate cheekbones. "I didn't realize you knew my parents."

That was a kick to the heart he hadn't been expecting. Not that he was particularly surprised. He knew some of what she'd been up to because he'd spent many hours working alongside her father. However, he couldn't have expected Russ to keep his daughter updated on everyone he knew and worked with in Rock Cove. There were too many people—and frankly, Jenna probably hadn't cared.

He rubbed his hand down the stubble on his jaw, suddenly wishing he'd shaved before coming. "Um, yeah. I used to work with your father. Several years ago, anyway." He wasn't about to go into the rest of the details of their relationship. Now wasn't the time, and Jenna didn't need to know.

She nodded, her gaze sliding away from him and focusing once again on the shiny mahogany of the nearby caskets. "Well, it was very kind of you to show up. I'm sure they would have appreciated it."

He opened his mouth, then closed it again. There was nothing he could say to help her, and his own grief was rising to the surface. He wished he had someone to share it with, but if Jenna didn't know what her parents meant to him, then she wouldn't appreciate someone else trying to horn in on her time of mourning.

It was time to go. He should leave her alone and find his own way to celebrate Russ's and Brooke's wonderful lives. Rock Cove wouldn't be the same without them. Denver imagined Jenna would sell the house and head back to wherever she lived these days. He would never walk into that sunny kitchen again, filled with the delicious scents of baking bread and snickerdoodle cookies. He would never again watch *Deadliest Catch* with Russ, both thanking everyone they could think of that lobster fishing wasn't nearly as fatal as fishing for king crab.

"I guess I'll see you around," he finally said, even while knowing it wasn't true. It was just one of those things that you said.

"You too," she said, her voice barely above a whisper.

As Denver walked back to his car, he fought the urge to go back and be with her. She'd sounded so broken. So lost. Losing one parent had to be bad enough, but losing them both at the same time had to be a shock that was nearly impossible to cope with.

He was surprised not to see her circle of friends around her. Sierra had been at the funeral itself, but she hadn't stuck around after it was over. Aura and Brigit hadn't shown up at all.

He glanced back at her slight form, his heart breaking for her—but knowing it wasn't his place to help. Maybe, if she stuck around for a little while, he could approach her in a few days and share some of his happy memories of her parents. For now, he needed to leave her be. He climbed behind the wheel of his truck and left, refusing to look behind him again.

Long after everyone else had gone back to their homes and lives, Jenna wandered the halls and rooms of her parents' empty and echoey house. It was the same house she'd grown up in, and it had been in her family for generations. It stood high on a hill overlooking the town below, a vibrant forest at its back. She never would have predicted inheriting it this early in life. She wasn't ready to say goodbye to the memory of her parents and the many generations that predated them.

The warm wood tones of the interior were complemented by the soft throws and cushy pillows, which made the house feel like a comforting, welcoming embrace. Even though this place hadn't been her home in more than a decade, she still couldn't imagine parting with it. Selling the house and the land would feel like cutting off a limb

It was also the source of her magic.

Power crackled across her skin as she breathed in the sandalwood and cinnamon scent that reminded her of her childhood. While she had her magical gifts when away from Rock Cove, they were dimmed, muted—nothing compared to the power she commanded at her fingertips when she spent time at home.

Well, there was one other time when she felt more powerful, but that part of her life was over now. The door had been slammed closed in her face, and she had to face that it was never going to reopen. Choices had been made—and not by her. She just reaped the consequences.

Jenna moved slowly through the house, running her fingers over her parents' knick-knacks and stopping to look at photos of the three of them from family vacations over the years. Partially burned candles and now-dried flower arrangements—almost assuredly from her friend Sierra's flower shop, the Petal Patch—were a reminder of the woman who had carefully selected them and placed them just so. Jenna knew better than to touch the crystals, at least without cleansing them first, but followed their trail up two flights of stairs into the walk-up attic.

Almost nothing had changed in the space since the last time she'd been in it. Her mother had kept her sacred space spotlessly clean and organized. The altar on the far wall was covered by a clean white cloth, which in turn had a mixture of white and purple candles on it and several stones that appeared to be lapis lazuli.

Her mother had apparently been looking for enlightenment, harmony, and inner peace. What on earth could her mother have been worried about that would have caused her to use this particular set of tools during her practice? Too bad Jenna would never know.

Jenna stood in front of the altar and bowed her head. She said a quick incantation to release whatever her mother had been seeking, then cleared the altar to start fresh.

She went to her mother's supply cupboard and selected candles in indigo—for cleansing—and brown—for honoring her family elders. She also grabbed a sage stick—for purification—and a large rose quartz to release emotional tension. She carried her selections to the altar and laid them out in front of her.

Jenna took a deep breath, clearing her mind as she closed her eyes. When she felt as centered as she could be, she opened her eyes and touched her finger to each candle in turn. The wicks caught instantly, sparking to life as if they had been merely waiting for her command. She lit the braided sage stick and placed it in a metal bowl so its smoke could permeate and cleanse the space.

> *"Ancestors of the chosen line,*
> *I call you to this sacred shrine.*

I give to you these two new souls,
their hearts aflame like burning coals.
Protect them now from dark and pain,
their mortal flesh too soon was slain.
Accept them now among your ranks,
and earn from me eternal thanks."

Jenna chanted the spell and bowed her head, sending her prayer into the world.

A moment of warmth and love surrounded her, her mother's presence almost a physical touch along Jenna's skin. With one last gentle squeeze, the sensation was gone, and Jenna knew her parents had passed on, their souls at one with her ancestors.

Jenna gently snuffed out the candles. The sage stick had already burned to a nub. "Goodbye Mom and Dad. I don't know what I'm going to do without you."

Tears hot in her eyes, she turned to flee the space, but her eye snagged on a lone piece of parchment awkwardly sticking out of her mother's book of shadows. It felt rude to pry into her mom's spells—akin to reading her diary—but in the end, curiosity won out.

She wiped her damp cheeks and flipped the spell book open to the marked page. The page contained a spell for seeking guidance. This could explain the altar setup. Her mother had been casting this spell.

The folded parchment fluttered to the ground. Jenna stooped and picked it up, flipped it open, and read the words on the page. It was titled simply "The Prophecy."

The day shall come when storms will rise,
Evil comes in friendship's guise.

Chaos reigns to ill effect,
Giving rise to an Architect.
While lives are lost and costs incurred,
He shall raise the Harbinger.
Yet hope remains while bonds stay strong,
Friendship rules and all belong.
Fire, Air, Earth, and Water,
Must stand against the endless slaughter.

What the hell?

Chapter Three

J ENNA WALKED INTO CINDER & Spice with curiosity. The cozy little café wasn't in Rock Cove during her childhood, and she'd never managed to make it there during any of her short visits home. The café sat right downtown, steps from the wharf. The owners had clearly remodeled one of the existing buildings, because it fit right in with all the other businesses in the cute city center. The brick exterior had been painted black, but it made it look sharp and clean, rather than dreary. There were cheerful yellow tables out front, even though it was still far too cold for anyone to take advantage of them.

The interior of the shop was light and airy, but the floors still had that old creaky character that couldn't be replicated in newer structures. The walls were pale ivory, full of shelves crammed with books, knick-knacks, and floral arrangements. A huge fireplace graced the rear wall, crackling merrily as it tried its best to stave off the bitter February chill.

Seated right next to the fire, hiding in a cozy booth, was Sierra Dalton—Jenna's best friend and the only person apart from her parents that she'd kept in touch with. Sierra was bundled up in a chunky green sweater, which flattered her long chestnut-brown waves and her sharp brown eyes, and jeans. Somehow, she still managed to maintain the appearance of a healthy tan even in the dead of winter. A thick down coat, a hat, a scarf, and a pair of gloves filled the space next to her on the bench. When Sierra saw Jenna come through the door, she launched herself out of the booth and into Jenna's open arms.

"Oh, Jenna. I'm so sorry I couldn't stay any longer at the funeral. The school called. I had to go pick up Lucas from kindergarten early," Sierra said into Jenna's hair.

"What did he do this time?" Jenna had to hold in a chuckle. Sierra's five-year-old was a handful. Sierra released Jenna and slid back into the booth. Jenna sat on the opposite side, slowly peeling off the layers of her winter gear.

Sierra let out a huff. "Apparently, he's been telling other kids on the playground that they need to *feel the flowers*. It's been creeping out the other students."

Jenna couldn't contain her laugh that time. "Like mother, like son, I guess." Jenna and Sierra had known each other since they were toddlers. Sierra had always had an affection for growing things and nature. It went hand in hand with being an earth witch, even if she didn't practice anymore. It also led to her current job, which was the owner of the Petal Patch—the most successful flower shop in Rock Cove and its surrounding area. People came from miles away to get one of Sierra's creations. "Is this all your work?" Jenna asked, gesturing to the flowers and greenery that spilled over every inch of the café's flat surfaces.

Sierra followed her gaze, her chest puffing with pride. "Yeah, I supply several of the shops around town. Cinder & Spice is one of my better customers, though."

The server—a perky blond named Corrine—came over to their table. They ordered sandwiches and soup, Jenna adding a mocha for an extra bit of warmth and caffeine. Her blood had definitely thinned since she hadn't had to live through a New England winter in several years.

After Corrine left, Jenna turned back to her friend, not even sure where to begin. Well, that wasn't exactly true. She thought about bringing up the prophecy she'd found in her mom's attic but immediately decided against it. She didn't even know if the prophecy was real, much less if it really applied to her and her former coven. No need to bring it up now. There was one thing, however, that she was dying to get out. "So, I ran into someone interesting at the funeral."

"Oh?" Sierra took a sip of her water and leaned in—clearly hungry for a tasty morsel of gossip. "Who might that have been?"

Jenna suddenly felt foolish. Denver Wallace was just a man, the same as half of the population of Rock Cove. Yes, it had been more than a decade since she'd seen him, but he said he used to work with her father. It made sense that he came to their funeral.

That wasn't why her heart had squeezed just a bit when she'd seen his handsome face. The face she'd drooled over in high school. The face she'd wanted to write sonnets about, even if she wasn't a poet. She'd had a mad crush on Denver all through high school, but he hadn't even known she'd existed. He had been a popular jock, and she'd been a mouse who lived in the library. Their paths rarely crossed.

"Never mind. It's nothing. So what have you been up to lately?" Jenna pounced on her mocha as soon as the server placed their order in front of them, hoping that Sierra would let her change the topic. No such luck.

"Oh, no. You're not getting away with that. It's obviously something, or you wouldn't have brought it up. I need details immediately." She rested her chin on her hands and batted her eyelashes.

Jenna threw the crumpled-up straw wrapper from her water glass at her friend. "Fine. You win. It was Denver." She studiously avoided looking Sierra in the eye.

"Ooh, hottie Denver? Denver of the doodles and hearts that lined your notebook freshman year?" Sierra teased.

Heat radiated off Jenna's cheeks. Her pale skin left nothing to the imagination when it came to embarrassment. "Yes, that Denver. Do you know any other Denvers who live in Rock Cove?" she hissed, glancing around to make sure no one was paying attention.

Sierra eased back, her teasing smile fading slightly. "Honestly, I'm not surprised he was there. From what I could tell, he got close to your folks after you left. Your dad, especially."

Her mouth dropped open as surprise ricocheted through Jenna. Her parents and Denver had been friends? How had she not known about this?

"Really?" It wasn't that her dad was hard to know or like—in fact, just the opposite. She'd just never imagined him making friends with someone her age. There was no way her parents hadn't known about her raging attraction to Denver back in the day—she wasn't exactly subtle about it.

"Yep," Sierra answered, taking a bite of her turkey club. She swallowed before continuing. "I don't know all the details, but I get the impression Denver didn't have a great home life. Your parents sort of stepped up when he needed someone."

That sounded like her parents. They were always loving and caring toward everyone. If they'd known that Denver needed someone in his life, it absolutely made sense that they would reach out and offer to be those people. And if what Sierra said was true and he had a less-than-stellar situation at home, it also made sense that they wouldn't have felt the need to spread that information around, even to her.

"Oh, well good for them." It felt like a canned response, but she wasn't sure what else to say.

"Are you going to see him again before you leave town?" Sierra asked as she munched away at her lunch.

Jenna wasn't sure which part of the question to tackle first—the assumption that she was only staying in town long enough to bury her parents and then taking off again, or the question about Denver. She chose the easier path.

"Who says I'm leaving town?" She arched her eyebrow and crossed her arms smugly.

Sierra paused, a spoonful of tomato bisque halfway to her mouth. She slowly lowered the spoon back into the bowl. "Are you serious? You'd consider moving back?"

It was something Jenna had been thinking about. As long as her parents had been alive, Jenna had a tenuous connection to Rock Cove and her ancestral lands. With their passing, she felt like it would be all too easy for that connection to snap. While she had some pretty bitter memories of this town—and a few of the residents in particular—she also had lots of great ones. She'd had a wonderful childhood growing up in this little hamlet on the water, which somehow managed to maintain its small-town feel despite being less than forty-five minutes outside Boston. Plus, Sierra was here. She'd get to hang out with her best friend and watch Sierra's son, Lucas, grow up—with her as his honorary auntie.

"I reached out to the Boston Aquarium to inquire about a position on their research team. Nothing is set in stone yet, but it's looking good. The whale research community isn't all that big. I would need to leave for a while—go sell my house and wrap up the work I'm doing for my current job—but I'm hoping to be back soon."

Sierra squealed and danced in her seat. "I would love to have you back. You have no idea how much I need adult conversation in my life. Spending long days with a stubborn five-year-old and a bunch of flowers isn't doing much for my social life."

"Well don't get your hopes up too high. Nothing has been finalized. I did let my team down in Florida know that I would be taking a few weeks off though. It's going to take me a while to go through my parents' effects. Either way, it looks like we're going to get in some quality girl time." Jenna was thrilled to hang out more with Sierra. As much as she loved her work and hadn't missed a lot of the baggage that went along with life in Rock Cove, Sierra was another thing entirely. Jenna missed her friend desperately. It would be phenomenal to have time to catch up.

"A few weeks, huh? Well, I guess you'll have plenty of time to reconnect with Denver then," Sierra said coyly.

Jenna rolled her eyes. "Why would I do that? I barely know the man, and he never even acknowledged my existence growing up. It's not like we were friends or anything." Much to her teenage disappointment.

"I wouldn't go that far. Rock Cove High School wasn't all that big. Everyone knew everyone else's name, even if they weren't close. Denver knew who you were."

Jenna shrugged. "Knowing my name and exchanging a conversation with me are two totally different things. Denver is a silly part of my past. He's not a part of my present or future. We're just two ships passing in the night."

It wasn't like he was in her league anyway. Being with him had always been an unattainable dream, and one she hoped he would never find out about. It was probably best if she just kept her distance from him. She didn't want to embarrass herself by drooling over him or anything.

Now, if Jenna could just get her schoolgirl crush to chill long enough to stop picturing his perfectly chiseled jaw, deadly smile, and neatly trimmed facial hair every time she closed her eyes. And his emerald-green gaze? Forget about it. It was nothing.

Yeah. Right.

Chapter Four

AS A BOAT CAPTAIN, it was rare that Denver found himself inside the Boston Aquarium, even though they were his employer. There weren't many boats to pilot inside a building on dry land. However, today was one of those rare exceptions that found him wandering around the building he usually didn't spend much time in.

The building itself wasn't enormous, and it was built vertically rather than horizontally. The first floor was his favorite part because it housed the penguin habitat. The cute little dudes wandered around looking like dapper little gentlemen in their tuxedos. He'd been lucky enough to show up during feeding time, so he spent an enjoyable few minutes watching the staff in their wetsuits feed the penguins as many fish as their little hearts desired. There was a relatively young one—not quite a chick but clearly not fully grown—that struggled to take the fish out of the staff member's hand, repeatedly falling off the rocks into the water each time it tried. Denver laughed as it once again plunged into the water, then swam back to the rock to try again.

Since he was early for his meeting with the aquarium director, he took the spiral ramp up around the central tank, which climbed several stories. He loved the enormous turtles that glided effortlessly through the water, despite their massive weight and cumbersome bodies. Shiny schools of fish flashed past as he finally reached the top of the exhibit and headed back down again.

He was just wondering if he'd have time to go outside and visit the seals when he heard his boss's voice. Trevor Clark was the director of the aquarium and a super nice guy. He really cared about preserving the oceans and aquatic life in general, but he had a soft spot for whales.

Most people didn't realize it, but the aquarium wasn't just a building full of fish. The Boston Aquarium had a research arm that employed various biologists and researchers to study marine life and help in conservation efforts. Denver was one of the captains who piloted their research vessels. Whatever the scientists were after, it was his job to get them there and back safely.

That was why Denver was there in person. Trevor had hired some hotshot new researcher and was pairing them with Denver for all their boat-related needs. Most of the researchers were friendly and passionate about their work, so Denver couldn't wait to meet the new guy.

"Ah, and there he is!" Trevor's voice was far louder than it needed to be considering they were indoors.

Denver turned to face the pair and sucked in a sharp breath. There, standing no more than twenty feet away, was Jenna. He hadn't seen her in three months—not since the funeral in February—so seeing her now was a shock to the system.

Jenna stopped in her tracks, her brilliant smile slowly fading into a slightly puzzled, if not outright concerned, look. "This is who I'm going to be working with?" she asked Trevor, skepticism clear in every word. She crossed her arms and squinted at Denver.

Denver nodded at her in acknowledgment. "Jenna, nice to see you again."

He took in her casual yet professional ensemble of trim chinos and a navy-blue polo that suited the icy blue of her eyes. He wasn't sure where her doubt was coming from, but there was no need to return it. In fact, he was quite thrilled to see her again. He'd had such a close relationship with her parents that it would be nice to get to know her better. She wasn't bad on the eyes, either. Not that he was ogling a colleague. Not much anyway.

"You already know one another? That's wonderful," Trevor said. He looked so eager that Denver wouldn't have been surprised if he started clapping like one of their sea lions.

Jenna's eyes narrowed as she continued her judgmental stare. "Yes, Denver and I are from the same hometown. We've met."

We've met? That's all she was willing to admit to? They hadn't been friends in school, but they also weren't strangers who met accidentally in the grocery store or something. He didn't want to bring up their history—or lack thereof—in front of their boss, however, so he just silently raised his eyebrow. Maybe he could figure out later what her deal was.

Trevor glanced between Denver and Jenna for a second before plowing on to cover the slightly awkward silence. "Yes, well, I suppose that means you'll have much to chat about on your excursions. Jenna, Denver here, captains the *Sea Bliss*, our fleet's largest vessel. I mean, we only have three boats, but the *Sea Bliss* is our pride and joy!"

Denver appreciated Trevor's vote of confidence and support. Denver had sort of fallen sideways into this career after spending almost a decade working lobster boats with Jenna's dad. He'd made his way up from crew to captain and then decided to get out of the fishing business entirely.

He couldn't leave the sea behind, though—that was just in his blood.

"I'm excited to be working with you." Denver wasn't just tossing out platitudes. He'd never had anything against Jenna but had never gotten a real chance to get to know her either. He knew her parents far better than he knew her, which seemed a bit odd considering they were the same age. Hopefully, they would get to know each other better while working together.

"What's your particular area of study?"

Her eyes narrowed suspiciously, but she answered readily enough.

"The North Atlantic right whale," she said as she gestured toward the large skeleton hanging from the ceiling, "that guy."

Denver knew the basics about the right whale, but he was by no means an expert on the subject. He was eager to learn more about them. "What sort of activities will you need to do?" Each researcher did slightly different things depending on the focus of their research.

She shrugged. "It depends on the time of year and what's going on at the time. It could be getting water and food samples, locating and acquiring feces samples, collecting sonar samples for other researchers to analyze, or, in emergency situations, a rescue mission to help save an injured or entangled whale."

He'd never been on a whale rescue mission before. That had to be intense and incredibly gratifying. "Well, I am at your service. Let me know what you're going to need and when, and we'll make it happen."

She nodded at him. "Thanks, I will."

Trevor beamed at them. "I'm sure this will be a match made in heaven. Now Jenna, if you'll come with me, there's a bit of paperwork I'll need you to fill out before you leave today." He ushered Jenna toward the office. Denver's eyes followed them until they disappeared around the corner.

A match made in heaven, huh? Denver probably wouldn't go that far, but who knew? Maybe he could win Jenna over. He wasn't quite sure why she treated him like an interesting bug she'd just stepped on, but he refused to let it get to him. She'd warm up to him sooner or later. He was a likable guy.

Since meeting Trevor and Jenna had been his only reason for coming to downtown Boston, Denver hightailed it out of the city before rush hour hit and traffic gridlocked. He liked that the city was less than an hour away from his home and that he could drive in for the occasional Red Sox or Bruins game, but he was very happy he didn't have to live in the mess that made up downtown. Give him small-town life any day of the week.

With some time to kill on the drive, he popped his cell phone into the holder attached to the dash of his 1986 Ford F-150 and hit the button to dial his best friend.

"Holden Kay speaking."

"You always sound so official when you answer your phone," Denver said, grinning.

"Oh, it's you. If I'd realized, I would have just sent it straight to voicemail," Holden snarked back.

Denver laughed. "Ouch, man. I love you too."

"Not that I don't love a good verbal sparring match, but is there a specific reason you called?"

"Boredom, mostly. I'm heading back to town from the city." Denver flicked on his blinker and smoothly changed lanes.

"Please tell me you're at least calling me hands-free. I'd hate to have to write you a ticket."

"I'm not currently in your jurisdiction but never fear. I'm being a safe driver."

Denver paused for a moment, trying to figure out why he'd really called. He knew the reason, not so deep down, but for some reason, he was reluctant to admit it.

"So, you'll never guess who I ran into at work today." Denver could just barely make out the rustling of paperwork over the connection.

"A mermaid? The Loch Ness Monster?" Holden asked.

Denver rolled his eyes, even though Holden couldn't see him. "No, you ass. Jenna Hastings. Apparently, she now works for the aquarium."

Holden let out a low whistle. "Does she know yet?"

"She knows that I was friends with her parents, but I don't think she knows the full extent of it." How exactly did you convey to someone you barely knew that *their* parents were better to you than your own?

"That's not what I was asking about. Does she know about your father? About what he did?" Concern laced Holden's voice.

All of Denver's muscles locked up. He hadn't forgotten that his father was the reason the Hastings were dead, but he did his best every single day to forget that Ken Nelson existed, much less that he was related to him in any way.

"You know I don't think of Ken as my father."

Holden scoffed. "Like that's what matters in this situation. I'm the one who had to call her and tell her that her parents were dead. That's never an easy conversation to have, and everyone handles it differently. So far, she hasn't started asking questions about the night of the accident, but you know it's only a matter of time. She's going to find out one way or the other."

Holden was probably right, but there was absolutely no way that Denver could confess that his asshole of a father had gotten drunk off his ass, climbed behind the wheel of his broken-down Chevy, and plowed into the Hastings' car, instantly killing them both. Denver had his own questions about the situation that would likely go unanswered, so he had no idea how to cope with Jenna's.

Had Ken hit the Hastings on accident, or had he deliberately aimed for the surrogate family that had adopted Denver as one more way to hurt his only son? Even if Denver was willing to speak to his father—who was currently locked up in the Rock Cove jail awaiting trial—he wasn't sure he would trust a word that came out of his old man's mouth anyway.

"Well, I'm not going to be the one to tell her, especially now that we're going to be working together moving forward." Denver pulled off the highway at the Rock Cove exit, and headed straight home. "Hey, I'm getting ready to pull into my driveway. I'll talk to you later, man." He hung up before Holden could get in any parting shots.

Denver pulled into the garage of his tiny bungalow and turned off the engine, enjoying the peace and quiet. He'd started the drive home excited to work with someone new and for the opportunity to get to know the beautiful Jenna a bit better. He'd ended the trip feeling about as tall as a slug. He knew he wasn't his old man, but somehow Ken's actions kept coming back to haunt Denver, and he was sick and tired of it.

"Damn it!" he yelled into his empty truck before slamming his way out of the vehicle and into his house.

Chapter Five

T HE LEAST GLAMOROUS, BUT arguably most important, part of Jenna's job was making sure she had enough money to fund her research. As an aquarium employee, her salary covered some of her living expenses, but research science always required more than that. If she wanted to do more than eat peanut butter and jelly—much less pay for the necessary equipment and fuel for the boat she would take out into the ocean—fundraising was crucial to her survival.

She contemplated setting up her laptop in the living room of her parents' house—she hadn't yet begun to think of it as her own—or even reclaiming one of the guest bedrooms as an office. Instead, she decided to treat herself. She headed into town and, just minutes later, walked into the welcoming atmosphere of Cinder & Spice.

She breathed in the heavenly aroma of coffee and cinnamon. Enormous pecan cinnamon rolls sat in the bakery display, and she couldn't wait to sink her teeth into one. She found an empty booth in the back and pulled out her laptop.

The server took her order, and by the time the young woman came back with her espresso and cinnamon bun, Jenna was already lost in a sea of grant paperwork. She absentmindedly bit into the sticky dessert and almost groaned in pleasure. It was amazing. Possibly the best one she'd ever eaten. If this was the quality of the baked goods in this place, Jenna could already tell she was going to be spending way too much of her paycheck in this café.

The jangling of the cheery bell attached to the door made her glance up from her laptop screen. She almost wished she hadn't. The woman who walked through the door was stunningly beautiful—long, glossy blond hair and a face made for a camera. Her stunning blue eyes stood out, even from twenty feet away.

Great, just great. Aura Burton was one of a small number of people that Jenna would have been perfectly happy to never see again. She wasn't the first person on that list—that honor was reserved for Brigit Westlake—but Aura was a close second.

Jenna tucked herself as far as she could into the corner of her booth, hoping Aura wouldn't look in her direction. She didn't need a confrontation with her former friend turned frenemy while she was just trying to get some sugar and caffeine. Hopefully, Aura would just grab a quick coffee and depart.

No such luck. Aura parked herself at a table right near the cash register and made herself comfortable. Jenna watched her discreetly while pretending she was doing no such thing.

Aura had gotten even more beautiful since high school, if that was even possible. She'd always been striking, but now she had just enough polish and glam to make her a knockout. She was wearing a trim skirt suit in pale pink that looked stunning against her glowing peachy skin.

There weren't a lot of reasons to wear a suit in Rock Cove, so at a guess, Aura probably worked somewhere in Boston.

Jenna had no idea what she was up to these days. She'd deliberately avoided asking either her parents or Sierra for updates on the people she'd left behind, but Jenna couldn't imagine her doing anything so mundane as working in an office or begging for funding like Jenna was doing.

Maybe if Jenna kept her head down, she had a chance of getting out of this situation without a confrontation. There was no reason why anyone would need to dredge up old wounds, right?

"There you are!" A loud voice came from the direction of the kitchen.

Jenna's stomach sank. No. It couldn't be. No way was fate this cruel.

She turned her head just enough to catch a glimpse of the red-headed woman making her way out of the kitchen at the back of the restaurant. She wore a wine-colored apron embroidered with the café's logo—a coffee cup sitting on top of a campfire like it was a cauldron or a giant soup pot.

Just the quick glimpse of the woman's hazel eyes and pouty pink lips threw Jenna back to the last time she'd seen her. They'd just graduated from high school, and what should have been one of the happiest days of her life turned dark as Brigit's smile twisted and became cruel as she plunged a metaphorical knife into Jenna's back.

"I know, I know. I'm late. Sorry," Aura said as Brigit joined her at the small table. "I got hung up at the station."

Jenna had known she was bound to run into Aura and Brigit eventually. She had just hoped that day would be much further in the future. She was still trying to find her footing now that she was back in town—especially without her parents around to serve as a sounding board.

She briefly considered packing up her laptop and making a break for it, but Brigit and Aura were sitting between her and the only door out of there. She'd probably draw more attention to herself. It was better for her to stay where she was. If she didn't cause a scene, maybe they wouldn't either.

Jenna focused intently on eating her delicious pastry and reviewing the document open on her screen. She tried her best not to look in the direction of their table, but her eyes kept straying without her permission.

Brigit looked happy, glowing even. The long red waves of her hair sparkled from the sunlight pouring through the windows. She threw her head back and laughed at something Aura was saying.

Jenna's breath caught in her chest, her heart suddenly aching for what she'd lost. At one point, she had been thick as thieves with Sierra, Aura, and Brigit. The *four* musketeers. The four elements. Together they had not only been a close-knit group of friends but a powerful coven of witches. Jenna had the power of water, Sierra the earth, Aura had air, and Brigit—fittingly enough for her temper—fire. Jenna wondered if either of them still practiced.

The four of them had grown up together and learned how to wield their powers at the knee of their mentor Roderick. They had been on track to be the most powerful group of witches on the planet, but then it all fell apart. Jenna still wasn't sure exactly what had happened, but one day everything was magical—literally and figuratively—and the next, Brigit had turned on her. They'd had a blowout fight and hadn't spoken to each other since.

Aura and Brigit finally wrapped up their afternoon coffee date and gossip session. Just when Jenna thought she was in the clear, Brigit stood from the table and glanced around the café, assessing everything with her sharp hazel gaze. Her eyes landed on Jenna like a missile with a tracking beacon. The smile slid off Brigit's face like raindrops off a glass window.

Power punched into Jenna's chest as if someone had hit her with a fist. She sat, pinned in place, as Brigit wound her way through the tables, Aura trailing behind like her shadow. *Yep, Brigit still used her magic.* Jenna thought about using her own magic to counter but decided against it. They had been taught early on not to do magic where ordinaries could see. She was honestly shocked that Brigit was breaking even that most sacred vow. Unless her life was at risk, she was bound by her duty and her beliefs to not cast in public.

"So, you're back. Interesting that you would show your face in here, of all places," Brigit said as she crossed her arms, covering the café's logo in the process.

Jenna took a long, soothing breath as the pressure around her chest loosened slightly. "Brigit, Aura, nice to see you both. Though if I'd known you were going to be here today, I might have picked a different restaurant." She didn't want to fight with them, but she wasn't going to let Brigit walk all over her either.

Brigit sneered. "Yeah, I can't imagine why I would show up at my own restaurant. Truly a puzzle if you ask me."

Oh. Cinder & Spice. The coffee cup cauldron in the logo. Brigit was a fire witch—the clues were all there and should have tipped Jenna off. Apparently, she needed to have a conversation with Sierra and ask her not only why she'd brought her here in the first place but also why she hadn't warned her who owned the place.

Jenna cleared her throat. "I didn't realize this was your restaurant. Now that I know, I'll make myself scarce. Do you mind?" Jenna glanced down at the invisible bands still holding her in place. She didn't particularly like the idea of letting herself be chased off—and the cinnamon roll really was to die for—but she also didn't see the reason to open herself up to bitter hatred from the shop's owner for no good reason.

"Do whatever you want to do. You always do anyway. Now that you're back, I assume you'll be living in luxury up in Mommy and Daddy's house?" Brigit cocked her head.

Jenna flinched like she'd been slapped. Whatever bad blood existed between her and Brigit was one thing. Throwing her recently deceased parents into the mix crossed a line.

"Brigit," Aura barked, her eyes narrowing at her friend.

A brief look that might have been regret flashed across Brigit's face before she once again masked it beneath a harsh glare. She dropped her arms. "Whatever. Your money is just as green as the next person's." Brigit spun on her heel and stalked back behind the counter and into the kitchen. An invisible cloud of heat followed behind her.

An awkward silence stretched between Jenna and Aura. Jenna was frozen in place, and Aura glanced between Jenna and the closed kitchen door. "That was uncalled for," Aura finally said.

Her body finally released from its paralysis, Jenna shoved her laptop into its bag and yanked the zipper closed. "Since when did that ever stop Brigit from saying or doing anything?" She rose with as much dignity as she could gather, left the café, and barely made it to her car before the tears started to fall.

Chapter Six

DENVER WALKED INTO THE dim but inviting interior of the Copper Lantern and glanced around for Holden. The Irish pub looked like it had been there for a hundred years, even though it had only opened in the last ten. The floors were slate, the walls a mix of drywall and brick, and all the furnishings were a warm brown. There was a huge stone fireplace off to one side of the crowded space, and unsurprisingly, Holden was parked in front of it at a high-top table near the end of the bar. It was their favorite place in the bar, even when it was far too warm for the fire to be lit.

Denver wound his way through the Friday night crowd to join his friend.

"You made it. Finally," Holden said, holding out his arm for a quick bro hug and pat on the back.

If the empty glass on the table was anything to go by, Holden was already on his second drink of the night, and even that one was almost gone. Denver had some catching up to do. He caught the eye of the man behind the bar and gestured for two more beers.

Killian O'Rourke had moved to Rock Cove ten years ago from Boston and opened the Copper Lantern less than a year later. He was a few years older than Denver and Holden, and since he hadn't been born in Rock Cove, they hadn't grown up together. None of that mattered though, because they'd become fast friends with the feisty Irishman almost immediately.

"We didn't think you were going to show up," Killian said as he delivered their pints. "Poor Holden was practically ready to pass out from boredom."

Holden gave Killian a light shove. "Oh, fuck off. I was not. There's plenty going on in here tonight to keep me busy," Holden said as his eyes roamed over the crowd and traced several of the very attractive local women.

"Are you sure there are any women left in Rock Cove that you haven't already slept with and tossed aside?" Denver asked, tongue-in-cheek. He got his own shove from Holden.

"Don't you start in on me too," Holden said. "Besides, there are at least one or two." His eyes slid to one of the nearby tables and focused intently on a redhead who had her back to him.

Denver had no idea how long Holden had been into Brigit Westlake, but for some reason, he refused to do anything about it. Instead, he watched her from afar, only speaking to her when politeness demanded or she said something to him first. Denver had repeatedly told Holden that he had a pretty good shot at getting Brigit to go out with him if he just made a move, but he never did. Denver had long since learned to keep his nose out of it.

As usual, Brigit was hanging out with Aura. It was rare to see the two of them apart, especially when socializing was involved. Denver was slightly surprised that Sierra wasn't with them, but perhaps she hadn't been able to find a sitter for her kid. The three women had been friends since high school. He hadn't run in the same crowds as they had, but in a town as small as Rock Cove, no one was ever really a stranger.

The door to the pub opened and blew in a gust of fresh air—along with Sierra, her wavy brown hair swirling in the wind. Right behind Sierra was Jenna, a smile on her beautiful pink lips and a look of keen interest in her bright blue eyes as she took in the pub.

Her eyes skated over the crowd of people and tables. Her gaze snagged his briefly before she gave him a quick head bob of acknowledgment. She didn't linger on him, however, and kept looking around the space. He saw the exact moment she realized that Brigit and Aura were there. She froze for a moment before she turned to Sierra and whispered something in her ear.

Jenna's delicate face was pinched with concern, and Denver found himself suddenly very curious about what she was saying to her friend.

"How's it going with Jenna?" Holden asked, startling Denver out of his one-sided staring contest.

"What?" He ripped his gaze away from the heated whisper debate happening by the front door.

Holden took a sip of his beer and glanced at the spot where Denver had been looking. A smirk crossed his face. "I asked how things were going with Jenna."

Denver's gaze was drawn back to Jenna as she and Sierra walked across the floor and snagged an empty table all the way across the room. Jenna sat with obvious reluctance as she glared at Brigit and Aura's table.

"Earth to Denver." Holden smacked his arm, breaking whatever spell Jenna had him under.

"Good, yeah. It's fine," Denver blurted out, which was total crap. He hadn't even seen Jenna in the two weeks since their meeting with the aquarium director. "Actually, to be honest, it's been a bit of a non-thing if you want to know the truth. I've taken a few of the other researchers out on the water, but she hasn't reached out yet with any plans for what she needs." He shrugged. He was there to help her, but he wasn't the researcher. She was. He was just there to drive the boat.

"Now's your chance. She's right there. Go talk to her." Holden gestured to Jenna's table.

Denver raised an eyebrow at his friend and gestured to where Brigit was sitting in the opposite direction of Jenna. "I could say the same thing, man."

"That's totally different," Holden said.

"Sure, it is," Denver said on a laugh.

They spent the next few hours shooting the shit and intermittently watching whatever sporting event happened to be playing on the TV behind the bar. Killian was a huge fan of soccer—or football, as he frequently liked to try to correct them—so more often than not, that's what was playing. Soccer wasn't really Denver's favorite sport, but he could appreciate it from time to time. Tonight it wasn't holding his interest.

Intentionally or not, Denver's eyes kept darting back to the table in the corner where Jenna and Sierra were clearly enjoying themselves. He watched surreptitiously as several former classmates, most of them male, stopped by their table. As far as Denver could tell, however, Jenna seemed to be immune to their attention. Was she that oblivious to what was going on? Or maybe that unaware of her own appeal?

"Just go over there, dude. I can feel your jealousy from over here," Holden finally said.

Denver's head snapped around to stare at his friend. "I'm not jealous. I barely know her, how could I be jealous?"

Holden shrugged and downed the last sip of his beer. "What's stopping you from getting to know her?" He slammed his glass on the high-top table and grabbed his phone. "I'm heading out. You should make a move before someone else does."

Holden wasn't wrong. Jenna was right there, and Denver really did want to get to know her better. Maybe this was as good a time as any to approach her.

Something about Denver's expression must have given away his thoughts, because Holden smacked his arm. "There you go."

Denver sucked in a steadying breath and took a long gulp of his craft beer before he shoved back from his table and headed in Jenna's direction. He wasn't even halfway to her table when he felt someone's arm snake around his waist. A head of fiery red hair showed up in his peripheral vision. "Brigit?" he asked in confusion. He had no idea why she was suddenly attaching herself to him like a clingy octopus.

"Hey there, handsome," she purred in his ear. "Can I buy you a drink?" She tried to tug him toward the table she had been sharing with Aura, who was suddenly nowhere to be found.

Brigit licked her lips in an overtly sexual way, making Denver swallow deeply and try to take a step back. Brigit didn't let him. It wasn't unusual for an attractive woman to flirt with him, but this felt out of the blue—and Brigit just didn't seem like herself.

Denver glanced at Holden as if his friend could tell him what was going on. Unfortunately, he was no help. Holden's suddenly stormy gaze closed off before he turned and fled the bar.

Denver was on his own.

"I'm flattered, Brigit, but I was actually just on my way to talk to Jenna." He tried once again to extract himself from Brigit's clutches. He glanced quickly at Jenna, but she was staring daggers at Brigit, and he was caught in that crossfire.

Brigit didn't release him. "Why would you want to talk to her?" She was practically pouting. She also glanced in Jenna's direction but unlike him, Brigit seemed to enjoy Jenna's apparent anger.

Trying to let Brigit down easy, Denver thought of a handy excuse. "It's a work thing. We both work for the Boston Aquarium."

She let out a huff. "Of course you do," she muttered under her breath. She cast another look at Jenna's table before she unwound her arms from around Denver's neck. "Fine, I know when to take a hint." She smiled and winked before sashaying back to her table.

Finally. Denver tugged at his shirt to straighten it and turned back toward Jenna. Except Jenna was gone.

Chapter Seven

WHILE THE OCEAN WAS always going to be Jenna's number one happy place, the forest surrounding her ancestral home was a close second. Her many-times-great-grandparents had settled in Rock Cove long before it had that name, and through the generations, her family had acquired dozens of acres that sat on the outskirts of town and bordered nothing but parkland. It not only made for a peaceful retreat, but also made it easier to hide things that were best kept a secret from the world.

Jenna trekked through the thick trees to the clearing she knew was there, even if she hadn't been there since she left. A few lone birds made for cheerful company as she trudged through the damp woods.

The grove came up suddenly and was in far better shape than she'd predicted. The trees formed a ring with an opening in the middle, but their upper branches curved over the top of the expanse like a living canopy. One of the many benefits of having an earth witch around—at least when Sierra had still been practicing magic—was that she could convince plants to do whatever she wanted them to do. Providing a bit of top cover was just one more way to keep their secret safe. No satellite was going to snap a photo through the dense tree cover. Not that there was a *reason* for satellites to be spying on her home, but you never knew.

Jenna stopped just inside the clearing, not yet venturing to the large stone circle in the center of the glade. She took in the well-maintained trees, the absence of overgrowth, and the lack of any moss growing on the stone. Someone had been coming out here regularly to care for this sacred space, even though Jenna and her coven had abandoned it after they'd split in such spectacular fashion. Her parents must have kept up with it on the off chance that Jenna and her former friends ever reconciled.

Fat chance of that. Jenna thought back to the night before, watching Brigit stake her claim on Denver the same way she'd done when they were seniors in high school. Nothing had changed. Nothing ever would.

Jenna shook her head, trying to clear it. That's not why she was out here. She needed to ignore Brigit and Aura and focus on herself and her craft. Witchcraft worked best with a clear mind. She closed her eyes and took a deep, cleansing breath. When she felt more centered, she opened her eyes and crossed to the stone circle in the center of the clearing.

The stone was ten feet in diameter and had been manipulated by an earth witch from a previous generation to be perfectly smooth and flat. It was the type of thing that didn't look natural, but it was. As elemental witches, they only worked with natural elements. Nothing artificial would have been able to act as a conduit for their magical energies.

At some point in her family's history, someone had meticulously carved a symbol—variously referred to as a quaternary knot or a witch's knot—into the stone. It consisted of a single line that twisted over and under itself, creating a series of interlocking half-circles without a beginning or end. The knot had four points, one pointing to each of the four cardinal directions. East represented air, the direction of sunrise and the personification of spring. South represented fire and summer, the same direction as the sun at its peak. West represented water and autumn, Jenna's favorite season. And North represented earth and winter, the time when the growing season was over, and the earth was rejuvenating itself for the following year. In the center of the witch's knot—overlapping the loops in each direction—was a complete circle that signified unity.

While plenty of witches had elemental powers, the four of them had been born on the exact same day, at the exact same time, in the exact same hospital—though to different parents. It wasn't a mere coincidence either. When witches of the four elements arrived simultaneously, a link was created between them that gave them the ability to combine their magic in a way that was impossible for other witches. They were known as the Elementa. The phenomenon hadn't happened in several hundred years, but it was always a sign of great change or upheaval. It's what had made her and her friends so powerful as a coven. They were the most powerful witches in generations. Together, they were supposed to do amazing things.

Instead, they were broken.

Jenna shook off her depressing thoughts and inspected the stone carving. Something was wrong. Just like it had been obvious to her that someone had been maintaining the circle in her absence, it was equally obvious to her that someone had used the circle in the recent past. Oh, it hadn't been that day or even that month. But it also wasn't all that long ago. Less than six months for sure.

The magic felt both familiar and unfamiliar the same time. She knew immediately that it didn't belong to one of her coven. She would have been able to instantly identify their magic as easily as if it were her own.

Something tickled the back of her mind, like she'd felt the sensation a long time ago. But there was a twist of darkness to the magic that she was 100 percent positive she'd never encountered. She would have known if her powers had ever brushed up against that choking sensation before, and they hadn't.

How had another witch even known about the circle? It wasn't like she advertised it online or anything. She tried to probe the magical residue she was feeling but came away with nothing. No hint of who had tarnished her sacred space. There was only one option. She needed to cleanse the area. To reclaim the circle for herself and her magic.

The western point of the stone carving called to her gifts, welcoming her back like an old friend as she took her assigned place. Trickles of energy flowed from the stone beneath her feet and into her body, smoothing out the cracks and crevices in her soul left by the last few months. She'd missed this. She knew she shouldn't neglect her power and vowed that from here on out, she would nurture it as it deserved.

With a deep breath, she began to chant.

"Mother, maiden, crone divine,
with your help my gifts align."

The trickles of energy became a steady hum throughout her veins.

"I join you in this sacred space,
by your will and with your grace."

The tips of Jenna's fingers began to tingle.

"Water ebbs and flows through me,

rain and river, lake and sea."

A light drizzle began to fall, which quickly turned into swirling flurries and then back to rain.

"I call upon this ancient land,
protect me now at my command."

Power rushed out of Jenna in every direction. The blue glow of her magic emanated from her body, flew around the glade, and cleansed the residual unknown magic. The witch's knot lit up. A burning blue shimmer started at the point where she stood and began to flow sinuously around the carefully carved stone grooves, stopping where it met the loops on either side that belonged to her sister witches. One-quarter of the carving was ablaze, the westernmost piece. The rest would stay dark unless or until her former coven joined her.

Jenna tipped her head and stared at the overcast sky barely visible through the thick branches above. Her arms were spread wide, welcoming the rush of energy and connection back to her ancestral land. It had been far too long since she'd done this. She hadn't ignored her gift in the dozen years that she'd been gone—it was as much a part of her as a limb—but neither had she felt this deeply connected to the power she wielded at her fingertips.

Practically buzzing with energy, Jenna lowered her arms. "As I will, so mote it be." She closed the spell and could feel a residual heat energy pulse in the talisman that she wore around her neck, tucked under her clothes.

"Impressive. Though you always were talented."

Jenna jumped at the unexpected voice. It was one she hadn't heard since before she and her coven had fallen apart. "Roderick," Jenna said, trying to calm her racing heart.

The man standing at the edge of the clearing didn't look like he'd aged a day. She guessed he was in his mid-fifties, with a strong widow's peak and closely cropped black hair. His angular face was almost cruel in its severity, and his dark brown eyes bore into her like he was trying to peer into her soul.

It wasn't a stretch, really. At one point, Roderick had known her more deeply than even her parents. Roderick was the most powerful witch in the Boston area, which is why the Circle of Thirteen—the ruling body for witchcraft in the United States—had appointed him as their coven's tutor. He'd been the only one strong enough to take on the role of mentor to the four of them. Though at their peak, and especially when their powers worked together, even Roderick had been no match for them.

Jenna had never really liked the man, but she couldn't deny that she'd learned a lot under his tutelage. However, no matter how much help he'd been over the years, he still just creeped her out.

"What are you doing here?" Jenna asked when she finally had her pulse under control.

He smirked. "Visiting you, of course. I heard you were back in town and figured I would drop by and say hello."

Roderick didn't live in Rock Cove. The only way that he would have heard that she was back in town was if he was still in touch with someone here. Brigit no doubt. He always did have a soft spot for her and vice versa.

"Well, the rumors are true. I'm back." She stepped down off the stone circle but stayed where she was, refusing to join him where he stood.

He gave her a nod and a small smirk. "Planning to get the band back together again?" He gestured to the stone behind her.

Jenna shrugged. "That's not really up to me. I wasn't the reason things fell apart in the first place."

He cocked his head at her like he was trying to decide if he believed her or not. Jenna wondered what lies Brigit had been spinning in his ear if he thought Jenna was the reason their coven went down in flames.

The silence stretched awkwardly between them, and Jenna couldn't figure out how to break it. It was rude to ask him to leave, but she didn't want to spend any more time around him than she had to.

Roderick finally shifted in place, breaking the weird trance they'd been under. "Well, if you ever want to practice again, just let me know. My phone number's the same as before." His gaze narrowed as if he was trying to pin her in place.

She did her best not to let him see how unsettled he made her. "Thanks for the offer. I'm sure I still have your number in my phone." And damn it all, she did. She'd never been able to fully cut ties with him. Removing his number or blocking him seemed like a bridge too far. He may have been mildly creepy and a bit heavy on the mansplaining, but it wasn't like he was evil or anything. Just not someone she wanted to subject herself to in large doses.

Roderick bobbed his head once and then marched off through the trees.

Roderick had almost, but not quite, managed to ruin the buzz she still had in her system from the spell. She took a deep, cleansing breath and let it out slowly. Jenna forced as much tension and negativity as she could out of her mind and body and into the sacred space. The clearing was not only a conduit for their elemental powers but a place of healing, at least for her. Jenna waited until she felt centered again before heading back to the house.

Chapter Eight

I T HAD BEEN SO long since the meeting with the aquarium director that Denver was half convinced Jenna would avoid him forever. He had no idea why she was distancing herself, or what he could possibly have done to make her want to steer clear of him, but he was starting to think that she would find a way to work with someone else.

Imagine his surprise when his phone rang and Jenna's voice was on the other end of the line.

"Denver?" Jenna's voice was almost hesitant.

Denver dropped the sandwich he'd been shoving into his mouth and quickly wiped his fingers with a napkin. "Jenna? Is that you?"

"Yes, it's me." She paused as if uncertain how to proceed. "There have been a few whale sightings in Cape Cod Bay, so if you're available, I'd like to head out and capture some water samples." As soon as she started talking about her work, her voice gained confidence. It seemed her work was her happy place, and Denver was happy to oblige.

"Sure thing. How does tomorrow work?" They wrapped up their call by working out the logistics for when and where they would meet.

It was ridiculous that he felt nervous about the situation—he had no reason to. He was an experienced boat captain and had been out on the bay hundreds of times. He also had plenty of experience working with scientists. All he had to do was show up and drive the boat wherever she wanted it to go.

Was he nervous about Jenna? Yeah, she was hot, smart, and happened to be the daughter of people he considered surrogate parents. But that didn't really mean anything. He was a grown-ass adult, and he could take care of himself. No unease necessary.

The next day dawned bright and clear, but Denver still dressed in layers. It was late May, which meant it would probably be in the sixties or seventies on land, but the wind off the water could make it much cooler. Always best to be prepared.

While they both lived in Rock Cove and the boat was moored forty-five minutes away in Boston, they'd decided to meet at the docks rather than drive to the city together. Denver got there in plenty of time to double-check that everything on the boat was set and that the *Sea Bliss* was fueled up and ready to go. It wasn't supposed to rain, but the iron-gray sky loomed ominously. Cloud cover or even mist wasn't out of the question. Hopefully it wouldn't affect Jenna's research.

Denver was just stowing the last of his gear when she approached. She stepped confidently aboard the ship, hauling several bags of equipment along with her. He rushed to grab them from her and helped her stow them.

"Thanks," she said as she shrugged her final bag off her shoulders.

Once she was all set up at the small table inside the boat's main cabin, he asked, "Where are we headed?"

She flipped her laptop screen around and showed him a general area in the bay. "The sightings from yesterday were in this area. If we head that direction, we may get lucky and catch them feeding."

"You're the boss," he replied with a smile.

Between the two of them, they cast off the mooring lines and set out into the open water. It was going to take them several hours to reach their destination, so they had a bunch of time to kill. Jenna seemed perfectly content to focus on whatever she was doing on her laptop and ignore him, but after an hour, Denver decided he'd had enough of the silence.

"What exactly are we after today?" Hopefully talking about her work would ease the conversation into a topic she was comfortable with.

She glanced up from her laptop screen, carefully tucking her long black hair behind her ear as she glanced at him. "It depends on what we find when we get there. If we see whales feeding, I'd like to grab water samples to see if we can figure out what they're feeding on. If we're lucky, we may be able to get some audio samples as well."

"Have you always been interested in whales?" Denver kept most of his attention on the water and the boat's heading, but he glanced at her as often as he could.

"Ever since I was a kid." Her expression turned sad briefly before she schooled her features. "When I was eight, my parents took me to the beach. It was supposed to be a fun day in the sun and sand. Unfortunately, when we got there, there was a dead whale washed up on the beach, and the whole thing was closed."

"That must have been pretty traumatic for a kid," Denver said. His heart went out to that little girl. He couldn't imagine seeing such a tragedy at such a young age.

Jenna shrugged, but he could tell she wasn't as calm about it as she was trying to make him believe. "I've always had a ... connection with the water. It was hard on me for sure. Such an enormous and beautiful creature. It had been struck by a ship's propeller and couldn't recover from the injuries. I made it my mission to learn as much as I could about whales and do whatever I could to help them."

Denver could picture a tiny little Jenna, all book smarts and indignation, wanting to help save the whales. The image made him smile. He wished he had known her better back then. "And here you are, all these years later, doing exactly that."

They lapsed into a comfortable silence, but at least this time Denver didn't feel like Jenna was ignoring him on purpose. Unfortunately, the closer they got to her chosen location, the denser the cloud cover became. Eventually, fog rolled in and almost totally obscured the path in front of them.

"I hate to break it to you, Jenna, but this trip might wind up being a total bust." He gestured out the front windows.

She got up from her seat and came to stand next to him. She sighed. "Well, that's obviously not ideal."

He killed the motor when they arrived at the location she'd pointed to on her map. They bobbed along in silence for a few minutes. "Should we head back to Boston? Or do you want to hang out and see if the fog clears up at all?"

She chewed on her lip and crossed her arms. "Let's not head back yet. We may still get lucky." She shrugged back into the windbreaker she'd removed earlier and zipped it up to her neck. She grabbed a pair of binoculars—which were probably going to be useless in the fog—and draped them around her neck. With a quick nod in his direction, she left the cabin and headed out to the aft deck of the boat. She wound her way around the various rigs and pieces of equipment and headed to the rails.

Denver followed her lead and tugged on his outerwear. He wasn't sure what she was hoping to see in the thick soupy fog, but they'd come all the way out there. It didn't hurt to give it a chance.

They stood in total silence. In fact, unless he was hallucinating, Jenna even closed her eyes like she was taking a quick nap while standing up.

"You bored already?" he asked.

Her lips twitched, but her eyes didn't open. "Not exactly. I'm listening."

Well, that explained almost nothing.

"Listening for what?" he prompted her.

Her eyes flew open, and a huge grin split her face. "That." Her excitement was obvious. Her whole face lit up.

Her beauty made him catch his breath, but he had no idea what she was talking about. "What?"

Jenna put a finger to her lips and then pointed at her ears. Denver got the point. He shut his trap and strained to hear anything that wasn't the sound of the gentle waves lapping against the side of the boat.

A deep moan broke the silence. It hadn't come from him or Jenna, so it had to be what she had been talking about. He glanced at her and raised his eyebrows. She smiled and nodded. "It's a right whale."

He glanced around, still not able to see more than five feet in front of him, much less far enough out to identify one marine mammal from another. "How can you tell?"

She glanced at him, then just as quickly glanced away and pulled the binoculars up in a vain attempt to spot the animal. "Right whales have a few unique vocalizations that other whales don't. It's a distinct noise only made by one species."

Jenna set down her binoculars and started prepping a piece of equipment. He had no idea what it was. It just looked like a box attached to a long cord. She slowly lowered it over the side of the boat and into the water. She secured it in place and grabbed her laptop. He watched her open a piece of software that slowly filled the screen with data.

He stepped closer to her and peered over her shoulder. "What are you doing?"

She sent him a distracted look. "I'm recording the sounds they're making. There are researchers at the aquarium who study whale vocalizations—there are still several that we don't understand the purpose of."

Denver watched in fascination as she set up her equipment then sat back to watch the data coming in. It was actually very relaxing. They sat in companionable silence listening to the whale song. Every once in a while, a whale would make a scream-like sound, which seemed to make Jenna very happy.

"Is that more than one whale?" he asked tentatively, not sure why he thought he knew enough about whales to even guess at what they were hearing.

"Yeah, I think it might even be a mom and her baby." Jenna pointed out two different lines on her audio software showing the different intonations being made. "I just wish I knew which whales we were hearing. If I could just catch a glimpse, I would be able to identify them."

Denver spent almost as much time studying Jenna as he did paying attention to the whales. She was so beautiful, and she clearly loved her work and the whales. Her delicate fingers flew over the keyboard as she worked, and she bit her lip in the cutest way when she was concentrating. This trip was the first time she'd managed to relax around him since they'd run into one another at the funeral. It was a nice change.

Eventually, she stopped focusing on her laptop screen and wandered over to lean on the rails at the side of the boat. She stared into the thick fog as if it held the meaning of life. Denver leaned next to her, just happy to be in her presence.

"It's Diamond!" She whispered with a yelp as she whipped the binoculars up to her face.

Denver squinted through the fog and just barely made out a black head with rough white patches breaching the surface about twenty feet from the boat. Seconds later, a smaller black head appeared next to the first. It was astonishing that she could identify a specific whale on sight, especially under these conditions and when she could only see a tiny portion of the animal's body.

With a flurry of energy, she tossed the binoculars on the table with the rest of her equipment and grabbed a camera with a telephoto lens attached. She frantically started clicking away. She put her hand out in front of her as if to brace herself from tipping over.

Even the bay was cooperating. The waves that had been rocking the boat suddenly stilled to almost placid calmness.

Eventually, the whales sank below the surface and disappeared into the mist, out of camera range. She slowly lowered the camera and started scrolling through the screen on the back to see what she'd captured.

"I can't believe I saw them again. I watched that baby being born," she confided in him. "Now that I've got the photos and the baby is a bit older, we can readily identify her. And she sang to us so sweetly that I think I'll name her Siren after the mythical creatures that lured sailors with their songs." As if in a dream, she drifted back to her laptop to transfer the photos from the camera.

Denver stayed where he was, almost hypnotized by the gentle slap of the waves that had picked back up and the experience of being that close to such powerful creatures. He had never had the fascination with whales that Jenna had, but he could admit it was a powerful feeling to see them up close.

"I wish I could have brought my dad out here." Jenna's words were so quiet he almost missed them. He hadn't realized she'd once again joined him at the railing. "He loved being on the water. He would have enjoyed listening to the whale song and seeing the baby."

Denver held his breath. It was the first time she'd brought up her parents around him. "I'm sure Russ would have been thrilled to come with us. That man was a natural on the water. It felt like a part of him."

Jenna turned her head and looked at him. "Were you close?"

Denver tried to read into her question. Was she upset that he had a relationship with her parents or simply curious? Jenna was impossible to read. "Honestly?" She nodded at him, so he continued, "Yeah. We were very close. He was a wonderful friend and a huge stabilizing influence in my life at a time when I really needed one."

Jenna smiled. "That sounds like him. Always there to help, and he never met someone he couldn't befriend."

A sharp pang hit Denver's heart. "That's not strictly true. There's at least one person he couldn't stand." He cleared his throat. Now was not the time to get into Denver's asshole father. "But in general, you're right. Russell Hastings never met a stranger."

Thankfully, Jenna didn't pry. "I miss them." Her arms came around her waist like she was giving herself a comforting hug. Denver wished he could be the one hugging her, but knew she wasn't ready for that. Instead, he gripped the boat's rails tightly to stop himself from reaching for her.

"Me too," he confessed. "Not in the same way, obviously, but I used to hang out with your parents several times a month. They were amazing people. It's tragic that they were taken from this world so early." A dark look passed over Jenna's face. *Way to go. You're trying to get to know her, and all you can do is make her sad.* Denver chastised himself. He quickly tried to redirect her thoughts. "What's it like being back in Rock Cove after all this time?"

The sadness receded but was replaced with a complicated combination of happiness and frustration. "In some ways, Rock Cove feels like it hasn't changed since I was born. It's the same small-town feel, and gossip seems to spread before you're even aware there's gossip to share. In other ways, it's changed a lot and in ways I wasn't quite expecting." She tangled her fingers together like she was trying to keep from fidgeting.

"How so?" He turned his back to the water and leaned against the railing so he could get a better view of her face.

Jenna looked at him but quickly glanced away again, as if she wasn't comfortable with his scrutiny. "Well, everyone I knew back then is all grown up now, for starters. Both Sierra and Brigit own businesses in town, and Aura is off doing whatever beautiful people do in Boston."

"She's a meteorologist for Channel Ten News," Denver supplied.

"That tracks," Jenna said. "It would be right up her alley."

Denver had no idea what she meant by that, but it didn't really matter. "And now you're back, and you're some hotshot whale researcher." He meant to cheer her up, but he didn't expect her laughter.

She had trouble reining in her giggles enough to speak. "I'm not sure there is such a thing as a hotshot whale researcher. In general, we're boring science nerds. Not much else to it."

Denver turned and locked eyes with her. "I happen to like boring science nerds. In fact, boring science nerds might be my new favorite thing."

A light pink blush climbed up her neck and made her cheeks flush prettily. She bit her lip again as she stared at him briefly before taking a quick sideways step away from him.

He glanced at his watch and realized how late it was getting. "Is there anything else you wanted to do while we're out here? Otherwise, we should probably start heading back in. We've got several hours ahead of us before we hit Boston."

Jenna easily accepted the change in topic. "Without a clear visualization of where the whales are feeding, it's not super helpful to take the water samples I was after. We'll have to come out another day and try again."

"Looking forward to it," he said with a grin. "I'll get us underway." He left her to pack up her equipment as he went back inside to restart the boat.

It wasn't exactly what he'd been hoping for out of their day, but it was a good start. She would warm up to him eventually—surely. He just needed to have a little patience. Unfortunately, he was used to getting what he wanted and had never learned to be patient.

So learn. Jenna was worth it.

Chapter Nine

THE PETAL PATCH WAS the only bright pink building in all of Rock Cove. If the color alone didn't make it stand out, the rose-bushes and ivy vines that started at ground level and climbed the full two stories up the exterior were a dead giveaway that it wasn't like the other shops. The riot of pink and white spring blooms was an instant mood-lifter to anyone who happened to drive past.

The bell Sierra had attached to the shop's front door jingled merrily as Jenna opened the door and entered the small store. Jenna had been to the shop before, but she never got tired of seeing what Sierra had built for herself. Every surface, both inside and out, was covered in flowers in every shade of the rainbow. The scent was heavenly. She wound her way around potted plants, coolers full of fresh-cut floral arrangements, and hanging baskets, each one as attractive and appealing as the last.

If Sierra didn't practice her magic anymore, no one had bothered to tell her plants that. Jenna had never seen such perfect blossoms in her life. One could be forgiven for assuming there was an extra something that made them just that much more amazing.

Sierra was just stepping out of the back room of her shop—no doubt drawn by the sound of the bell—when Jenna reached the counter that hid the cash register behind yet more potted plants. "Jenna! What are you doing here?" Sierra asked with a grin.

The truth was, Jenna wasn't sure. She'd been feeling unsettled the last few days, and none of her usual meditation or breathing exercises had worked to dispel the feeling. In the end, she decided that she needed to get out of her head, and who better to help her with that than her best friend?

"Roderick came to see me," Jenna said as she leaned against the glossy wood countertop. Not exactly where she'd thought this conversation was going to go, but her subconscious had other ideas.

Sierra rolled her eyes, grabbed a rag, and started wiping down her counters. "Oh? What did he want? You didn't attack him, did you?" she asked in exasperation.

"No, I didn't attack him—and thank you very much for that vote of confidence. He offered his services if I ever wanted to practice with him again."

"What did you tell him?" Sierra stopped wiping her counter and stowed the rag.

"What do you think I told him? I blew him off. Politely, of course."

Sierra shrugged. "Well, that tracks. You never were a fan of his."

A loud crash came from the back room. Sierra's eyebrows furrowed and her eyes narrowed. "Lucas, is everything all right back there?" She walked the short distance to the doorway and flicked open the curtain that blocked the view of the back room, allowing them to see inside.

"It's fine, Mom." Lucas's guilty-sounding voice let both Sierra and Jenna know that it definitely wasn't fine. "The vase just fell over on its own."

Jenna had to struggle to keep a straight face. It was obvious from the lack of crying that Lucas wasn't hurt, so now he was probably just trying to figure out how much trouble he was in.

Sierra took a deep breath and let it out slowly, then crossed the floor to where a ceramic vase lay in several pieces. Lucas reached for it, but she abruptly cut him off. "No! Don't touch that. It's sharp." Sierra grabbed the bigger pieces of the vase and tossed them in the trash, and then quickly and efficiently swept the floor to get any of the remaining smaller pieces out of the way of the little boy's fingers and toes.

It was wild watching Sierra as a mother. It was one thing to hear about it over the phone or via text message, but it was totally different to see it in person. Riding herd on a five-year-old was hard enough, but doing it as a single parent made it twice as difficult.

"Mom, I thought you said I could go to Cameron's house today." Lucas's voice had taken on a whiny tone.

Sierra had the look of a woman praying for patience. "Cameron's mom is coming to pick you up in an hour. Until then, can you please stay out of trouble? Don't you have a new video game you could be playing?"

"Yeah, I guess," Lucas scuffed the bottom of his shoe against the cement floor. He grabbed a well-worn backpack off a nearby stack of boxes and dug through it before producing a handheld gaming console. Seconds later, dings and bings from the device indicated he was doing exactly as his mother suggested.

As soon as they headed back to the front of the store, a frantic-looking man came in asking for help with the best flowers for apologizing to his girlfriend after he missed a date. The bad boyfriend was followed by someone looking for a potted plant as a birthday gift and someone else looking for a bouquet to lay on a grave. The Petal Patch did brisk business on weekends, that much was obvious.

Once the crowds had died down and Lucas was out the door with Cameron and his mom, Sierra speared Jenna with a piercing look. "Why are you hovering around my shop instead of doing something fun?"

Jenna had sudden sympathy for Lucas. Sierra definitely had the mom glare down pat. "Can't I just want to hang out with my friend?" Jenna asked innocently.

Sierra rolled her eyes. "Of course we can hang out. But that feels like something better done after working hours, don't you think? That's not what's making you hover in the corner of my shop like a creepy vampire."

Put on the spot, Jenna decided to prove her friend wrong. She started winding a meandering path through the store, stopping every once in a while to smell the intoxicating scent of the various blooms. Unfortunately, the store wasn't all that big, so on her third trip around the small space, she admitted defeat and went to stand by Sierra. Sierra said nothing, just watched calmly.

It was the serene stare that finally did her in. Somehow, Sierra's quiet support did more to get Jenna to talk than thumbscrews would have. "It's Denver," Jenna finally blurted.

Sierra smiled knowingly. "And what did our favorite hottie boat captain do this time?" She waggled her eyebrows.

Jenna's shoulders slumped. "He's nice."

Silence stretched between them.

"Um, okay. Isn't that a good thing?" Sierra finally asked.

It was. Of course it was. But Jenna hadn't been expecting it. In high school, he'd been untouchable and slightly aloof. Not mean, really, just not aware of Jenna's existence. He'd never tried to engage her in conversation back then. She'd assumed that it would be the same now.

She'd also been hoping that the crush she'd harbored for Denver would have been long dead and buried by now. She was a professional. A scientist. She should be able to do her job without mooning over her coworker. Being trapped on the relatively small boat with him, just the two of them, had been an exercise in avoidance. She'd kept her head down and focused on her laptop long after she'd had anything useful to do, simply because if she didn't, she would have spent the entire time staring at his gorgeous face. Not that she hadn't done that anyway whenever she thought he wasn't looking.

And she couldn't believe she'd let her excitement over seeing Diamond and Siren get the best of her. She'd used her water magic to still the bay enough that she could get clear photos of the pair. It was unforgivable. Even if Denver hadn't realized what she'd done, it was still a risk. She'd done magic without thinking about it. Who knew what would happen next time?

But Sierra didn't know about that, and Jenna wasn't about to tell her. Instead, she let out a frustrated huff and answered her friend. "I guess it's good." It came out as more of a question than a statement.

Sierra gave her a sympathetic smile. "Jenna, what's the issue here? You're being forced to spend time with a superhot guy who also happens to be nice. That seems like a great opportunity. Flirt a little. See where it goes."

Jenna was already shaking her head. "We work together. Even if he was interested in me, which I highly doubt, dating a coworker is never a good idea."

"If you've already made up your mind, then that's that. You won't be budged. Nothing to stress about anymore, right?" Sierra gave Jenna some side-eye that conveyed she didn't believe a word she was saying.

Jenna's mind was made up, though. She did not need to be pining over a guy who was clearly out of her league. Her attraction to Denver was her problem, and she just needed to get over it. Or at the very least keep it to herself. The last thing she needed was Denver figuring out she was interested in him. Well, the *last* thing she needed him figuring out was that she was a witch, but her attraction to him was a close second. Talk about embarrassing. She was going to be strictly professional. She could do this.

Now, if she could only make herself believe it.

Chapter Ten

Denver stepped out of his house and stretched. The air was always slightly fishy this close to the water, but it was like a drug to him. He couldn't imagine living anywhere else. The sun was not quite at its peak, and the sky was clear, without a cloud in sight. It was a beautiful day for a stroll with his best girl.

He grabbed Rosie's bright purple leash and clipped it to her collar, causing her to spin in place with excitement. Rosie loved going on walks. She loved being off-leash more, but since he was taking her into town, a leash was safest for everyone.

It was Saturday, which meant he had the whole day in front of him to do whatever he wanted. He was planning to meet up later with Holden and Killian to watch the Red Sox game, but in the meantime, he was planning on spending time spoiling his dog and eating way too much food.

Rock Cove had a cute park not far from downtown that had a dog run. Rosie loved to play with the other dogs and was a huge fan of fetch, so that was their first stop. Her step got an extra swagger the closer they got to the park entrance, making him chuckle out loud. Thankfully there weren't many other dogs already there, so as soon as the gate latched behind them, Denver unclipped Rosie's leash and let her explore. She immediately turned around and started sniffing his pockets like she was looking for something.

"All right, you caught me," he said as he ruffled the fur on her head. Denver reached inside his pocket and pulled out a tennis ball that had seen better days. Her butt immediately plopped on the ground, though it was still wagging enough that she vibrated with excited energy.

He pulled his arm back and let the tennis ball fly. Rosie barked once in response and took off after it. She brought the ball back to him and gently spit it out at his feet. With a grin, Denver grabbed the now-damp ball and did it all over again. They played fetch for twenty minutes before Rosie plopped herself on the ground in front of him, panting contentedly. He crouched next to her, and she rolled over to let him give her belly scritches.

"Ready for lunch, big girl?" At the word lunch, she immediately came to attention, and her ears perked up. Anything involving food was sure to get an immediate reaction. Denver clipped her leash back in place, and they headed into the heart of town.

There were several restaurants in Rock Cove, but most were sit-down places, and their menus leaned heavily on fish. He was in the mood for something heartier and more substantial, so he headed to Cinder & Spice. Brigit definitely knew her way around the kitchen.

"Now Rosie," he lectured his dog, "I can't bring you inside when I order food, so you be a good girl and I'll be right back." He tied her leash to the metal fence that separated the café from the next building over and ducked inside.

The teenager behind the counter, Corrine, looked harried when he stepped up to place his order. And no wonder, the place was packed. Thankfully there were still a few open tables out front.

"Table for one? There might be a bit of a wait." Corrine asked, tucking a lock of blond hair behind her ear.

"I'm going to take it outside, actually. I'll take a Reuben sandwich and a plain hamburger, both with fries." He glanced at the glass case next to the register. "And two of your chocolate chip cookies." He'd peel the patty off the hamburger and toss it to Rosie as an extra special treat. He was keeping the fries though.

Denver kept glancing anxiously out the front window of the café as he waited for his food. He didn't like leaving Rosie all alone. Rock Cove was a safe town, but you never knew what was going to happen. Thankfully, she seemed perfectly content to people watch, her tongue hanging out of her mouth with a doggy grin.

He was grateful she wasn't a reactive dog. She wasn't wary of strangers per se, but she wasn't immediately everyone's best friend either. You had to earn her trust and loyalty, but once you did, she was your best friend for life.

"Denver?" Corrine called his name, drawing his attention back to the counter where the girl was holding a large plastic bag full of food.

He stepped up to grab it. "Thanks." He nodded in her direction.

He spun back to the door to head outside just as Rosie lunged at someone. He couldn't see who it was, since the woman was crouched down and had her back to him. Denver almost threw the bag of food in his haste to get outside and see what was going on. He would never forgive himself if Rosie attacked someone because he wasn't there to prevent it.

It wasn't the sound of growls that greeted his ears when he stepped outside. Rosie was barking and yipping excitedly as she reared up and tried to lick the face of the woman who had stopped next to her. Once Denver registered who it was, his brain was able to tune in to what was going on.

"Look at you, pretty girl. Who would leave you all tied up out here? That's not very nice of them," Jenna crooned to his dog. Rosie gave her a few licks before dropping back to all fours and then proceeding to sprawl herself on the pavement, asking for belly scritches. "You just want some love and attention, don't you. Aren't you the sweetest thing?" Jenna scratched Rosie's chocolate colored belly, which made Denver's jaw drop open in shock. It had taken months for Rosie to trust him enough to let him scratch her belly, and here she was, letting a total stranger do it.

Not that Denver really blamed her. He would totally roll over and let Jenna scratch his belly if she were interested.

"Playing the woe is me card, are you Rosie? You make it seem like you never get any attention," Denver said as he came up behind Jenna.

Jenna obviously hadn't heard him approaching because her shoulders stiffened and she slowly rose to her feet. "She's your dog?" Rosie shot upright at the sound of his voice and stared intently at the bag of food in his hands.

Denver sent his dog an affectionate look. "Yep. Shameless flirt that she is. Her name is Rosie. Rosie, this is Jenna." He introduced his dog to the woman next to him, though her warm brown eyes barely flicked in Jenna's direction, instead focusing intently on the food.

"She's very sweet. What sort of dog is she? Her fur looks too shaggy to be a lab, but she's not quite a golden retriever." She sent the dog a warm look. Jenna was much more relaxed than she'd ever been around him. Maybe he was onto something.

"She's a Chessie. A Chesapeake Bay Retriever," he clarified at her blank look. "She's a great water dog. They're great hunting dogs too, though I'm not a hunter myself."

Silence stretched between them for a moment before Jenna shifted like she was going to move. "Well, I should let you get back to your lunch." She gestured to his takeout bag.

"Stay," he impulsively offered. "I have plenty of food here." He mentally adjusted his plans. *Sorry, Rosie. No hamburger for you.*

Jenna hesitated, glancing from him to Rosie. He could tell she wanted to spend more time with his dog, so he pressed his advantage. "Rosie could always use the extra company. She spends too much time cooped up by herself. It does her good to get out and meet people."

"All right, if you're certain."

Denver untied Rosie's leash from the fence and led her over to one of the bright yellow tables the café had on the front sidewalk. He unpacked the bag and handed Jenna one of the Styrofoam containers. "I hope you like Reubens."

He took the plain hamburger for himself, popped open the container, and immediately munched on a french fry.

She opened her food more reluctantly, but she took a big bite anyway and then practically moaned in pleasure.

"Good right?" he asked as he took a bite of his much blander food. Oh well, the company was worth the lack of condiments and toppings.

Jenna finished chewing her bite and daintily wiped her mouth. "Say what you will about Brigit, but she's a hell of a cook."

Denver had been wondering for a while what had happened between them, so he took her opening and ran with it. "What happened between you? You guys were thick as thieves back in high school. Now it seems like you can't even be in the same room." He tossed Rosie a fry, which she caught in midair.

Jenna couldn't quite meet his eyes. "You remember that?"

Remember that? Why wouldn't he remember that? "High school wasn't *that* long ago, you know." He quirked his brow at her.

"No, I know," she wiped the grease off her hands then unnecessarily tugged on her shirt. "But you and I weren't friends." She met his eyes briefly, then deliberately turned her focus to Rosie. She carefully fed her a fry, which Rosie gently nipped from her fingers before gulping it down.

Denver shrugged. "That might be true, but it's not like we were strangers. The school wasn't that big." In fact, he might have been slightly more aware of Jenna than he was letting on. She'd been shy and timid back then, but she'd always had some sort of appeal to him. Maybe he just liked the quiet nerdy types. "What happened?" he prompted her again.

She shrugged. "She betrayed my trust. Kind of hard to stay friends after that."

That only intrigued him more. "That's both specific and vague. What sort of juicy high school drama did she stir up?" He took a bite out of his plain hamburger and carefully chewed. It wasn't as bad as he'd been afraid it would be.

Jenna glanced at him and then immediately looked away again. "Um, there was someone I liked. Brigit swooped in and got to him first."

"Ouch, not cool." Denver was both surprised and not surprised. Brigit had always had a slight mean streak to her, but he wouldn't have thought she'd deliberately hurt her friend like that. It showed how people could always shock you. He could see how uncomfortable Jenna was, and now he felt bad for pushing her. "Did you ever plot your revenge?"

Her eyes flew to his. "Revenge? No. What do you mean?"

He flipped another fry to his dog before stuffing a few in his own mouth and chewing. "I don't know, I was never a teenage girl. Whatever you do to get back at one another. Hang her underwear outside on the electrical lines. Spread nasty rumors about her at school. Pants her in the locker room. That sort of thing."

Jenna chuckled weakly. "I'm pretty sure pantsing is far more common for teenage boys than girls, but no. I never did anything like that. It happened right before I left for college anyway, so there wasn't much time to carry out any convoluted schemes." She started eating again, which made Denver happy.

They continued to catch up on their lives and what had happened in the decade since they'd been in school together. By the end, Jenna was laughing and a lot more relaxed. A pool of warmth settled in his stomach. *He'd* made that happen.

"And finally, no meal would be complete without dessert," he said as he reached into the bag one last time and pulled out the cookies with a flourish. "Who can possibly resist chocolate chip?"

"Anyone who could resist is obviously a monster," she said with a smile as she accepted the cookie and bit into it.

This time her moan of pleasure went straight to his crotch. It should be illegal to make a noise like that in public. He shifted uncomfortably on the metal chair to relieve some of the sudden pressure on his dick. He cleared his throat and said, "Sinfully good, right?"

Jenna nodded her agreement before catching Rosie's hopeful stare. "None for you, sweet girl. Chocolate is bad for doggies." She polished off her cookie and then reached out to scratch Rosie's silky ears. She sent Denver a shy smile as she stood. "Thanks for this. It was lovely."

"Anytime." And he meant it. If he had anything to say about it, he was going to make sure they spent time together as much as possible.

Just as Jenna was getting ready to leave the café she jerked oddly, lunging in front of him, her back to his front. She swept her arms out parallel to her chest like she was cleaning an invisible window.

"Jenna, what the hell?" he asked as he stood from his chair.

"Denver, don't move!" she barked, using her arms to keep him behind her.

He glanced over her shoulder and saw a young woman—probably in her early twenties—staring at them with interest. The woman was tiny and waif-like, with hair that was halfway between dark blond and light brown, and she had an intense glare. The woman moved her hands in a complicated swooping gesture that Denver was fairly certain wasn't American Sign Language, but if it wasn't ASL, then he had no idea what she was doing. Was this some new social media dance craze? Was he going to go viral right now?

Jenna's arms once again made the same sweeping motion, but this time she followed it up with a punching gesture, palm out toward the other woman. The blond woman stumbled sideways a few steps, despite being thirty feet away from them.

Denver had no idea what was happening. Jenna hadn't touched the other woman, wasn't even anywhere near her, but the other woman was rubbing her chest like she'd taken a physical blow.

A crowd was starting to form outside the café, the townspeople glancing from Jenna to the stranger and back again. More than one person grabbed their cell phones to begin recording the incident. The other woman realized they had an audience and let out a frustrated huff before turning and sprinting away.

Jenna's hands dropped to her side as her breathing slowed. She didn't budge from her position in front of him until the crowd began to dissipate, and it was clear the other woman wasn't coming back.

He cleared his throat. "Friend of yours?" he asked tentatively.

Jenna finally turned to glance back at him. "I've never seen her before in my life."

"So what was," he gestured from Jenna to where the other woman was no longer standing, "that all about?"

Jenna's eyes narrowed. "I honestly have no idea, but you can bet I'm going to figure it out."

Chapter Eleven

H OLY CRAP. SHE'D JUST used magic in front of Denver. Again. Actually, scratch that, it hadn't just been Denver but seemingly half the town. Yes, the strange woman had attacked them first, and if Jenna hadn't thrown up a shield to block the other woman's spell, Jenna and Denver could have been seriously hurt, but still ... the code.

She vividly remembered the day her coven had turned sixteen—the day when every witch was required to swear an oath to the Circle of Thirteen, promising to abide by the code to protect the secret of magic from the non-magical community and not use magic in public. Thankfully, there was an exception in the code if the witch thought their life or the lives of others were at risk. It had been clear that the woman was coming after them, so Jenna was well within her rights to defend herself and others. Officially, she should be covered. Hopefully, the Circle agreed. She could only cross her fingers that they didn't come knocking on doors around Rock Cove asking questions.

What had all the people in town thought? What had *Denver* thought?

And who in the hell was the bitch who thought it was a good idea to attack her and Denver in broad daylight in the middle of town? Jenna had never seen her before, but that didn't mean anything. There were plenty of witches in the world, and Jenna had only met a small handful of them.

Even more important than the woman's identity was why she had attacked them at all. Had she been after Denver or Jenna? Or someone else at the café? Jenna didn't have run-ins with nefarious people. This was outside her wheelhouse.

She rushed home, hoping to regroup and figure something out. Maybe she could cast a locator spell or some other spell that would give her more information than the *none* she currently had to go on. She wanted to pick up the phone and call Sierra, but she also wanted to respect her friend's choice not to practice magic anymore.

She was on her own.

She pulled up in front of her house and hopped out of her car. Before she even touched the front door, Jenna knew something was wrong. She'd never felt the need to ward her house against intruders, but now that seemed like a glaring oversight. In a town as small as Rock Cove—with a crime rate that at times barely seemed to justify having its own police force—it seemed like overkill to add a magical layer of protection on top of the usual locked doors.

Something just felt off. It was like the house was trying to tell her something. All the doors and windows were still locked, and everything was just the way she left it.

Was she being paranoid?

A sudden wave of *wrong* slammed into her as she crossed the threshold. She froze in place and instinctively slammed her own protective mental shields up just in case. No sense in being caught unaware for the second time in an hour. When she wasn't immediately attacked by someone—or something—she took another cautious step inside.

She stretched her magic slowly through each room of the house, searching for the presence of anything that shouldn't be there. A few moments later, she had her answer. She was alone.

She was only sort of relieved. Even though there wasn't anyone currently in her house, it seemed obvious that someone had been, recently. There was a strange, magical residue that she couldn't explain. It was like someone had tried to wipe out any trace that they'd been there, but hadn't done a good enough job at it. They'd left traces behind.

That alone told her she was dealing with a person of power. An ordinary thief wouldn't have the knowledge or ability to hide their presence from a witch. At a guess, it was probably the same wannabe witch she'd just run into in town.

Jenna considered calling the police, or more specifically, calling Holden, but what was the point? If she were dealing with someone using magic to get in and out of her house undetected, the police weren't going to find anything.

Jenna focused her magical senses on the spell's residue and tried to trace its presence. She wandered from room to room, following the likely path the intruder had taken. In most rooms, the remaining sensation was weak, as if the person hadn't stayed very long. Unfortunately, there were two rooms where the trickle was more like a flood. The first was her bedroom, and the second was the attic. The two most intimate places in her house. Where she slept and where she practiced her craft.

A dark, slimy sensation crawled down her spine. This wasn't a random break-in, though that should have been immediately evident by the fact that magic had been involved. Whoever this creep was, they had been looking for something.

Jenna started with the attic, since the unknown intruder seemed to have lingered there the longest. The oily residue was thick in the air, almost like she could touch it with her fingers. Yet it was entirely magical, not physical, and it was everywhere. It was like they had picked up and examined everything in the entire space. They had rifled through every shelf, opened every closet and cabinet, and touched every flat surface. Unfortunately, no one location stood out among the rest, making it unclear what the intruder was after. Everything was equally tarnished and would need to be cleansed. After a futile hour of searching and trying whatever magical tricks she could think of to pinpoint anything specific in the attic, Jenna gave up and moved on.

While it was disturbing that the thief had been in the attic, which was a sacred space, it was downright creepy that the person had spent considerable time in her bedroom. She felt so violated. This was her personal space, and no one should be in there who hadn't been expressly invited.

Once again Jenna stretched her senses, following the flow of residual magic. Like the attic, the oily smear was everywhere. Unlike the attic, however, there was one spot where it was thicker than anywhere else—her dresser. What would someone want with her clothes? They weren't high fashion, and they weren't worth anything. It didn't make much sense.

There were only a few items on the top of the dresser, a handful of receipts she'd pulled out of her purse, a bottle of perfume she'd been given as a gift and rarely wore, and her jewelry box. With a sinking swoop in her stomach, Jenna grabbed the jewelry box and yanked the top open. She'd stored her parents' wedding rings in there after they'd passed, and she would be devastated if they'd been stolen. But, they were exactly where she'd left them, the white gold and diamonds sparkling in the dim overhead lights.

Jenna wasn't much of a jewelry person and tended not to wear it. She didn't have any worth stealing. The only accessories she wore on a regular basis were her watch and the necklace currently hanging around her neck under her T-shirt.

The necklace. That had to be what the thief had been after. It was a small silver charm on the end of a sterling silver chain. The charm was that of a witch's knot—the same symbol as the stone circle in the forest.

It wasn't the monetary value of the necklace that made it worth stealing. The charm was her talisman—a connection point between her and the magic of the sea. While she didn't need the talisman to use her magical gifts, she was *much* stronger with it. It was also inextricably linked to her magic and hers alone. It didn't make sense that another magic user would want her talisman. As far as she knew, a witch's talisman couldn't be used by anyone else.

That was, in part, why each of the members of her coven had been given their own identical charm when they'd turned sixteen. The talisman helped them hone and focus their powers. The shape of the charm was to represent what the four of them would be when they came together. Not just four equal parts, but more than that. Greater than the sum of their parts.

While each pendant had been identical when they'd received them, after years of being worn and used to help shape their individual powers, the charms became unique to the wearer. Sierra's wouldn't work for Jenna the way her own did.

Jenna reached for her necklace, pulled it out from under her T-shirt, and clutched it in her fist. It was a good thing she'd been wearing it. She couldn't imagine what she would have done if someone had stolen it.

Another thought raced through her mind, and Jenna grabbed her phone. She tapped Sierra's name in her contacts and waited impatiently for her to answer.

"Hello, Jenna dear. Are you calling to give me all the juicy details about your impromptu lunch date with tall, dark, and dreamy?" Sierra's voice purred through the airwaves.

With everything that had happened since she'd arrived home, Jenna had almost forgotten about the wonderful meal she'd shared with Denver and Rosie. He'd been perfectly charming company, and his dog was an absolute sweetheart. She also didn't even bother to ask how Sierra had heard about their shared lunch, since that was the nature of living in a small town. Someone had probably seen it and run to the flower shop to tell Sierra all the hot gossip.

"Sadly, that's not why I'm calling, though we may need to come back to that later." Especially about the attack at the end. Jenna couldn't keep the tension out of her voice as she asked, "I need to ask you something, and you might not be comfortable answering."

Sierra's voice immediately lost all teasing as she asked, "What's going on?"

"I know you stopped practicing after our eighteenth birthday—after the Trials."

"Yes." Sierra's drawn-out word made it obvious Jenna was treading on a sensitive topic.

Silence stretched between them, and Jenna knew it was on her to break it. "I don't want to push you because I know you went through a really rough time, but someone broke into my house." Jenna described the attack at the café, everything she'd seen and felt in her house, and her suspicions that her mystery assailant was also after her necklace. "Do you still have your talisman? Has anyone ever tried to take it from you?"

"Not that I know of. I'm pretty sure it's exactly where I left it. Let me go check." There was rustling and banging on the other end of the phone for a few moments before Sierra's voice came back. "Safe and sound and still in my possession."

Jenna breathed a sigh of relief. "I have no idea why someone would want them but forewarned is forearmed. Keep it safe just in case."

"I'll guard it with my life," Sierra said. "Now can we talk about the cute boy?"

Jenna let out an unguarded laugh, more tension draining from her. "The cute boy with the even more adorable dog?"

"That would be the one."

"Well for starters, if the way Rosie was eyeing our food tells me anything, I'm pretty sure Denver gave me his lunch while he settled for the burger that was meant for her."

"Aww, now that's true love. Buying your girl an overpriced, but super tasty, lunch on a sunny afternoon."

Jenna's stomach clenched. Love? They'd only been in each other's lives for a few weeks and barely knew one another. She didn't want to draw attention to the *L* word though, so instead she asked, "His girl?"

"Rosie, duh. That dog is just the sweetest, smartest thing."

Rosie. Of course. That should be a weight off her shoulders, right? It wasn't like she was interested in starting something with Denver. He was out of her league. She'd spent several of her formative years pining after Denver, and she wasn't about to start up again. But maybe they could be friends. And maybe he would let her hang out with his dog some more.

She could be just friends with Denver, *right*?

Chapter Twelve

"WHAT IN THE HELL were you thinking?" the Architect yelled. "You confronted one of the Elementa in broad daylight in the middle of a crowd. That was just about the stupidest thing you could have possibly done!"

Danika Salvato stood in front of him with her head bowed slightly and refused to look him in the eye. This stupid witch had no idea what could have happened. She had no idea that the Circle of Thirteen could have discovered what she'd done and arrested her for it. Of course Danika didn't know that. He'd never even told her of the Circle's existence. Maybe it was time he did. Perhaps they would scare her into compliance.

The Architect paced a tight circle inside the empty warehouse he called a workshop. The cement floor wasn't attractive, but it didn't need to be. It was functional, and it allowed him to use chalk to draw whatever shapes or runes he needed to cast his circle. The lighting was also quite dim, but he'd never felt the need to spruce the place up. The workshop was for function, not form. It allowed him to be near his targets without drawing attention to himself. It was more than adequate.

Danika stood motionless, not even bothering to glance in his direction as he tried to walk off his agitation. While he appreciated the fact that she wasn't talking back, it also simultaneously pissed him off that she was such a pushover.

He needed to make it very clear to her what was at stake. "You know that we need their magic. I have a plan in place to make that happen, and I don't need you screwing it up for me—us," he quickly corrected. He needed her on his side and couldn't afford to push her away. She was a key element of his plan, and he wouldn't be able to succeed without her. He couldn't afford to send her packing, as much as he sometimes longed to.

When he'd taken Danika in, when she was fifteen, he'd had such high hopes for her as a witch. He'd sensed power in her that others had overlooked. He took her under his wing and taught her how to use her magic. She'd become like a daughter to him, though one that was a source of constant disappointment. She did have magical abilities, but they were nothing like he'd hoped for when he'd first found her huddled behind a dumpster doing her best to keep warm in the bitter New England winter.

Danika finally peeked at him from under her lashes. "You need her talisman, right?" she asked, her voice a whispered, barely there sound.

The Architect stopped pacing and crossed his arms. "Yes, I've explained this before. We need all four of them." He glared at her. He shouldn't have to explain this again.

A small ray of hope lit up her elfin face, and she brushed her mousy-brown hair behind one ear to get it out of her way. "I was trying to get Jenna's talisman for you. I was hoping to surprise you with it."

He was both impressed by her initiative and royally pissed-off that she'd taken matters into her own hands. "What do you mean?" He enunciated each word carefully so there would be no misunderstanding.

She flinched slightly but squared her shoulders. "I figured that Jenna likely kept the talisman at her house, so I went there and tried to find it. I searched her workspace and her bedroom but didn't find the necklace. When I couldn't find it at the house, I assumed she had it on her. That's why I confronted her outside. I was hoping to get it from her."

"That is not your responsibility!" he thundered at her. He grabbed a jar of red potion from the nearest table and threw it across the warehouse. It smashed into a metal wall and sent the red liquid everywhere. Every place the liquid touched began to hiss and smoke. The metal wall melted slightly under the onslaught of the potion.

Danika immediately dropped her head until she was staring at her shoes. "I'm sorry, sir. It won't happen again."

He took a step closer to her, and she flinched away from him once more. Good. Maybe she finally understood the consequences of her actions. "Yes, it will. Your incredibly shortsighted actions have forced me to move up our timetable. You have exposed yourself to the water witch, and it's safe to assume that by now she's also aware that someone broke into her house. The element of surprise is no longer on our side, but we can't allow her to dwell too long on you or your actions. We need to force her hand."

When he didn't continue, Danika glanced at him quickly before immediately dropping her gaze once more. "And how are we going to do that, Architect?"

"In the most public way possible."

Chapter Thirteen

IF YOU IGNORED THE strange confrontation at the end, lunch with Jenna had been a success. A key part of that success was Rosie. It was clear Jenna was a huge animal lover. Not only did she seem to enjoy petting his dog, but she was also a marine biologist for heaven's sake. If he wanted to spend more time with Jenna, then animals were the way to make that happen.

He couldn't take her to the aquarium—no one wanted to go to work for a date. And as much as she'd seemed to enjoy spending time with Rosie, he couldn't count on her being a convenient distraction forever. He needed another idea.

Luckily his boss, Trevor, accidentally presented him with the perfect opportunity the next time Denver stopped by the aquarium.

"Denver, have you been to this yet?" Trevor waved a colorful, glossy piece of paper in Denver's face.

Denver grabbed the paper to hold it still. It was an invitation to an exclusive gala event, with plated dinners and an auction to raise money for the Boston Zoo. Normally, Denver would have run away as far and as fast as possible. Dressing up in suits wasn't really his thing. This event, however, was not only raising money for the zoo, but also taking place there. It even featured animal "guests" and promised that the attendees could interact with the animals up close.

Jackpot.

"No, I've never been to this. I've never even heard about it before."

Trevor shrugged. "They send the aquarium a few complimentary tickets every year as a show of support. My wife and I have been several times, but in recent years I've started giving the tickets to other employees if they're willing to represent the aquarium at the event."

"Yeah, sure."

Trevor hummed in satisfaction. "Great. Let me see. Who else can I rope into this—I mean invite." Trevor chuckled at his own joke. "Maybe I can give the other ticket to Jenna. She definitely hasn't been before, considering she's a new employee. I haven't seen her around here today, though. Maybe I can call her."

"I can take care of that. We live near one another." Trevor had just unknowingly given him the perfect opportunity to spend time with Jenna. Denver wasn't sure what Trevor would think about his employees getting involved, but what his boss didn't know wouldn't hurt him.

Trevor gave him one raised eyebrow but immediately shrugged it off like he didn't care. "Suit yourself. How's it going with her, by the way?"

"Good," Denver told him about the trip they'd taken out into the bay and their plans for future trips. "Hopefully she's getting the data she needs."

Trevor just grunted. "I'm sure she'll let you know if she isn't. Okay, well I'm off to call maintenance about a broken water filter." His boss disappeared as quickly as he'd shown up.

Now all Denver had to do was figure out how to ask Jenna on a maybe-date to the zoo. The event was the next day, so he didn't have a ton of time to come up with anything super creative to convince her to say yes. Maybe the truth was the best option. Or at least, a version of the truth.

Which is exactly how Denver found himself knocking on Jenna's door early the following morning. He'd always loved her enormous house with its wraparound porch and the cedar shingles that had long since faded to gray. It was so perfectly New England, and it suited both Jenna and her parents. He'd been there countless times for dinner or drinks with Brooke and Russ, but it felt different now that he was shuffling his feet on the porch waiting for their daughter to answer the door.

Jenna finally answered, seeming somewhat surprised to see him. The small smile showed that his visit wasn't an unwelcome surprise at least.

"Denver?"

Suddenly nervous, he ran his hand through his hair and shifted his weight from one foot to the other as he tried to figure out what he should say. Maybe he should have given this more thought, or maybe he should have brought Rosie with him to soften her up. "Trevor wants us to go to the zoo."

Jenna's eyes narrowed, and a slight vee appeared between her eyebrows. "Um, what?"

He had apparently lost all the game he'd ever had. He didn't blame her for being confused, and he backtracked to try to clarify. "Sorry, let me start over." He reached into his pocket and pulled out the glossy invitation to the gala event and handed it to her. "I ran into Trevor, and he said that every year they send a few staff members to represent the aquarium at the zoo's annual fundraising event. He suggested we might want to go this year since neither of us had attended in the past." There, hopefully that seemed more like a work-related event and less like he was asking her on a date. Even though that's exactly what he wanted to be doing. Baby steps.

Jenna took her time reading the invitation, chewing on her pale pink lips in concentration. "This is tonight." Her pale blue eyes met his, and he could see the hesitation in her gaze.

"Yeah, I know it's last minute, but I've never been before. I figured it would be a fun activity, and we could get brownie points with the boss since he said he'd been a million times already." He had to physically stop himself from shifting on his feet. He hadn't been this nervous around a woman since he was a teenager. What was it about her that got to him? "Plus, we get to meet some of the animals up close. I think we can even feed the giraffes."

It was the giraffes that did it. He could see the moment she made up her mind. Her eyes softened, and she tucked her hair behind her ear before giving him a shy smile. "All right. I guess I need to find something to wear to a gala."

Instant relief flooded his body. She'd said yes. He could feel a wide grin split his lips and didn't even try to rein it in. "Great. The event starts at four, so why don't I pick you up around three this afternoon? It'll give us time to drive into the city and navigate parking and whatnot."

"Sounds good. I'll see you then," she said with a wave as she handed him back the invitation, then stepped back inside her house and closed the door.

He tried not to take it too personally that she'd practically shut the door in his face. It was obvious that Jenna was shy and slightly uncomfortable around him, but the more time they spent together, the more that seemed to ease. Hopefully this non-date date at the zoo would help even more. Now he just needed to dust off his suit and hope for the best.

"Is it a date? Do you think it's a date? It feels like a date, right?" Jenna found herself pacing in circles around her bedroom while Sierra lay sprawled across her bed, surrounded by piles of discarded clothing options.

She had to admit that she'd been surprised to find Denver on her porch that morning, but not unpleasantly so. It was never a hardship to see his gorgeous face, and he'd seemed adorably flustered for some reason, which was totally out of character for him. The hot, confident, former-football-star persona had been nowhere to be seen, and in his place, she'd seen the cute, friendly boy next door who got to her almost more than the hot jock did. It made him more real. More approachable. Less out of her league—even if he still was.

Sierra rolled her eyes. "Do *you* think it's a date? That's probably the more important question here."

Jenna dug through a pile of discarded dresses. She picked up a purple one, stared at it for a few moments, then tossed it back on the pile with the rest.

If Denver hadn't mentioned Trevor's name, she would have immediately assumed that an invitation to a swanky dinner event was obviously him asking her on a date, and she probably would have immediately shot him down. Not that she didn't want to go with him—and hello, adorable animals—but really, he was still way out of her league, and it felt awkward. But when he'd told her that it had been their boss's idea, her anxiety level had instantly lowered. An event where she represented the aquarium, she could do. She was more than accustomed to the glad-handing and baby-kissing aspects of fundraising, having had to do it herself on more than one occasion. Who was she to begrudge the zoo?

But then there was the image of Denver looking devastatingly handsome in a suit—like the one he'd worn at her parents' funeral—and she started to doubt all over again. "I don't know!" she yelled in frustration before face-planting on her bed.

"Would it be so bad if it was?" Sierra asked as she pulled Jenna's hair away from her face so she could see her more clearly.

Jenna turned her face to the side, making eye contact with her friend, but really so she could breathe in air instead of the comforter. "No?"

Sierra laughed. "Is that a question or a statement?"

"A statement?"

"Jenna my darling, I love you to pieces, but you need to lighten up. You're going to be spending an enjoyable night petting cute animals with an attractive man. Whether it's a date or a work function doesn't really matter. Just enjoy yourself. Get to know Denver. Who knows, maybe next time you go out with him you'll know for sure that it's a date and you won't have this much angst about it." She waved her hand toward where Jenna was sprawled on top of her rapidly wrinkling pile of clothes. "And wear this one." Sierra fished a little black dress out of the pile and handed it over.

Jenna rolled over onto her back and glared at her friend. "I can't wear that one. It's my sexy dress."

A wide grin split Sierra's face. "Exactly."

"But what if it's a work event?" She chewed on her bottom lip.

"Who says it can't be both?"

Chapter Fourteen

THE DOORBELL RANG, AND Jenna's stomach immediately flooded with butterflies. She'd kicked Sierra out of her house half an hour ago, not wanting her to still be there by the time Denver arrived. That meant she had spent the last thirty minutes pacing her living room, debating whether to yank off the slim-fitting black dress that hit her mid-thigh and put on something looser that didn't show off quite as much skin.

The bell rang again, and Jenna realized she was out of time. No going back now. She slipped into her heels, grabbed her small purse, and opened the door.

Denver's broad smile slowly faded as his eyes went wide, and his gaze raked her up and down. If she didn't know better, she could have sworn that lust flooded his eyes, but that couldn't be right, could it?

"Jenna, you're absolutely stunning," Denver finally said.

Well, maybe she hadn't been wrong. As hard as it was for her brain to process, it seemed that Denver was attracted to her after all. Fourteen-year-old Jenna was squealing inside her head. Adult Jenna was trying to figure out how to respond to his compliment. It wasn't exactly her forte.

She went to brush her long locks behind her ear before she remembered she'd twisted her hair into a loose French braid. She dropped her hand limply before it reached her ear. "Thank you. You look great too."

Great was an understatement. Denver was looking scrumptious in a medium-gray suit, crisp white shirt, and a green tie that made his green eyes pop. For someone who spent all his time on boats, he sure cleaned up remarkably well.

"Are we ready to head out?" Denver asked, offering his elbow to walk her to his older-model blue truck. The vehicle wouldn't be winning any awards for attractiveness or modern amenities, but it suited him down to the ground.

Jenna hesitated for a moment or two before gracefully placing her slim hand on his arm. This was creeping closer and closer into date territory every second that passed. Denver pulled open the door to his truck and ushered her inside before gently closing the door behind her. She tried not to wiggle in the seat with nerves.

The drive to the zoo took them about an hour. Their conversation flowed surprisingly smoothly, but Jenna kept sneaking glances at Denver out of the corner of her eye. He was so incredibly handsome, it was hard to believe she was sitting here with him, heading out to a fancy dinner.

They arrived amid a flurry of other cars but thankfully found a parking space that wasn't too far from the zoo's entrance. Jenna was slightly regretting her choice of footwear. The strappy black heels might look amazing, but they weren't particularly good for trekking long distances through a zoo. Though she could swear Denver kept raking his gaze up and down her legs, which made her think the heels might be worth the minor torture after all.

Denver presented their tickets to the attendant at the entrance and mentioned that they were employees from the aquarium. They were greeted warmly and given special badges that identified them as such. Apparently the two venues had a history of helping each other out, and the zoo was happy to have them in attendance.

"Who knows," the attendant said with a wink, "you may even get asked about your aquatic friends by some of the other guests."

Jenna smiled politely. "I doubt you have any whales in your zoo, but I'll see what I can do."

They were handed a fancy, numbered card attached to a stick for the auction that would take place during dinner. Then they were ushered into the zoo to enjoy the festivities.

It had been years since Jenna had visited a zoo, and even longer since she'd visited this particular zoo. Her love of animals was universal—no matter if they had fins or feet—and she was excited to learn about the conservation efforts the zoo did to help save some of the more exotic animals in their care.

Guests in fancy dresses and suits swirled along the concrete paths, mingling with zoo employees, who wore khaki pants and green polo shirts. One of the first animal experiences near the entrance was a zookeeper standing with two brightly colored parrots on a perch. The docent talked about the birds as they flapped their blue, green, and red feathers. Denver snapped pictures with his phone as they went.

As they rounded a curve in the path, a few of the roaming peafowl walked out in front of them. Just as they were about to skirt around the birds, one of the peacocks decided to fan out its magnificent tail.

"That's a mating ritual," Jenna said as she admired his colorful plumage.

Denver smirked. "Are you saying that the peacock wants to mate with you? I mean, it's not like I could blame him."

A fiery blush flooded Jenna's pale skin. She could feel the heat climbing from her chest to her neck and then up into her cheeks. She wouldn't have thought that spouting pedantic animal facts would have led to her being hit on by her maybe-date, but here they were.

"You should get closer. I'll take your picture with him." Denver made a shooing gesture with his hand.

Jenna did her best to crouch down in her tight dress and high heels, making sure her skirt didn't ride up too high on her thighs in the process. No need to put on a show. Denver snapped several quick photos and then walked over to show her. She was surprised by how large her grin was. The zoo event had been a great idea.

They wandered past the Serengeti area, spotting the zebras and warthogs. At the end of the exhibit was the ostrich pen.

"Ostriches are kind of like whales, when you think about it," Denver said thoughtfully.

She chuckled, not following his logic. "How do you figure?"

Denver gestured to a nearby tree, which had a robin cheerfully singing away. "You have birds like that. Tiny, pretty, but fairly common. And most bird species are probably closer in size to the robin than the ostrich. You also have birds like the parrots we saw earlier. Bigger, still pretty, but still relatively small in the grand scheme of things. Then you have the ostrich." He gestured to the awkward-looking six-foot-tall bird on the other side of the glass, currently pecking away at something on the ground. "It just doesn't fit in with its buddies. It's large, weirdly shaped, and not nearly as attractive as the rest of them. But they're fascinating to look at."

Jenna could almost see where he was coming from. "I guess. I mean, comparing a whale to a fish—which is what I think you're doing—isn't really a fair comparison to either of them. Whales are mammals. Fish aren't."

"Ok, fair point. But then that's even weirder. My brain can't really compute comparing a whale to Rosie."

That tickled another laugh out of her. "Well, you've got me there. Dogs don't have all that much in common with whales. Hippos are the closest land mammal to the whale."

He gave that some thought. "I guess I can see that. They're both enormous and love the water."

The ostrich chose that moment to take off running to the other side of its enclosure, so they continued meandering around the zoo. They listened to a few of the zookeepers talk about the animals in their care. They wandered past the lion pen just as the majestic cat decided to climb to the highest rock and let out an earth-shattering roar. Denver whipped out his phone and caught it on video. Jenna could honestly say she'd never heard a lion roar before, and it was seriously impressive. Eventually the giant cat gave up his yelling, flopped over on a warm rock, and sunned himself. The gathering crowd disbursed and moved on to other animals.

"Did you ever want to do anything other than be a whale researcher?" Denver asked her as they headed over to the giraffe pen.

She thought about it for a moment, but she didn't really need to. "No. It's pretty much what I've always wanted to do. What about you? Did you always want to be a boat captain?"

He took much longer to think about it than she had. "No, I can't say that was my life's plan when I was growing up. When I was a teenager, all I could think about was football, but even back then I knew I wasn't good enough to go pro. Add to that the fact that I couldn't afford to go to college to keep improving my skills at the collegiate level, and it was a dream destined to die on the vine."

They had reached the giraffes and—much to Jenna's infinite joy—the zoo was offering the opportunity to feed the magnificent creatures. They patiently waited their turn to be handed a branch of leaves.

Just as Jenna was about to ask another question, Denver surprised her by continuing.

"Your dad was the one who got me into lobster fishing. He helped me a lot after high school. My dad"—he paused as if looking for the right words—"he's not a good man. My mom raised me by herself, but she had to work two jobs just to keep us afloat. I didn't have a lot of great influences growing up. Russ sort of adopted me. He took me under his wing at a time in my life when I was feeling lost. He mentored me and helped me find work on his lobster boat. I don't know what I would have done without him."

The zookeeper gestured them forward, handed them each a branch covered with leaves, and cheerfully waved toward the two giraffes whose heads were eagerly trying to get to the plants. Jenna used the distraction of the gentle giant carefully snuffling her hand to gather her thoughts and emotions.

"You mentioned on the boat that you were close?" Tears threatened to spill, but she was able to hold them back by focusing on the beautiful animal in front of her.

Denver glanced at her as if gauging her reaction. "Very. He was one of my closest friends." He held his branch up for the second giraffe to nibble on. "And your mom was amazing. The snickerdoodle cookies she made were my absolute favorite thing ever."

That brought a smile to Jenna's face. "Mine too. I probably have her recipe somewhere, though I can't promise I'm nearly as good a baker as she was."

"I may just take you up on that offer."

The thought of baking cookies for Denver was a nice one, but she had an even better idea. It popped out before she could stop herself. "Or we could make them together." She couldn't believe she was brave enough to invite him over to her house, and for baking cookies of all things. She was about to backtrack and find a way to apologize for the strange offer when he beat her to the punch.

"Name the day and time." The flash of his perfect teeth as he grinned at her was almost blinding.

She needed to do this before she chickened out. "How about Monday night. Around six?"

"I'll be there with bells on."

After the giraffes had eaten all the leaves, Denver and Jenna were ushered away by the zoo attendant. It had been amazing being that close to such a regal creature, but Jenna could hardly focus on the experience because her stomach was swirling with butterflies for a whole new reason. While she still wasn't certain if this zoo event was a work event or a date, she was 100 percent positive that Monday was a date. And she'd been the one to ask him, not the other way around.

They wandered over to the gorilla enclosure to watch the enormous animal chowing down on a bowl of fruits and vegetables the zookeepers had clearly just given him. The enclosure was quite large, with a pond, several boulders, and a few wooden structures and fake trees for him to climb or explore. However, he seemed perfectly content sitting on the ground, munching away and watching the humans on the other side of the glass just as they were intently watching him.

Jenna was so distracted by watching the fascinating creature that she almost didn't sense the strange shift in the atmosphere. The hair on her arms rose, and she spun around, instantly scanning for the threat. Someone was using magic in their vicinity, she just didn't know who or where. The zoo was crawling with people. Guests in formal evening attire were everywhere, but nothing seemed out of the ordinary except that her instincts were screaming at her. Whatever was happening was going to be big.

A loud crack had her whipping back around toward the gorilla enclosure. All eyes were on the fake tree in the center of the enclosure that was suddenly swaying hard in a nonexistent wind. One of the limbs hung precariously, seconds away from dropping to the ground. With another huge crack, the limb separated from the trunk, but instead of dropping straight to the ground like logic—and gravity—should have dictated, the enormous branch was picked up in a sudden breeze and flung toward the edge of the enclosure. With a deafening smack, the branch hit the glass wall and smashed it into tiny fragments of safety glass.

The gorilla pen gaped wide open.

Jenna glanced around at the stunned faces of the other zoo patrons. Absolutely none of what they'd just seen was natural. There's no way any breeze could have broken that tree branch and hurled it with enough force to break a glass partition specifically designed not to break. Denver looked as shocked as she felt, his hand grasping for hers as if on instinct. The zookeepers looked stunned, frozen in place and unsure of what to do.

The gorilla had no such issue. It roughly shoved the bowl of food away and got up on all fours. It danced in place, darting this way and that, roaring loudly and doing its best to intimidate everyone around him.

He absolutely succeeded.

"Go for the tranq gun," one of the zookeepers yelled at his coworker. The other man scampered off toward the small shed at the rear of the enclosure.

"We need to get out of here," Denver said, yanking Jenna's arm as he tried to pull her away from the danger.

The gorilla lunged at the broken glass partition, using the downed limb as a convenient bridge from where he'd been sitting to where the humans were gathered less than fifty feet away.

Jenna reacted before she knew what she was doing. She felt the magic surge within her and called to the nearest body of water, which just so happened to be the pond in the gorilla's enclosure. The water immediately responded, rose into the air, and slammed into place in front of the gorilla, taking the place of the broken glass panel.

The gorilla reached the watery partition a second after her makeshift wall rose in front of him and smacked his hand into it. The water wall shook, but held firm, which only seemed to enrage the gorilla more. He started pacing and jumping, smacking into the barrier and making the glass panels rattle in their frames.

The gorilla was pissed.

Time and again, the silverback paced and slammed himself into her makeshift wall. Each time it did, Jenna felt the strain against her magical reserves, but each time, she held strong. She was getting weaker—the gorilla testing her strength—but she was the only thing standing between these people and that enormous beast.

What felt like hours later—but was logically only minutes—the second zookeeper was back, tranquilizer gun in hand. He lifted the gun to his shoulder just as Jenna felt the last of her strength leaving her. The wall of water fell with a splash, and the tranquilizer gun popped several times.

Jenna could only hope they'd subdued the creature as she sank gracelessly to the ground.

Chapter Fifteen

D ENVER'S EYES FELT LIKE sandpaper, probably because he hadn't managed to get a single minute of sleep the night before. Bright sunshine was pouring through his bedroom window, but he wasn't sure he could move.

More than half a day later, and he still had no idea what he'd witnessed at the zoo.

He'd watched the terrifying incident with the gorilla, in frozen shock. It all went down so fast that it was hard to make sense of exactly what had happened. If it hadn't taken place in front of dozens of other equally terrified people, he would have assumed he'd hallucinated the whole thing. The screams of the other zoo patrons and the pop of the tranq gun had assured him that everything he'd seen was real.

Jenna's arms had made some of the same weird sweeping motions he'd seen her make back at Cinder & Spice, only this time it was as if—as impossible as it seemed—the water had responded to her, and she'd somehow used it as a temporary barrier to block the gorilla from escaping.

Right before she'd passed out.

Thankfully she hadn't been out long, but when she'd come to, she'd been very tired and somewhat confused about what was going on. Unsurprisingly, the zoo had decided to postpone the rest of the gala event and had asked everyone to leave while they dealt with their situation.

Denver hadn't hesitated. He'd scooped Jenna into his arms and strode back to his truck and tucked her inside. The ride back to Rock Cove had been almost silent, each of them in their own minds and needing peace and quiet. He'd dropped her at her house and watched as she got safely inside, then came straight home and sprawled on his bed with his laptop, where he'd been ever since. Yet he had no more clue this morning than he'd had the night before about what he'd seen.

He'd started the night with his laptop, googling magic tricks, wind patterns, gorilla behavior, and the weight of a tree branch, all in an attempt to come up with a plausible scenario that would have caused what he'd seen. But science supported his belief that there was no way the tree branch could have done what it did in anything short of hurricane-force winds. And since he didn't think Jenna was trying to pull one over on him by setting up some elaborate hoax, he had to stretch his mind further into what might have been possible.

He'd shifted to looking for anything out of the ordinary about Jenna, her family, or Rock Cove. Apart from a quick report about Jenna's million swimming trophies and ribbons from when she was a kid, he couldn't find anything about her in the local newspaper. Her parents had been upstanding citizens who hadn't caused any trouble worthy of reporting either. Nothing strange had ever been reported about their house or land, and Rock Cove seemed to be exactly what it was. A small town on the coast of Massachusetts with a cute downtown and a busy tourist season. He couldn't even find any local YouTube videos of people claiming to see Bigfoot or a giant sea monster.

At two in the morning, his brain had started contemplating some of the more far-fetched explanations he could come up with. Maybe she was telekinetic. Or an alien. Maybe she had the gift that Magneto from *X-Men* had, except instead of being able to manipulate metal, she could manipulate water. Perhaps she was a waterbender like from *The Last Airbender*. His brain immediately rejected each ridiculous thought as soon as it popped into his mind, but that didn't leave him much of anywhere by the time his alarm went off in the morning, startling both him and Rosie.

He let out an exasperated sigh, rubbed his burning eyes and realized that he wasn't going to get any rest. He threw off the covers and shuffled his way to his small kitchen in nothing but his boxers to start a pot of coffee and let Rosie outside. He was going to need the caffeine. He took a quick shower while the pot was brewing, then stared at his mostly empty refrigerator without much hope of finding anything worth calling breakfast. He should just go out. His exhausted brain couldn't contemplate how to make something edible out of what was in his house.

Maybe Holden would meet him for a late breakfast. It was always fun dragging him to Cinder & Spice. Holden spent most of his time casting hopeful glances at the kitchen on the off chance that Brigit would make an appearance. Denver could also get the added benefit of a sane mind that he could bounce some ideas off regarding Jenna. Holden wouldn't hesitate to call him on any crap.

He picked up his phone to text Holden, who—after the expected amount of over-the-top groaning about Denver's choice of restaurant—agreed to meet him. He also texted Killian, who was barely awake after closing the bar the night before. He begrudgingly agreed to come too.

Holden was already there by the time Denver showed up and, unsurprisingly, he'd snagged the seat with the best view of the kitchen door. Denver pretended to scratch his chin to cover his smirk as he sat down at his friend's table. Killian walked in a few minutes later, looking a bit worse for wear.

"You okay, man?" Denver asked.

"Rough night at the bar. I'll be fine," Killian responded.

The server came and poured them each a cup of coffee. Denver fell on his like it was the key to life itself.

"What happened? Someone get rowdy or something?" Holden asked as he sipped his coffee much more sedately. "I didn't hear about any emergency calls."

Killian was already shaking his head. "Nah, nothing like that. I'm breaking in a new bartender, and let's just say he needs a lot of training. He dropped and smashed an entire tray of pint glasses, spilled red wine on the mayor, and broke one of the beer taps so that it started spraying beer everywhere."

Denver couldn't help the laugh that fell out of his mouth. "Seriously? Did you fire him?"

Killian just rolled his eyes. "Not yet. I came really close, but instead I just sent him home. I'd say that his leaving was more work I had to do, but honestly, I was doing my job and his at that point anyway, so it wasn't a huge loss. Not exactly a typical Saturday night, but not the worst I've had either."

It was almost the perfect setup. Denver pounced on it. "Speaking of atypical Saturday nights, that's actually why I asked you guys to come here." Denver stopped talking while the server took their order.

As soon as the server left, Holden turned to him. "Didn't you have a date with Jenna last night?" He wiggled his eyebrows suggestively as he took another sip of coffee. "What sort of atypical did you two get up to?"

Denver wished he were just here to share details about their work date. "Yeah, unfortunately, not anything close to what you're thinking." Denver walked Holden and Killian through the evening from the moment he'd arrived at Jenna's house to when he'd dropped her off and headed home.

The other two sat there in silence as if processing what he'd told them. Thankfully the server arrived with their food, and they dug in, chewing in silence for a moment.

"I have no idea what to make of that," Killian finally said.

"Oh, and I forgot to mention what happened outside the other day," Denver gestured to the outside eating area of Cinder & Spice and recounted the weird situation with Jenna and the other woman. He'd been able to brush it off at the time, but now he was looking back on it with a new lens.

Jenna's arm motions had been similar both times, but he'd seen her making a punching gesture, and the woman—who was easily thirty feet away—had stumbled backward.

"I mean there's no way any of it is real, right? Am I losing my mind? Am I seeing things?"

Killian was busy swiping away on his phone, but Holden finished chewing a bite of food and calmly said, "If you're seeing stuff, then I am too."

While those weren't the last words Denver would have expected from Holden, they were close. "What do you mean, you've seen stuff too?"

Holden glanced around the café to see if anyone was listening in, then leaned across the table and dropped his voice. "I don't think it's just

Jenna. You know how she used to be tight with Brigit, Aura, and Sierra, right?"

Denver nodded his agreement.

"Well, weird stuff used to happen when they got together. Flowers bloomed outside in February. During one of the fire drills, one of the teachers was trying to do roll call, and the paper with everyone's names on it was just ripped right out of his hand by a gust of wind that came out of nowhere. There was a rainstorm sophomore year when we were waiting for the bus, and somehow the four of them were completely dry even though the rest of us were soaked."

The door to the kitchen opened with a bang, and Brigit came out loaded down with several plates of food. Holden stopped talking and watched her deliver the food with a smile before she returned to the kitchen. "And just this past winter, I was in here getting a cup of coffee right as they opened, and I swear to you, Brigit lit the fire in the fireplace with nothing more than a wave of her hand. I don't think she realized anyone was around to see it."

"So you think that whatever is going on with Jenna is also true for the other three." Denver puzzled it over. "You realize this sounds crazy, right? Like, lock-us-up-in-an-institution level of out there. We can't possibly have seen what we thought we did, right?"

"Several dozen people from the zoo and most of the internet would disagree with you," Killian finally chimed in as he flipped his phone around to show them what was on his screen.

The cell phone video unmistakably showed the gorilla enclosure at the zoo. Denver wasn't sure why, in all his googling the night before, he hadn't thought to search for incidents at the Boston Zoo. Either way, the video showed everything that had happened the night before, exactly how he'd described it. He watched the giant limb snap off the fake tree and fly at the glass panel, smashing it into pieces. Whoever was taking the video hadn't been that close to the action, but Denver still distinctly heard the zookeeper yell for the tranquilizer gun. And right in front of the missing glass panel, you could clearly see him and Jenna. They were probably the closest people to the enclosure, not counting the zookeeper himself.

With a huge roar, the gorilla charged the glass wall. Denver watched the water rise up and slam into place in front of the gorilla, causing him to roar in anger.

Though recorded from afar, it was clear how much strain it put on Jenna to hold the wall of water in place and prevent the gorilla from escaping. Her knees shook, and she slowly crumpled. The second man arrived with the tranq gun just as Jenna passed out. Denver watched himself lunge for her, catching her before she smacked into the paved path.

"Holy shit," Holden said. "I can't believe that was caught on video. That's nothing like what I remember them doing in high school."

The clip ended, and Denver slouched back into his chair, all thought of breakfast forgotten. "What. The. Hell."

Chapter Sixteen

Jenna didn't wake up until the afternoon on Sunday. She'd emptied her magical stores the day before at the zoo, and the only cure for that was rest and food. After Denver had dropped her off, she'd gone straight to bed and passed out for at least fifteen hours straight. Her rumbling stomach finally woke her and forced her out of bed in search of food.

Not even bothering to change out of her pajamas, she shuffled her way to the kitchen to find the easiest way to consume as many calories as possible. She wasn't really up for making anything complicated, so peanut butter and jelly with a side of chips was going to have to do. She slapped it together and shoved the food in her mouth while hovering over the kitchen island, not even bothering to take the food to the dining room table. As soon as she finished the first sandwich, she made another one and wolfed that one down too.

She took the chips into the living room and slumped down on the overstuffed steel-gray couch to contemplate the mess that her life had become in such a short amount of time. The first instance of her using her magic in public could have been explained away. None of the bystanders had quite figured out what was going on, and the confrontation ended almost before it had begun. She'd been briefly worried that the Circle of Thirteen would send a representative to talk to her and remind her of the code, but she hadn't been particularly shocked when it hadn't happened. The zoo incident wouldn't fly under the radar as easily. The Circle was bound to find out somehow.

The Circle was made up of the thirteen most powerful witches in the country. It was their job to make sure that the magical world was kept a secret from the ordinaries. They had various ways of ensuring it, including matching new witches with experienced mentors. Each witch, upon coming of age at sixteen, was put in front of a member of the Circle and required to swear an oath to uphold the witch's code, which, in part, said they would not use their magic in public. They were also assigned to a mentor. That was how Jenna and her coven had gotten saddled with Roderick. The Circle members were also the enforcers who were sent to deal with anyone who broke the code.

With a groan, Jenna finished the last of her lunch and curled into a ball on the couch, burying her head in her arms. She was so screwed.

The Circle was terrifying. She'd only met one of them—and only once on her coven's shared sixteenth birthday—but she remembered the day like it was yesterday. The woman's name was Mabel Hexley, and she'd looked like someone's sweet, elderly neighbor who always had chocolate chip cookies for anyone who stopped by. At best guess she was a retired librarian or maybe a teacher. She had short gray hair and wore lipstick just a tad too red on her thin lips.

Jenna had been excited to meet Mabel and had been looking forward to it for weeks. Jenna had met other witches before—her mother was one after all—but members of the Circle were another thing entirely. Each element was represented evenly, with three witches specializing in each of water, earth, air, and fire. The thirteenth witch was the leader of the group, and the position rotated from one element to another during each transition of power.

Mabel Hexley wasn't an ordinary earth witch. She was one of the three most powerful earth witches in America. When she'd stepped out of the back of the dark sedan as her driver held the door open for her, Jenna had held her breath, hoping to make a good impression. Brigit, Aura, Sierra, and Jenna had each been looking forward to and dreading that day in varying degrees. Jenna had been on the more hopeful end of the spectrum, with Sierra being outright terrified. Mabel had looked so sweet that Jenna thought it seemed impossible for anything to be less than perfect.

Much to Jenna's shock, as Mabel approached their foursome, Jenna found herself cowering, unable to look the older woman in the eye. Mabel's mere presence was commanding enough that Jenna found herself involuntarily sinking to her knees. The elderly witch's earth magic washed over her in wave after wave of almost suffocating power. None of her friends had fared any better than she had.

Jenna had tried to choke out an introduction, but her tongue hadn't wanted to cooperate. Mabel's eyes narrowed and her lips pursed, but she didn't seem surprised by the reaction. Instead, she cut right to the chase. "Jenna Hastings, Sierra Dalton, Aura Burton, and Brigit Westlake, as initiate witches under the jurisdiction of the Circle of Thirteen, you are bound to our code, our honor, and our legacy. Do you swear, upon threat of punishment or death, that you will uphold the beliefs and teachings of this ruling body?"

Jenna's tongue loosened enough for her to reply, "I do," as her friends did the same.

Mabel had clearly not expected any other answer. She nodded her head sharply once, then said, "Then by the authority granted to me, I grant you each the status of apprentice witch. You will train with your mentor until your eighteenth birthday, at which point you will take your Trials. If you successfully pass those, you will be granted the status of full witch. Good luck to you." With those brief words, Mabel spun on her heel and departed, blowing out of Jenna's life no more than ten minutes after she'd arrived.

That had been a simple formality, and she'd still been dropped to her knees by the mere presence of the other witch's power. Now, after everything that had happened in the last week, Jenna was almost assuredly staring down another visit from a member of the Circle, and this time, it wasn't for a simple initiation ceremony.

She should probably do something to prepare for the imminent arrival of the Circle, but she couldn't bring herself to do anything but stew on the couch. She had no idea what was going to happen to her after the little situation at the zoo. There was no way it was going to stay under the radar. She half wondered if she should try to find a way to contact the Circle preemptively so it looked like she was cooperating rather than trying to hide what had happened. It wasn't like she could claim there hadn't been any witnesses—there were dozens of them, including Denver.

Oh God, Denver. He must think she was certifiable. What had gone through his mind when the glass broke and she'd used her magic to protect them? There was no way to just hand wave over the situation of a bunch of water rising into the air and forming a wall directly in front of them. Denver wasn't dumb, nor was he gullible. He'd seen exactly what she'd done, but unlike her, he didn't have any backstory or knowledge that could explain it.

The entire drive back from the zoo, the truck had been completely silent. She'd been too tired to try to make up lies to cover up what had really happened, and he hadn't even tried to ask. They'd only just started to become friends, with the slight possibility of more than friends, and she'd ruined it.

Not that she'd had another option. If she had to choose between Denver being injured but blissfully unaware of what she was, or him being safe and whole yet freaked out by what she'd done, she'd take safe and whole any day. As much as she wanted to give things a shot with him, it was far more important that they were both there to live another day.

On Monday morning, she emailed her boss, Trevor, that she was taking a sick day. She wasn't going to be able to concentrate on her research, and there was no way she was picking up the phone to call Denver to head out onto the water. She'd mentally resigned herself to going back to distant colleagues who saw each other only for work-related situations, but her heart and her libido weren't quite ready for that yet. She needed some distance so she could figure out what to do next.

She was in the middle of making chicken Parmesan for dinner when the doorbell rang. She double-checked that everything in the kitchen was safe and nothing would catch fire if she stepped away to see who it was. She opened the door and froze in place, surprised to see Denver standing on her porch in the evening light.

"You said six, right?" He said when she didn't immediately greet him.

Oh God. The cookie date.

Jenna was dumbfounded he'd shown up. The manners her parents had ingrained into her brain kicked in before her thoughts did, and she stepped back and waved her arm for him to come inside. She closed the door with a small click and stood with her back to it, uncertain where to go from there.

"Are you back to not talking to me?" Denver asked with a small smile.

The verbal nudge was what she needed to break out of whatever trance she'd fallen under. "Of course not, please come in."

He chuckled. "I think we've already gotten past that part." He gestured to where they were standing in her entryway.

She shook her head to try to clear it. "Right. Of course." A timer went off in the kitchen, and she suddenly remembered the food she had cooking on the stove. "I have to deal with that," she said as she gestured toward the kitchen.

He swept his hand out like he was giving her permission to walk through her own house. She gave him an awkward glance and then fled down the hall to turn off the burner under the boiling water and drain the pasta.

"Smells delicious," Denver said as he entered the kitchen and set a small bag on the counter. She wasn't sure how out of it she'd been that she hadn't noticed him carrying it, but he wasted no time opening the bag and pulling out a bottle of wine.

"Thanks. Are you hungry? I made chicken parm." She was suddenly thankful she'd made enough to have leftovers because she'd totally forgotten about their date.

"Sure, sounds great."

Jenna retrieved two plates, covered them with spaghetti and sauce, then grabbed the crisp breaded chicken breasts out of the pan to place on top. She covered each with a huge serving of cheese and called it good. She turned around to find Denver staring at her. "We can eat in here," she said as she walked to the table on the other side of the kitchen island.

"Do you have glasses?" he asked, waving the wine bottle in her direction. She set the plates of food down and went back for wine glasses and silverware.

They dug into the meal with gusto. Jenna had finally recovered her magical stores after Saturday's energy drain. Now she was eating for comfort and had prepared one of her favorite dishes. But why was Denver here eating her food and making yummy noises? She wanted to ask, but it felt rude.

"Why are you here?" Apparently, her mouth hadn't gotten the same memo her mind had.

A concerned vee formed between Denver's eyebrows. "Do you not want me here?" He slowly put his silverware down and wiped his face on a napkin. "I thought you invited me. If I misunderstood, I apologize." He started to stand.

"Of course I want you here," Jenna blurted out before she could stop herself.

Denver dropped back in his chair with an audible plop. "I have to admit, I'm pretty confused right now." He made no move to pick his silverware back up.

Jenna grabbed her wine glass and drained it. Denver watched her without comment. If he wasn't going to bring up the elephant—or rather, gorilla—in the room, then she would have to. "I meant why are you here, given everything you saw on Saturday?" Jenna tensed, her muscles locking. A lot was riding on what he said next.

"Oh, you mean the magic?" he asked nonchalantly as he picked up his silverware and once again dug into his food.

Magic? What? How did Denver know about magic? How did a perfectly logical and rational person with no experience with magic just assume that it exists? More to the point, how did they willingly accept it?

"Um, what?" she finally asked as she slowly grabbed her own silverware and took a nibble of food.

Denver started gesturing wildly with his hands as he talked. "See, the best we could figure was that it had to be some sort of magic. Of course, we considered alternatives like psychic powers or that maybe you were aliens, but magic seems like the most logical choice out of all those options. And yes, I realize how odd that sounds coming out of my mouth." Denver chewed a piece of chicken and sauce.

"When you say 'we,' exactly who are you referring to?"

"Holden and Killian. We had breakfast together yesterday and talked it out."

Jenna's stomach dropped out. It was bad enough that she'd done magic in public and that the Circle was likely going to show up on her doorstep to question her about it. It was so much worse that people in town were discussing it casually at a restaurant. This was a nightmare.

She wasn't sure how to ask what she wanted to know, but she gave it a shot anyway. "I get why you would assume something weird was going on after the incident at the zoo, but how do Holden and Killian know anything about ... magic?" She had a hard time spitting out the last word. It felt so wrong discussing her powers with someone who wasn't even supposed to know they existed.

Denver seemed to have finally caught on to the fact that she was freaking out about the situation. He slowly put his silverware down again and looked her in the eyes. "Apparently Holden has suspected something since we were in high school. I guess you all weren't subtle about some of the stuff you did back then. Killian on the other hand, well it's probably best if I just show you."

Denver dug his cell phone out of his pants pocket and tapped at the screen for a few seconds before spinning it around so she could see it. He tapped the play icon, and Jenna's horror was complete. There was a video taken by one of the bystanders at the zoo that showed everything that happened. She watched right up until she saw herself pass out into Denver's arms.

The video was posted to social media, and if her eyes could be trusted, it already had over a million likes and shares. That number would likely only grow. This was bad. So bad that she didn't even know what to do.

She needed to protect Denver. If the Circle was coming—and there was no doubt in her mind that they would be here as soon as they could get on a flight—Denver needed to not be here when they arrived.

"You should leave."

Chapter Seventeen

Jenna was kicking him out? Denver had to admit he hadn't seen that one coming.

"Did I do something wrong?" he asked tentatively.

Jenna stared at his phone as if it was about to bite her. The video kept playing on repeat, and her eyes were fixed on the small screen as if she couldn't tear her gaze away. He pulled his phone back and paused the video, which finally succeeded in breaking her trance.

"You can't be here. It's dangerous." She stood up from the table and frantically started clearing away the dinner they hadn't finished eating. Her movements were jerky and erratic, like she was verging on a panic attack.

Denver slowly stood but didn't approach her. The frenetic way she raced around the kitchen was concerning, but he had no idea what had caused her sudden mood swing. He took a tentative guess about what might have caused it. "I'm not afraid of you. Or your power." He put his hands out like he would if he were approaching a wild animal.

Jenna froze in place and then spun to meet him. "Maybe you should be. You have no idea what I'm capable of or what you're getting yourself into." She started wringing her hands.

Denver slowly inched closer to her, giving her plenty of time to back away. She watched him warily but didn't budge from her spot near the sink. "Jenna, do you want to know how I know you would never hurt me?"

She eyed his hands as he reached out to grip her shoulders. "Sure, let's hear it."

He leaned down slightly so he could meet her eyes and make sure she heard every word he was about to say. "You are the kindest, most loving person I've ever met. You wear your heart on your sleeve and have a passion for caring for animals that I've never seen in anyone else. You even won over my picky dog, and she's no slouch as a judge of character. The fact that your first reaction at the zoo was to protect everyone else from a possible rampaging gorilla shows that you think of others before yourself. You did everything in your power—whatever that might actually be—to save a bunch of strangers from a very dangerous situation. You wouldn't hurt a fly."

Jenna slumped, all the energy seemingly draining from her in an instant. Denver took the opportunity to pull her into his chest and wrap his arms around her. After a moment's hesitation, he felt her surprisingly strong arms lace around his waist and hug him back.

"And what if I'm not the source of the danger?" Her voice was muffled by his shirt, but he was still able to hear her question.

He ran one of his hands up and down her back, trying to soothe her. "I doubt Sierra, Aura, or Brigit would hurt me either. Well, maybe Brigit." He pretended to give it some thought in hopes of getting a smile out of Jenna. It didn't work.

She pulled away from him enough to meet his gaze. "It's not them I'm talking about either, though it's even worse that you know about their powers too."

"What is it then? What are you afraid of?" What could possibly scare someone as powerful as she was?

She bit her lip. "I can't tell you."

"Oh." He pulled back slightly. "I get it." She didn't trust him. Even though he was here, and he was trying to show her that he didn't care about whatever extra stuff she had going on, he still wanted to be with her. How much more of a clue should he need? Maybe he should take her advice and leave. "Maybe I'll take off after all." He stepped out of her arms.

"Wait," she called as he turned to leave. "It isn't that I don't want to tell you, it's that I can't. I swore an oath not to say anything."

Who on earth swore oaths in this day and age? Was this some sort of pinky swear with her friends? "An oath." His voice was flat.

She nodded. "Yeah, an oath to prevent the ordinaries—non-magical people—from finding out about the magical world."

Denver crossed his arms and stared at her. If she was telling him the truth, he could see why she refused to say anything. Even more, he could see why she'd freaked out about the video. Going viral on the internet wasn't exactly doing a great job of keeping things on the down-low.

"Well, not to point out the obvious here, but that cat is already out of the bag. I already know about the magical world, even if I don't really understand the full scope of what I'm dealing with. How much worse could it really get?"

Jenna appeared to contemplate this for a moment. Finally, she seemed to come to some sort of conclusion. "Honestly? A lot, but you're right about the fact that you're already at risk. If you want to know the full scope, I'll tell you. You deserve that at least."

"I want to know. But maybe somewhere more comfortable than this?" He gestured to where they were standing in the middle of her kitchen.

She nodded. "And with more wine." She refilled both their glasses and then led the way into the living room and over to the overstuffed gray couch. She carefully perched on the edge of the cushion for a moment before she melted backward into the deep cushions, slugging back her wine like she needed the courage it provided. "Sierra, Aura, Brigit, and I are hereditary witches—we inherited our powers through the lines of our ancestors who also had this power."

Jenna paused as if to gauge his reaction. He did his best not to react at all. While he hadn't known about the witch thing exactly, it made about as much sense as any of the rest of this did. "Okay."

"A witch's powers develop at puberty. For the first several years, you are considered an initiate and mostly learn from your family at home."

"Wait, so Russ and Brooke were also witches?" Denver interrupted her. It felt impossible that someone he'd be so close with had been able to keep such an enormous secret from him. It made him want to dig through his memories of all the time he'd spent with Russ and look for clues he may have missed.

Jenna shook her head. "My mom yes, but not my dad."

Oh. So Russ hadn't been a witch after all. The sudden rollercoaster of emotion was wild. Denver wasn't sure if he should be happy or sad that his friend and mentor hadn't been a witch. He settled on conflicted. "Right, sorry to interrupt."

"Yeah, sorry. I know this is a lot. Do you want me to stop?"

He shook his head. "No, keep going."

"There are witches all over the world. Not so many that you'd notice them generally, but it's not a tiny population either. It's a large enough community to require a governing body, which we call the Circle of Thirteen. It's made up of the thirteen most powerful witches in the country, and it's their responsibility to make sure that magic stays a secret. To do that, they must ensure that witches are kept in line.

"When a witch turns sixteen, they take part in a ceremony that's presided over by one of the Thirteen. During that ceremony, you swear your allegiance to the Circle and promise to maintain the secret of magic. You spend the next two years training with a mentor, and when you turn eighteen, you take the Trials. If you pass, you become a full-fledged witch. If you don't, the Circle strips your powers from you." Jenna pointed to a photograph on a nearby bookshelf. "That's the four of us with our mentor Roderick."

"Looks like a charming guy," Denver said, which was anything but the truth. He looked more like a thug than a witchy mentor.

"He's not. Though to be fair, he was dealing with four hormonal teenaged girls, all hopped up on magic. If you think regular puberty is bad, try dealing with it when you can accidentally set something on fire or crack a building foundation in half. The four of us were a lot to manage, and Roderick was the one that got to deal with it. Not to mention, our coven fell apart shortly after our Trials. It was basically chaos. But, that's not the point."

There was far more to this situation than Denver had assumed, and he definitely wanted to know more, but he didn't want to interrupt her story. "Okay then. Makes sense so far. Keep going."

"The problem is that my use of magic is now out there in a very public way." She gestured to where his phone was sitting on the coffee table. "The Circle will have no choice but to come here. I broke the code and exposed magic in a video currently going viral on the internet. Saying they won't be happy about that is about the biggest understatement I can make. They can strip my powers, or worse, and who knows what they will do to an ordinary who suddenly has knowledge the Circle tries to keep a secret."

Denver swallowed thickly. He was finally grasping how much danger they were both in. "My knowing about magic is making this situation worse." He had no desire to make Jenna's life any more difficult than it already was. Maybe it really was time for him to go. "Maybe I really should leave you alone. I don't want to put you in any more danger than you already are." He put his half-full wine glass on the coffee table and stood.

Jenna reached out and put her hand on his arm, stopping him from leaving. "At this point, you're just one of dozens of people who know my secret, though you know more than most. Honestly it's been nice to have someone to talk to about all of this." She patted the couch cushion right next to her. After a tiny hesitation, he accepted her invitation and joined her.

"You can't go to Sierra, Aura, or even Brigit to talk about this?" he asked quietly. He hated to see her suffering, and it didn't make sense that she had to when she had three people so close by who would understand everything she had been going through.

She shook her head. "I meant what I said about Aura and Brigit. We're not close, and it would take something momentous to fix that rift. I don't see how bringing trouble to their doors would help repair what broke between us. And Sierra doesn't practice anymore for her own reasons."

Until that moment, he had no idea how lonely she truly was. "I'm sorry your friends aren't willing to be there for you when you need them. But you've got me. In whatever way you might need."

Jenna surged forward and fused her mouth to his. The move took him by surprise, but he quickly got on board. His arms snaked around her and tugged her closer to him as he slanted his mouth against hers. He ran his tongue along her luscious pink lips, and she gasped, opening under his ministrations. He dove into her mouth, his tongue swirling and mingling with hers.

She was like a breath of fresh air. He couldn't remember ever enjoying kissing someone as much as he was enjoying kissing Jenna. Eventually he tired of the few inches of distance between them and tugged her until she was straddling his lap. His cock woke up and took notice as she settled across his thighs.

Her hands plunged into his hair as she gave as good as she got. She might be introverted in her daily life, but nothing about the way she responded to him was timid or shy. She started rubbing up against him, teasing his cock into full hardness as she wriggled in place.

His hands settled on her hips and squeezed. He tentatively slid them under the hem of her shirt and around to the silky soft skin of her lower back. When she didn't stop him, he got bolder, running his hands up and down her entire back and teasing her lacy bra strap. He traced the delicate fabric around to her front and cupped her breast with a groan. She fit his hand perfectly.

Jenna's nipple perked up, turning into a hard nub. He teased her with the lacy fabric, rubbing it over the stiff peak over and over again.

A flash of realization ripped through him. They'd gone from zero to sixty in seconds. As much as he didn't want to, he tore his mouth off hers and dropped his hand back to her waist. "Jenna, stop for a second. Are you sure this is what you want?"

Jenna's lust-drunk blue eyes confidently met his gaze. "I've wanted this since I was fifteen." Her mouth crashed down on his once more with an almost tortured moan.

Denver didn't have the strength to say no. It was clear they were both on the same page. Instead he stood, encouraging her to wrap her legs around his waist. "Which way to your bedroom?" he managed to gasp out between kisses.

"Upstairs, first door on the left."

She didn't have to tell him twice.

Chapter Eighteen

Jenna couldn't believe that she was finally kissing Denver. All of her teenage fantasies were coming to life, and she couldn't be happier about it. She felt featherlight in his arms as he somehow managed to navigate his way up the stairs without dropping her. Now that she'd started kissing him, she never wanted to stop.

He gently kicked open her bedroom door and crossed the thick carpet to her bed. He tipped her backward and laid her on the plush white and blue comforter. He stood up, putting a slight separation between them.

"Jenna, you're going to have to tell me what you want here. I know what my brain is hoping for, but you need to tell me how far you're willing to go. I don't want to push any of your boundaries." He swiped his hand absently across his lips, which happened to be puffy and slightly red from their kissing.

Jenna sat up and leaned on her elbows. Consent was so sexy. "I appreciate you double-checking, but I'm sure. Get naked and get over here."

Denver didn't waste another second. He whipped his shirt over his head and exposed his absolutely amazing muscles to her ravenous gaze. Jenna sat up fully and reached out to run her fingers over his pecs and down the bumps of his abs. He clearly kept himself in good shape.

Denver cocked an eyebrow at her as his hands went for the button on his jeans. "You going to be joining me here?" He popped the button and went for his zipper.

Jenna licked her lips and ripped her shirt over her head, then tossed it in the general direction of her closet. She fixated on him as he shoved his jeans and boxer briefs down his legs. His cock sprang free of its confines and slapped lightly against his stomach.

Denver cleared his throat, and she glanced at his face. He was smiling. "Your turn."

Right, she was supposed to be undressing too. She reached behind her to flick the clasp of her bra open before she flung it in the same direction as her shirt. She rocked back onto the bed and wiggled her pants and underwear off, then tossed them too.

"God you're beautiful," Denver whispered as he climbed onto the bed next to her. He planted barely there kisses on her lips as his hand cupped her jaw. Before long, his hand started to wander. He dragged it down her neck and then cupped her breast, this time without the lace barrier.

Jenna arched like a cat as he petted her. Her hands landed on his shoulders and made their way to his well-muscled biceps, which were currently flexed as he leaned over her. She explored the expanse of warm skin at her disposal, running her hands down his back and around his sides to his stomach and pecs once more. He was a perfect male specimen, like the statue of David come to life.

His hands wandered lower, sliding in between her legs to rub her core. She bucked under his touch, encouraging him without words to keep doing what he was doing. His finger found her clit, and she let out a moan before she could even stop it. Not that she wanted to stop it. Denver was making her body sing in ways that she hadn't felt before.

Wanting to share the pleasure he was bringing her, Jenna grasped his cock, which felt like silk over steel in her hands. She gave it a few experimental pumps, and he let out a groan loud enough that he had to stop kissing her to let it out.

"Denver, please." She wasn't entirely certain what she was begging for, but he seemed to know.

"Do you have condoms?" he asked as he placed delicate kisses all the way around her collarbone.

"Bedside table."

He stopped what he was doing long enough to suit up and rolled on top of her. He carefully lined himself up with her entrance and pushed inside. The sensation was like the most welcome kind of invasion. He slowly slid home and bottomed out, pausing long enough for them both to get used to the sensation.

His green eyes were soft as they met hers. She gave him a nod, and he began to move. He went slowly at first, as if trying to find their natural rhythm. He gradually picked up speed, and Jenna threw her head back against the pillows as sensation swamped her body. She hadn't done this in a long time. The connection between them felt almost overwhelming and certainly stronger than she'd felt with any of her previous partners.

Her hands roved over his arms and torso, gliding over as much of him as she could reach. Her legs wrapped around his waist, and her heels dug into his butt to hold him in place.

Sensation built, coiling inside of her, tighter and tighter like the string of a bow being drawn. She was so close she could feel it.

Denver reached one hand between them and rubbed her clit, instantly sending her into oblivion. As lost in sensation as she was, she still noticed when moments later, Denver gave one last pump and froze, his body shuddering through his own completion.

It could have been minutes or hours later when Jenna came back to herself. Her body felt limp and exhausted in a totally blissful way. Denver was sprawled on top of her, breathing heavily into her neck. "I'll move in a second, I promise."

She smiled into his hair, even though he couldn't see it. He was heavy, but she was in no rush to push him away. "Take your time." She absently ran her hands down his back, enjoying the way his muscles responded to her touch.

He rolled to the side but didn't go far. He wrapped his arm around her waist and tugged so she was tightly snuggled up against him. "I can't say this was how I was expecting the evening to go," he said. Jenna stiffened, but before she could pull away from him, he continued. "I mean, I hoped it would, but I hadn't been expecting it."

Jenna relaxed back into the mattress. She could understand that. She couldn't even explain the amount of relief that had flooded her system when she realized that not only had he shown up for the date she'd forgotten about, but he also claimed he wasn't scared of her and her powers. Of course, he still didn't really know the full extent of what she was.

Could she show him? It sort of felt like in for a penny, in for a pound. He already knew about her magic, and he knew she was a witch. What difference could it make if she showed him what she could really do? It wasn't like he hadn't seen it at the zoo.

"Did you mean what you said earlier? About not being afraid, I mean," she asked, then cleared her throat, suddenly feeling incredibly exposed and insecure.

Denver leaned up on his elbow so he was looking down at her. She felt like a bug under a microscope. "Every word."

She fidgeted for a moment before making up her mind. "Come with me." She rolled out of bed and grabbed the clothes that she'd thrown haphazardly on the floor.

Denver raised one eyebrow but didn't question anything. Instead, he ducked into the bathroom to dispose of the condom, then tugged his clothes back on. It was a shame to cover up all those delicious muscles but necessary since she was taking him into the woods.

The sun still had a little while before it set, and she headed out the back of the house and into the depths of her property. He walked next to her in a comfortable silence but tangled his fingers in hers with a soft squeeze. They approached the clearing in the woods where the stone circle was, but she veered away from it. They tromped along for a few more minutes before a break in the trees revealed a small lake with a dock and a floating pontoon. She could clearly remember the last time she'd been swimming in the lake. It had been just before graduation, when she, Sierra, Aura, and Brigit had still been close friends. They'd loved lying out in the sun and trying to get tan, occasionally slipping into the water to cool off. It was a place with a lot of history for her.

She was a water witch, and this water belonged to her.

Jenna stopped on the small bank of the lake and looked around. It looked and felt pretty much the same. Maybe there was a bit more debris than before, but that was something she could easily take care of. This was her lake to maintain and care for, and she'd been neglectful. It was time to rectify that.

"It's beautiful out here," Denver said as he looked around and breathed in the damp air.

"It sure is. Through the decades, my family has acquired dozens of acres of land, including this lake." She stopped and turned to face him. "I told you I was a witch, but I didn't really elaborate on what that means." At Denver's nod, she continued. "Sierra, Aura, Brigit, and I are elemental witches, which means we each have a unique ability to manipulate the natural elements of the world. Sierra's power is tied to the earth. Aura's is tied to the air. Brigit has the power of fire, which leaves mine as..."

"The power of water," he finished her thought for her.

"Exactly. As elemental witches, our powers get stronger the more we're around the elements we draw our abilities from."

A light of understanding dawned on his face. "So you being a whale biologist isn't an accident."

Of course he understood. "No, it's not. I mean, yes, the story of finding a dead whale on the beach is still true, and I have a passion for helping the animals of this world that have a hard time helping themselves. But beyond that, I'm stronger on the water. The power of water flows through me and gives me strength and powers I wouldn't otherwise have."

"Okay, tracking that. You draw your power from water, so you choose to be around it as much as possible."

"Yes, and as odd as this may seem, ownership of the elements matters. The major difference between the four of us is this property. All our families have been in Rock Cove for generations, but while they lived in the city, or even moved frequently in some cases, mine has been entrenched in this land for generations. My power is intrinsically tied to this land. And that means—"

He once again finished her thought before she could say it. "That you're the most powerful one of the four of you."

"Gold star for you. And don't think that didn't cause a level of jealousy and petty squabbles while we were growing up."

Jenna lifted her hand from her side, and water from the lake rose and hovered in midair. She spun her hand in circles, and the water formed into a vortex. With a flick of her wrist, she sent the waterspout racing across the lake toward the other side, where it caused enough wind damage that leaves were sucked off trees and pulled up into the spinning chaos.

The damaging side of her abilities was awe-inspiring enough, but despite bringing Denver out into the woods for her little demonstration, she really wasn't trying to scare him off. She dropped her hand and let the spiraling water splash back into the lake. She made a complicated swirling gesture with her hands, and out of the depths of the lake rose a stallion made of water. The horse raced across the surface of the lake toward them. Just before it hit the beach, Jenna flicked her wrist again, and the horse dissipated into a mist that blew lightly in their direction.

"Holy shit," Denver said, but to his credit, he hadn't flinched or moved during her entire show of power.

"Scared yet?" she asked lightly.

"Hell no. That was amazing." He sent her the biggest grin she'd ever seen in her life.

Jenna laughed, a lightness flowing through her. She hadn't realized exactly how stressed she'd been lately. Yes, she had Sierra and could talk to her about most things, but she never wanted to push her when it came to magic. Being able to share this part of her with someone so openly was freeing in a way Jenna had never anticipated. She had never imagined how it would feel to bring someone along for the ride, however bizarre it might be to *them*.

"Seen enough?" she turned to head back to the house.

Denver stopped her with a hand on her forearm. "Never. Last one in is a rotten egg!" With that, he stripped down to nothing, raced to the end of the short dock, and launched himself into the water.

Chapter Nineteen

DENVER'S HEAD POPPED BACK above the surface of the lake as he stared at Jenna. She hadn't moved from her spot on the shore, but she was laughing in amusement. He used his arm to fling water in her direction, hoping to entice her into playing with him.

He should have known better than to provoke a water witch. A wall of water rose in front of him and gently rolled over him like a wave. He came up spluttering but laughing. "Hey, you have an unfair advantage."

She stuck her tongue out at him. "You started it."

He slicked his wet hair back from his face. "What are you, ten?"

She walked to the end of the dock. "Says the man who tried to splash me with water."

He shrugged, unrepentant. "Whatever works." He swam to the dock and held on to it. "Come on," he urged. "The water feels great."

She glanced around like she was expecting someone to stumble on them this deep in the woods that she just so happened to own. She seemed hesitant but tugged at the bottom of her shirt like she wanted to do as he asked.

With a sudden flash of inspiration, he realized the problem. "Jenna Hastings, have you ever been skinny dipping before?"

She blushed, a pale red creeping slowly up her neck and to her cheeks. She nibbled on her lip. "Um, no."

Denver ran a finger along her ankle in a soft caress, then pushed away from the dock. He spread himself out so he was floating on his back, which exposed all of his nakedness to her view. A view she was eagerly devouring. "Come play with me," he whispered.

With a resolute nod, Jenna ripped her shirt over her head, pulled off her bra, and then dropped her pants and underwear in one fast move. His mouth watered at all the luscious skin she was revealing, her firm, high breasts, and the dark thatch of hair between her trim legs. He couldn't believe he got to see her like this. And because she was who she was, Jenna didn't make a cannonball entrance into the water like he had, but rather took a step out onto the lake, which supported her like she was the Second Coming of Christ. She walked to where he was bobbing in the lake before she slowly let herself sink beneath the cool, clear water.

He'd been dumbfounded when she'd first shown off what she could do. Her powers could be both beautiful—like the racing stallion—and deadly—like the monstrous vortex that could have torn trees down. He'd done his damnedest not to react as she revealed the extent of her power—it had been a make-or-break moment for them. If he'd let on that she intimidated him, she would have shut down and pushed him away, and there was no way he would have her spending this intimate moment with him with her naked body gliding along his.

It was simply astonishing how much power she packed into her relatively trim body and borderline shy personality. She was so unassuming in her daily life that no one who didn't know the truth would expect her to have the amount of *oomph* she possessed. She was awe-inspiring.

She wrapped her arms around his neck, and he tugged her closer until her curves were plastered against him without any space between them.

"You're amazing. Never let anyone tell you otherwise," he whispered in her ear as he ghosted kisses along her jaw and her cheek. "And no matter what happens with the Circle or the zoo incident, I've got your back. I may not be a witch or have magical powers, but I can drive a mean getaway boat should it come to that. Not to mention I happen to have a police officer on speed dial." He winked at her and was pleased when she laughed.

"Denver, never in a million years did I picture myself here with you, doing this." She dropped barely there kisses on his lips.

"Well lucky for me then, because I wouldn't want to be anywhere else right now." He claimed her mouth, his arm leaving her waist to cup her breast beneath the water.

She arched into him and made a small mewling noise. Her hands plunged into his hair as she angled their mouths to take their kiss deeper.

Denver pulled back just enough to drag in a deep breath. "Don't let us drown."

"Not drowning is sort of my specialty." She claimed his lips again, even as she pulled him under the water.

Denver started to panic for a moment before he felt a strange sensation move around his face, and Jenna's hands tapping his eyelids.

"Wakey wakey." Her voice, which should have been garbled and incomprehensible, was clear and right in front of him.

Putting all his faith in her, he opened his eyes, expecting to be greeted by fish and aquatic plants. Instead, he saw Jenna up close and personal. She'd created a bubble of air and wrapped it around their heads that allowed them to talk and breathe normally under the water, even while their bodies were still submerged and floating weightlessly.

"This is by far the coolest thing I've ever done," Denver said as he glanced around. It was like being in an inverted fishbowl, where the fish were on the outside and he and Jenna were cocooned together on the inside.

"We can't stay down here forever, or we'll eventually run out of oxygen, but it's a nice escape. I used to come out here and do this just to think through things. My brain goes quiet under water, especially since it often floods with thoughts and feelings up there." She pointed toward the surface of the lake.

"I imagine you probably weren't usually naked when you did it," he teased.

That brought a pretty blush to her cheeks. "No, can't say I ever was."

"All the more for me," he said as he tugged her snug up against him again. Not that she'd floated far away in the first place. He ran his hands up and down her ribs, skimming the underside of her breasts before skating away toward her mound below. Jenna let out a frustrated huff, and Denver swallowed his amusement.

"Just touch me already," she finally said as she reached between his legs and grabbed his incredibly interested cock.

"As the lady requests," he winked and used one hand to cup one of her breasts while simultaneously plunging his other hand between her folds below.

Jenna moaned loudly in their tiny bubble and wrapped her legs around his waist. She kept them bobbing gently beneath the water's surface as they devoured each other, tongues clashing and hands frantically searching for each other's trigger spots.

Denver thrust one finger inside her tight folds as his thumb came to rest on her clit and rubbed tight circles on the sensitive bundle of nerves.

Her hands flew over his cock, pumping him so fiercely he was already on the verge of coming. "I need you inside me."

He desperately wanted that too, but there was just one problem. "No condom." He gasped out between kisses.

She paused, a frustrated growl coming from deep inside. "I'm on birth control and I'm clean."

He lifted one eyebrow. "I'm clean too, but are you sure you want to risk it?"

She nodded once. "Yes, now do it." She leaned forward and clamped her mouth on his neck where it met his shoulder. She sucked hard enough to leave a bruise, a claiming mark that made him far happier than it had any right to.

Jenna used the grip she had on him to guide him to her entrance, and he sank inside.

Without a solid surface beneath them to push against, he couldn't move as much as he wanted to, but they made it work. He had a sneaking suspicion that Jenna might have been using her control over the water to give them more leverage than they might otherwise have had, but he'd take it. He gripped her hips and rocked back and forth, using the additional pressure of his thumb to take Jenna apart.

Just when he was certain he was going to come before he'd managed to send her over the edge, she groaned out her release and went slack in his arms. He pumped two more times and joined her in ecstasy.

In the back of his mind, he realized they were moving, but he only realized what was happening when their heads broke the surface of the lake and he breathed in the clean air of the clearing. He blinked the water out of his eyes and glanced around.

Nothing outside of the water had changed, but what they'd shared under the gentle lapping waves had been profound. He'd put his life in Jenna's hands, and in return, she'd given him everything. He glanced at her blissed-out expression and placed a light kiss on her lips. "You can drown me anytime."

Her eyes shot open like she was about to yell at him before she realized he was teasing her. Her features immediately relaxed. "Yeah well, you keep doing that to me, and we might have to make sex in the lake a regular part of our schedule."

"Sign me up. Maybe even ocean sex and river sex too." He wiggled his eyebrows at her.

Jenna splashed him lightly before she propelled them gently toward the dock. They climbed out, but since they hadn't thought to bring towels with them, they were stuck tugging their clothes on over their wet skin.

They started trudging back through the woods toward her house. "I guess we never really got around to the cookie-making part of the evening."

He bumped her hand gently with his own. "I'm not in a rush. Lead on."

If her small smile was anything to go by, that was exactly the right answer.

Denver had never been much of a baker, or even a cook, really, but he was all in. Any activity that put him in the same room as Jenna was a win in his book. Besides, nothing was wrong with being the newbie. All the more reason to ask her for help along the way.

The cookie-making process was a lot messier than he anticipated—he probably should have taken Jenna up on her offer of an apron, but clothes could be washed. A little flour wasn't a big deal in the grand scheme of things, and the end product had been warm, chewy, and delicious. Sneaking kisses between the mixing and the baking was an added bonus.

As much as Denver would have loved to stay the night—maybe even go for round three—he sensed that Jenna needed some time to think through what she wanted to do next. With no small amount of reluctance, he headed toward the door.

"When can I see you again?" he asked. Screw playing hard to get. He wanted Jenna, and he wanted her to know it.

She blushed lightly as she stood next to him in the doorway. "Maybe later in the week. I have some data to crunch over the next few days, so no need to head out on the water again quite yet."

A few days. He could wait that long if he had to. Jenna wasn't going anywhere, so if he wanted to be in this for the long haul—and he was starting to think he did—he needed to take things at her pace. "I'll be counting down the hours." He winked and left.

Chapter Twenty

R ock Cove, Massachusetts, didn't have a big enough population or crime levels to justify a prison, but it did have its very own jail. Denver had never seen the inside of it before, for which he'd counted himself lucky. His childhood had been spent on school and football, not delinquency, and as an adult, he'd never even gotten a parking ticket, much less spent the night in jail.

Thankfully, he wasn't there because of anything he'd done. He was there for something far worse.

His father.

Ken Nelson was Denver's biological father, or sperm donor really, since he'd never done a fatherly thing in his entire wasted life. He'd been a drunk when Denver was growing up, and he was a drunk now, despite the forced sobriety that went with spending months in jail pending trial for vehicular manslaughter.

Denver's mom, Noel, had met Ken one night at the Dockside Diner, where she worked waiting tables. Supposedly he'd been nice and had tipped well, though Denver had no idea how either of those things could possibly have been true. Either way, his mom claimed she'd been lonely—trying to make it on her own at nineteen with only a high school education. She had no job prospects beyond the late shift at the diner and the Tideway Inn motel, where she cleaned rooms during the day.

Regardless of how it had happened, Denver's mom walked away pregnant, and Ken had just walked away. Once every decade or so, he came back around, pretending like he cared about the child he'd created then abandoned—but Denver knew the truth. Ken Nelson didn't give a shit about anyone other than Ken Nelson.

Which is what made it especially odd when Holden called to tell him that Ken had been asking to see him. Denver couldn't fathom why. They'd spent a total of a few hours in each other's company over the thirty-one years Denver had been alive. They had nothing to discuss, as far as he was concerned.

So why was Denver walking up to the police station on a dreary Tuesday? Honestly, he couldn't even answer the question for himself. Ken was in jail for the hit-and-run that had killed Jenna's parents.

Maybe that was why Denver had reluctantly agreed when Holden asked him to come. He felt no obligation whatsoever to Ken. He did, however, feel an obligation to Brooke and Russ Hastings. If Denver's bio dad had killed them, Denver wanted to know what had happened.

"Thanks for coming," Holden said as Denver entered the small police station. "And once again, I'm sorry Ken is still stuck in our tiny jail. Hopefully he can get better accommodations once a spot opens up at County."

Denver waved off the apology. Honestly, he didn't care what sort of accommodations Ken had. Jail was jail.

"I'm not sure exactly what's going on, but Ken is insisting that he needs to talk to you. He's being quite loud about it," Holden continued.

It was always a kick to see Holden looking official and wearing a badge. It absolutely made sense that Holden became a cop—especially with what had happened when they were kids. Denver just liked to tease him about it.

"Anything for you, Detective Kay."

"Asshole," Holden muttered under his breath as he let Denver back behind the half-wall divider that separated the visiting area from the rest of the station. "But seriously though, how are you doing with this?" Holden asked as they made their way through the labyrinth of desks to the rear of the space.

Denver had no idea. He wanted to say he was unaffected, but that wasn't true. He'd never been comfortable around Ken and had no intention of making this—whatever this was—easy on him. He couldn't quite sort through his own emotions though. Was he angry? Upset? Depressed? He ran his fingers through his hair as Holden stopped outside the door that led to the cells. He finally settled on saying, "Ask me afterward."

"Fair enough." Holden pulled a swipe card out of his pocket and waved it at the reader next to the door. There was a slight click of the latch before Holden pushed the door open.

There was a utilitarian hallway on the other side of the door with three cells off to the right. The cells were separated by plain cement walls, but the front wall of each was made of sturdy bars. The cells each contained a small bed, a toilet, and a sink. Nothing else. Denver couldn't help but think how boring it must be to spend day after day staring at these same walls with nothing to entertain yourself and only occasionally having people to talk to.

Ken was in the last cell. He was pacing in agitation as he yanked his fingers through his hair, tugged at his orange jumpsuit, then started all over again.

"Come knock on the door when you're done," Holden said quietly before he left Denver to his fate.

"Finally," Ken said as he came close to the front wall, stuck his arms through the vertical bars, and leaned on the horizontal cross pieces. Denver took an instinctive step back.

Ken's brown hair was starting to turn gray, and his face was covered by a scruffy beard. It seemed more like he was refusing to shave than deliberately growing facial hair. He looked almost gaunt and slightly haunted, but Denver doubted very much that the police were starving him. His looks had more to do with years of hard drinking and an unhealthy lifestyle.

"Aren't you going to say hi to your old man?" Ken asked.

Denver shrugged. "I would if I had one." The man in front of him was borderline pathetic-looking. There was no way he was claiming him in any capacity.

Ken tipped his head to the side and gave him a glare. "Fine, if that's the way you want to play this."

Denver sighed and crossed his arms. "That's the thing, Ken. I don't want to play this at all. I'm not even sure why I'm here." He wasn't obligated to stay, and the longer he looked at this man's face, the more he realized he felt no connection to him whatsoever. He turned on his heel and started toward the door.

"Wait, don't go yet," Ken said, his voice losing some of the snark that seemed so instinctual.

Denver froze in place halfway to the door but didn't turn around. "Give me a reason not to leave."

"I want to talk to you about that night. About the accident."

That caught Denver's attention. He turned around and took a few steps back toward Ken. "The accident? Is that what we're calling it now? You mean the night you got drunk, climbed behind the wheel of your busted truck, and proceeded to smash it into the Hastings' car, killing two of the nicest people I've ever met?"

Ken flinched but otherwise didn't react to Denver's tirade. "I'm telling you it was an accident. I don't even remember getting behind the wheel."

Denver scoffed. "Yeah, you don't remember it because you were close to blackout drunk. You wouldn't have remembered anything at all."

Ken shook his head as if shaking off the accusation. He started wringing his hands. "No. That's not what happened. Well, I mean, it is what happened, but I don't know why. I know I'm a fuckup and a drunk. I get that's all you see in your old man. But I'm telling you I would never have gotten behind the wheel. Even while drunk, I know enough not to do that. I would have found someplace to sleep it off."

"Drunk people aren't exactly known for their smart decision-making skills. While it's a nice story that you think you wouldn't have gotten behind the wheel, the fact is you *did*." Denver leaned against the wall with his arms crossed and glared at Ken.

Ken yanked his hands back through the bars and started pacing in agitation again. "Someone must have made me do it. I swear to you I wouldn't have done it otherwise. Do you think I *want* to be in here?" Ken yelled as he gestured around at the spartan jail cell.

Denver swiped his hand to cut him off. He had heard enough. "Ken, you need to take ownership of your bad decisions. The fact is, you got drunk and killed people. No one made you do anything. Because of your choices, I lost the only man I ever considered a father." Denver stopped to catch his breath and fought back tears. "Russell Hastings was the best man I knew—he took me under his wing when I needed someone in my life. And you, the asshole who managed to knock up my mother, then run away, are the one who took him from me. We're through. Never contact me again. I hope you spend the rest of your life in prison."

Denver stormed down the hall and slammed his fist into the door to let them know he was ready to leave. Ken called after him, but Denver tuned him out.

Holden opened the door from the outside, and Denver couldn't get out of that hallway fast enough. "How did it go?" Holden asked.

"I need a drink." Denver wound his way through the desks and toward the front door of the police station.

"That well, huh? Well, I've got a few things I need to finish up here, but I can meet you at the Copper Lantern in thirty minutes."

"I'll be there."

Chapter Twenty-One

JENNA SPENT THE WHOLE week waiting for the other shoe to drop. For once, the research she was doing for work wasn't enough to hold her attention. She called Denver and arranged another trip out onto Cape Cod Bay, but as if sensing her agitation, the whales stayed away.

Being out on the water had helped soothe her rough edges slightly, but not nearly enough. She finally decided to call Sierra on Friday and invited her over for a girl's night. Maybe Sierra could help take her mind off things.

Honestly, it was lucky that Sierra hadn't seen the viral video yet, but Jenna was hoping it would stay that way. If Sierra didn't want to be around magic, Jenna wasn't about to drop her smack in the middle of a magical shitstorm.

The knock at her front door made Jenna jump like a startled rabbit. She'd been expecting her friend at any moment, so the noise shouldn't have been a surprise. It was a testament to how wound up she was.

Jenna yanked open the door. Instant relief flooded through her when she saw Sierra's smiling face on the other side. Sierra also happened to be holding a bottle of strawberry daiquiri mix in one hand and rum in the other. Even better.

"Thanks for coming," Jenna said as she stepped away from the door, giving Sierra room to pass.

"Always. It feels like you have some big news to share, which I'm totally here for. I dropped Lucas at my dad's house, so we've got all night." As Sierra crossed the threshold, she froze and immediately scanned the doorframe.

Jenna sighed. She knew exactly what had made Sierra stop.

"New wards on the house?" Sierra asked as she continued into the foyer.

Jenn shrugged lightly. "Times have changed. You can never be too careful."

Sierra made a noncommittal sound as she walked to the kitchen, but Jenna didn't immediately follow. Sierra mentioned big news. Did that mean she'd seen the zoo video? Jenna's stomach sank. She wasn't sure she wanted to face how badly she'd screwed up. She'd invited Sierra over to try to take her mind off the magical catastrophe, not dig into it.

Reluctantly, she followed her friend down the hall and grabbed a blender and some ice. "Big news?" she prompted.

Sierra looked up the drawer of measuring cups and rolled her eyes at Jenna. "The zoo. Duh."

Jenna froze. "You know?"

Sierra obviously didn't hear the tension in Jenna's voice, because she kept going. "Know? Obviously not. That's why I'm here talking to you. So was it, or wasn't it?"

Jenna was lost. "Was what what?" She leaned back against the counter and watched as Sierra grabbed two glasses out of the cabinet.

"The zoo. Was it a date or not?" Sierra measured ice, strawberry mix, and rum into the blender and started grinding.

Jenna sagged with relief. Sierra wasn't talking about magic or gorillas at all. She was talking about Denver. On that topic, Jenna had a lot to share. As soon as the blender cut off, she said, "Honestly, Saturday at the zoo is still undetermined, but he came over for dinner on Monday, and that was *definitely* a date."

Sierra did a little shimmy as she poured her frozen concoction into the glasses and handed one to Jenna. "Just dinner?" She wiggled her eyebrows.

"No, not just dinner." Jenna could feel herself blushing. She'd never been super comfortable describing the dirty details, so she gave Sierra the highlights of her and Denver's evening. "Oh, and he, uh … knows about me. About what I am." She paused to wait for Sierra's reaction.

"He knows you're a witch?" Sierra's voice rose in surprise.

Jenna nodded. "Yeah, it was a bit hard to hide after the other day." Jenna skipped over the incident at the zoo, but told Sierra about the incident outside of Cinder & Spice. That one already had to be relatively common knowledge around town, considering how many witnesses there were and how fast small-town gossip spread.

"How did he react? Did he freak out or anything?" Sierra asked as she took a large gulp of her frozen drink.

"He was shockingly reasonable about the whole thing. He told me being a witch made more sense than some of his other theories, like being an alien." She laughed.

Sierra snorted and almost choked on her drink. "Thank you for not being some sort of little gray humanoid."

"I do what I can." Jenna took a big gulp of her drink.

Hanging out with Sierra was exactly the sort of thing that Jenna had missed living across the country. She was extremely glad she'd chosen to move back to Rock Cove, even if it did come with the unfortunate side effect of having to deal with Brigit every once in a while. She needed to unwind like this more frequently, though with Lucas around, Sierra couldn't always get away for a whole night like this. That just made their time even more special.

A loud knock on the door interrupted their fits of giggles.

"Oooh, maybe it's Denver," Sierra said as she grabbed her daiquiri and sauntered down the hall to answer the door. "Maybe he'll want to join us."

Jenna hadn't made any plans with Denver, but that didn't mean he wouldn't randomly stop by. They hadn't seen each other since the boat ride a few days ago, and she wouldn't mind seeing him again.

"Jenna Hastings?" a stiff voice asked from the front porch. A voice that was most decidedly not Denver's. It was, however, one that was burned into her brain and had been since the day she'd turned sixteen. Mabel Hexley was standing outside her house.

"Just one moment, please, I'll go get her," Sierra said, closing the door in the woman's face. Sierra came speed walking back into the kitchen and almost slammed her glass onto the kitchen island. "What on earth is a member of the Circle of Thirteen doing on your porch?" Sierra hissed.

This was it. The moment Jenna had been dreading. "Um, I better go see what she wants," Jenna responded. She really hadn't wanted Sierra to be anywhere near this situation. Jenna had been keeping it from her for her own good. However, she also felt awful for lying to her best friend and couldn't keep doing it. "But if you google gorilla incident at the Boston Zoo, you'll probably have a good idea."

Sierra gasped quietly as she dove for the phone that she'd left sitting on the kitchen counter. Jenna ignored her and went to meet her fate. She took a deep breath to settle her nerves—like that was going to help—then opened the door.

Mabel Hexley looked exactly like Jenna remembered. She was tiny, probably no more than five foot two, and had short wavy gray hair. Her brown eyes narrowed and her nose turned up as she glanced Jenna over from head to toe, clearly unimpressed by what she saw. It had been fourteen years since she'd seen Mabel, but she didn't look a day older than ancient.

"Ms. Hastings, I presume?" Mabel asked in her clipped but indescribable accent. "May I come in?"

Jenna wasn't about to try to explain why the answer to that question was going to always be, "Hell no." She'd warded her house for a reason, and the reason was standing there staring at her impatiently. "It's a lovely night, I think we can talk on the porch," Jenna said as she gestured to the comfortable wicker furniture covered with thick cushions and flanked by a decorative but relaxing water feature.

Jenna stepped outside, leaving the safety of her wards and shutting the door on Sierra's "Holy crap!" She must have found the video. Oh well, Jenna would have to deal with her later. She had bigger problems right now.

As soon as she stepped outside her own protections, she could feel Mabel's magical aura. It was every bit as powerful as Jenna remembered. She'd been half hoping that her sixteen-year-old untrained witch's mind had made her into more than what she really was. It hadn't. The woman standing three feet from her was incredibly powerful and dangerous. Even if she looked like a doting grandma.

Mabel huffed quietly, then walked to one of the wicker chairs and perched delicately on the edge. Jenna followed a few steps behind and took the other chair.

"I presume you know why I'm here?" Mabel folded her hands primly on her lap.

Jenna wasn't about to offer up anything. No sense incriminating herself if she didn't have to. "Why don't you explain it to me?" She crossed her legs and leaned back against the soft blue cushions, the picture of someone without a care in the world. She was surprised her heart wasn't pounding out of her chest.

"As a full-fledged witch, you are aware that the Circle of Thirteen has a duty to protect the magical community in this country. It is our responsibility to keep the non-magical world from finding out about the magical one, and we do that through whatever means we need to. You also agreed to abide by the code, which means you also have an obligation to uphold that responsibility." Mabel lightly tapped her fingers on her knees like it was an instinctive gesture.

Jenna swallowed thickly but didn't respond.

Mabel continued her story as if she were almost bored with the proceedings. "A certain video has come to the attention of the Circle. A video that shows you using your magic in full view of dozens of people in broad daylight. I believe the video is up to more than a million views online. Congratulations on your spectacular failure at keeping our secret." Mabel glared at Jenna as if expecting her to immediately cave and confess everything.

"If you've seen the video, which I assume you have, then you can see that I was protecting those people. The gorilla would have escaped and could have injured or killed the zoo visitors. Even you have to admit that there are exceptions to the code that allow for the protection of life." Jenna had checked. And double-checked.

Mabel twitched her hand like she was brushing away a fly or an annoying comment she didn't want to hear. "Be that as it may, you were protecting them from a situation of your own making. The protection caveat doesn't come into effect if you were the one who put them in harm's way in the first place."

Jenna bolted upright. "What are you talking about? I didn't put anyone in harm's way. I was the one saving them by containing the gorilla long enough for the zookeepers to tranquilize it."

"The branch, Ms. Hastings. If you think the Circle didn't notice that the tree branch flew across the enclosure in an unnatural way, then you must think we're a bunch of simpletons. Only magic could have carried that branch far enough and hard enough to shatter the glass wall. As the only witch in the area at the time, who else could have made that happen?" Mabel brushed an invisible piece of lint off her perfectly pressed pantsuit.

It hadn't even occurred to Jenna to wonder about that. She'd realized, even at the time, that the branch had to have been moved by magic, but she'd been so wrapped up in her own situation and impending doom that she hadn't taken a moment to contemplate who had sent the branch flying. And more importantly, *why* they had sent it flying.

"That wasn't me," Jenna said. Even to her own ears it came out weak.

Mabel stood and tugged her suit coat back into place. There wasn't a wrinkle in sight. She gestured to a man standing beside a dark sedan who Jenna hadn't even noticed. The man approached the front steps. "I'm afraid you'll have to come with me for questioning. The Circle will hear your testimony and then convene to determine your fate."

"I said it wasn't me." Jenna's voice came out much stronger this time. She knew she was innocent, at least of causing the incident in the first place, and she wasn't about to let the Circle drag her off to God knows where. Who knew if she would ever come back from that. Her money was on no.

"That's for the Circle to determine, my dear," Mabel said as she came to stand in front of Jenna's chair. "Now up you get." She made a lifting motion with her hand, and Jenna felt a strong tug in her abdomen urging her to stand.

"No," Jenna said as she held her ground. She fought with every fiber of her being to ignore the urge to move and follow this woman. "I wasn't the witch that sent that branch flying and broke the enclosure. I'll admit to being the one to use my water magic to create the barrier and protect all those people, but I am not the person who caused the problem in the first place. I refuse to let you accuse me of something I didn't do."

Mabel's eyes narrowed. She made her hand gesture again, and Jenna felt an even stronger tug wrap around her insides and pull. She still resisted, staying exactly where she was.

The front door opened, and Sierra poked her head outside. "Jenna?" her voice was laced with fear.

"Sierra, get inside now!" Jenna hated yelling at her friend, but with Sierra out of practice with her magic, she was nowhere near ready to take on a witch of Mabel's power.

Sierra ducked back inside the house and behind the wards but didn't shut the door or go anywhere. Instead, she stayed and kept watch.

Fine. The more witnesses the better. The problem was that now Mabel had a second target, and if she couldn't get Jenna to cooperate, it wouldn't be that far-fetched to assume she'd target Sierra. Jenna couldn't let that happen.

Jenna stood from the chair, doing her best to loom over the shorter woman. She had about six inches on Mabel, and she intended to use every one of them.

Mabel smirked, as if she thought she'd won—convinced Jenna was only following her magical command. Mabel's smile faltered as Jenna took several steps sideways, putting herself between Mabel and Sierra.

"Derrek, the cuffs, please." Mabel gestured to her driver-slash-muscle, who tossed her a pair of metal cuffs far thicker and wider than any normal police handcuffs. The dull pewter color reflected the porch lights and Jenna could just barely make out runic inscriptions on them.

Nullifiers.

No way was Jenna going to allow anyone to slap her in cuffs that not only bound her hands but also nullified her magic. Time to take matters into her own hands.

"Derrek, why don't you head back to the car," Jenna said in an almost pleasant voice. Pleasant, but powerful. She'd learned a thing or two since her sixteenth birthday. Derrek shook his head as if he wasn't sure what was happening but did as she commanded, returning to the car and climbing behind the wheel.

Mabel watched the interaction with annoyance. The nullifiers clenched tightly in her wrinkled grip.

Jenna turned back to Mabel. "Did you think you were the only one that could order people around?" she asked sweetly.

"You're only making this worse for yourself. Put these on and come quietly and I'll forget about that little spell you worked on Derrek," Mabel said, holding out the cuffs.

As if Jenna was going to go anywhere near them. "I have a better idea. Why don't you get back in the car with Derrek and leave this place. And since apparently the Circle is now in the business of accusing innocent people, I'll stick around here and do your job. Someone needs to figure out who caused the situation at the zoo."

Sierra's gasp from behind Jenna meant Jenna had probably gone too far. It didn't matter. She was right, and the Circle was wrong. The truth would prove that eventually.

Mabel's heavily lipsticked smile turned cruel. "If you think I got to my current position by kowtowing to upstart witches like you, then you've clearly underestimated me." She swirled her hands in a circle, and the nullifiers began floating. They clicked open like they were just waiting for a set of wrists to wrap themselves around.

Right, Mabel was an earth witch. Manipulating metal was second nature to her.

With a flick of her finger, Mabel sent the cuffs flying in Jenna's direction.

Jenna ducked sideways while simultaneously using her magic to pull on the water that trickled out of the nearby decorative water fountain. The water responded instantly to her command and shot through the air, knocking the cuffs away before they could come anywhere near Jenna. She heard the metal skid across the wooden porch planks but didn't stop to see where they landed.

"This is my house. I dare you to try me," Jenna said, reaching deep within herself. She reached her mind through the porch and into the ground below. She could feel the centuries of magic her family had both taken from the land and fed back into it in return. The talisman around her neck radiated heat against her skin, a sign of her building power.

Mabel lifted her hands, but Jenna didn't give her enough time to get off a spell. Instead, she funneled the power she was channeling from the earth into the wards behind her. With a swell of rising power, the wards rapidly expanded outward and took Mabel with them. She slammed to the ground about twenty feet away.

Jenna held her breath. As much as she wanted Mabel gone—and Derrek too—she didn't want to kill either of them.

Mabel let out a pained groan, and Jenna was finally able to breathe again. She wasn't dead. Though Jenna might be as soon as the Circle found out what she'd done.

Derrek shot out of the car and raced to Mabel's side. He gave Jenna a terrified glare before hoisting Mabel into his arms and tucking her into the back seat.

"I'll let you know when I find the bad guy!" Jenna yelled after them as Derrek slammed his door and peeled out of the driveway.

Jenna felt a warm presence at her elbow and turned to give Sierra a tired glance.

"You've been holding out on me," Sierra said. It wasn't an accusation, but Jenna felt ashamed nonetheless.

"I thought I was protecting you." Jenna tilted her head to rest on Sierra's shoulder.

"Well, stop it. You're my best friend. If you're in this, then I'm in this. Mabel Hexley or not."

"Then I guess I should tell you that Denver and I also had sex under water," Jenna said with a small smile. "I promise to tell you everything, but I could really use that drink now."

Chapter Twenty-Two

D ENVER TURNED ONTO JENNA'S street and immediately swerved out of the way of a dark sedan flying down the road like the hounds of hell were chasing it. He only caught a quick look at the driver and the license plate in his headlights but sincerely hoped that, whoever they were, they wouldn't be heading downtown. Driving like that could kill someone, and Rock Cove was in the middle of tourist season.

He pulled into Jenna's driveway as she and Sierra were heading inside. They turned at the sound of his car. A tense look passed between them before Sierra continued inside and left Jenna standing in the same spot.

She looked exhausted.

He climbed out of the car and approached the house slowly, uncertain what he was walking into but positive it was more than just two friends hanging out on a warm summer night. About halfway between the driveway and the porch, an electric current raced across his skin. A wall of energy stood between him and the house, with Jenna on one side and him on the other. The closer he moved to it, the more the hair on his arms rose and the hair on top of his head stood on end. He stopped, uncertain if he should take another step. He was still getting used to this whole magic thing and had no idea if the energy was going to hurt him or not.

"It's okay. It won't hurt you," Jenna said.

Denver reached out his arm, slowly pushing against the current. With a zing of sensation that flew across his whole body, his arm came out the other side. With more confidence, Denver stepped forward through the barrier. The electricity raced across and around him, but didn't cause him any pain. With a shrug, he kept walking but stopped at the bottom of the steps leading to the porch.

"So that was new," he said as he ran his hands over his hair and arms, trying to discharge whatever static still clung to him.

"Yeah, sorry about that," Jenna said as she shifted closer, standing just out of reach at the top of the stairs.

"What was that all about?" He tucked his hands into his back pockets and rocked back on his heels.

"I added some wards to the house for extra protection. Just in case," she replied like he had any idea what she was talking about.

"Wards?"

She sent him a sheepish smile. "Right, I forget how new you are to all of this. A ward is a protective barrier. This one creates a dome around the entire house, and it won't let anyone through that intends to harm me."

If she had gone to those lengths, there was a reason. "That's a neat trick. You going to tell me why you felt the need to ward your house since the last time I was here?" He tentatively climbed the first few steps but stopped just out of arm's reach.

She chewed on her poor, abused lower lip. He had the sudden urge to capture her mouth to stop her from hurting herself. "It was protection against the Circle of Thirteen."

Right, the secret cabal of witches that somehow ruled the entire United States. The group Jenna was afraid of. An image of the black sedan speeding away from Jenna's road popped into Denver's mind. He was suddenly certain that he'd barely missed some sort of showdown. "And did it work?" he asked lightly.

Jenna slumped slightly as if all the energy was leaking out of her body. "A little too well, honestly. I almost killed one of the Circle members by flinging her across the yard."

Denver climbed the rest of the stairs and pulled Jenna into his arms. She leaned into his chest and wrapped her arms around his waist. "Whoever she was and whatever she did, I'm certain she deserved it." He didn't doubt it for a moment. Jenna was a lot of things, but murderer wasn't one of them. If she'd used her magic on the other witch, she'd had good reason.

The porch light glinted dully off a hunk of metal teetering on the edge of the porch as if deciding whether it wanted to hang on or fall into the bushes. "What's that?" he asked.

"What's what?" Jenna asked as she lifted her face to meet his gaze.

He nodded in the direction of the metal, which appeared to be some sort of circle—or make that two circles connected with a chain. "Are those handcuffs?" his voice rose in surprise. "What the hell happened?" He reluctantly released Jenna and crossed the porch to examine the handcuffs more closely.

"Don't touch them," Jenna almost shouted.

He paused, his fingers inches away from the pewter colored metal. "Why not?"

"They're nullifiers. Their sole purpose is to nullify any magical power the wearer may have."

"Then it's a good thing I don't have a lick of magic in me," Denver said as he reached out and grasped the cool metal. He stood and held the cuffs up to the porch light, trying to get a better look at them. They were thick bands, each cuff around two inches wide. Engraved across the metal were a series of carvings, but he had no idea what they meant. He took a step closer to Jenna, and she flinched and shied away from him. Another certainty slammed into him. "Did someone try to use these on you?" His voice was deadly quiet. He'd never been a violent man but suddenly wished he could strangle whoever had threatened Jenna with these.

"Um," Jenna hedged but didn't answer.

"Yes." Sierra's voice came from the open door. "One of the Circle members tried to arrest Jenna and take her in for questioning." She glanced at Jenna but shrugged at her disgruntled look. "You were taking too long. Plus you said he already knew about you being a witch."

Jenna sighed. "Denver, you might as well come inside. It's probably safe to assume that the danger has passed for the evening. They're going to have to retreat and figure out another option if they want to get to me." She gave the cuffs one last mistrustful look and then headed back inside.

Not sure what else to do with the magical shackles, Denver brought them inside and shut the door. He followed Jenna and Sierra into the kitchen, where a blender and the remnants of drinks spread across the counter. "Having a party?"

"It started out as a girl's night," Sierra said, "But that sort of went out the window when the bitch from the Circle showed up."

Denver set the nullifiers down on the kitchen table, and both women gave them a wide berth as they grabbed glasses and poured new drinks. "Should I leave you to it? I'd hate to interrupt." He probably should have texted before coming over, but he'd been too excited at the idea of seeing Jenna to realize that she might have plans.

Jenna grabbed an empty glass from the cabinet and set it next to the other two on the counter. "Might as well drink with us. Maybe we can puzzle through what happened at the zoo together. The Circle member accused me of being the one to break the glass partition in the first place, which I most certainly did not do. So who did?"

Sierra got the blender buzzing and poured a fresh round of drinks for everyone. They meandered into the living room where Jenna turned on the TV and pulled up the video on her phone, then cast it so it displayed on the large TV screen.

The three of them sat and watched in silence, the detail rendered in higher definition on the big screen. The evening had been lovely and warm, with only a gentle breeze in the air. But with the enhanced image, it was easier to see the moment the wind picked up. It was also more obvious that the wind had only gotten stronger in a very limited area—around the fake tree inside the gorilla enclosure. The leaves in the distance were still barely moving.

Denver watched again as the large limb snapped under the pressure of the heavy gusts and then flew through the air—picking up speed as it went—before smashing into the safety glass and shattering it. It should have been impossible. Even if the branch had broken naturally—which it clearly hadn't—it should have fallen straight to the ground. It had to be extremely heavy. No way would it have traveled more than a foot or two from the base of the tree.

On the screen, the gorilla got agitated and charged the hole in the glass, then Jenna used her magic to form the barrier made of water. Even now, a week later and knowing that no one had gotten injured, his heart pounded in his chest. He had no idea how Jenna had kept her cool enough to not only not freak out in the face of a charging gorilla but also react and instinctively protect others.

The three of them watched the video over and over again, and while they all agreed it wasn't natural, they couldn't figure out anything more than that.

"I mean, whoever caused this," Jenna waved her hand at the television where the video was paused on the moment the tree branch broke, "what would they even stand to gain? I mean, what's the point? Simply causing chaos?"

Denver had been asking himself the same question. They'd been discussing this for the better part of an hour—and were already on their third round of daiquiris—and he still couldn't figure it out. "How many witches or otherwise magical people are there in the Boston area?" He took a sip of his fruity drink. It wasn't his usual choice, but he had to admit that it wasn't bad—if a little sweet for his tastes.

Jenna and Sierra looked at one another and shrugged. "No idea. There's not a register or anything. Well, at least nothing we could access. The Circle would know, of course," Sierra said.

"But if you had to guess. A handful? Thousands?" Denver prompted.

"Maybe a few dozen?" Jenna said. "The community isn't really all that big."

A few dozen in all of Greater Boston? That was a very small community. He got up and paced, an idea forming in the back of his mind. "Okay, so hear me out. There are only a few dozen witches in the entire area. One of them decides to make trouble. They just so happened to pick the zoo as their target, and on a day when there were actually *fewer* visitors than there normally would be, because the zoo was closed for a private event."

Jenna's eyes narrowed, and she leaned forward on the edge of the couch. "Right. That sort of stretches the idea of a coincidence, doesn't it?" She glanced at Sierra, who was already nodding in agreement.

Energy coursed through Denver as his idea took shape. "That's weird enough, but then this witch just so happened to attend *this specific* event that Jenna was also attending. If you were this unknown magical person, what is the worst possible time you could cause chaos if that was, in fact, your end goal?"

"Right in front of another witch," Sierra excitedly answered his semi-hypothetical question. "Because the second witch might be able to stop you."

"Then why would the first witch do it if they knew another witch was in the area?" Denver asked.

"Maybe they didn't realize I was there?" Jenna suggested.

"Or maybe they did know, and that was why they did it. To expose you." Denver stopped pacing and stared at his rapt audience. He could already tell that Jenna's mind was going a mile a minute.

Now Jenna was the one pacing back and forth in agitation. "But to what end? What did that accomplish for them?"

Sierra's eyes shot back and forth between Denver, standing by the couch, and Jenna, who paced in front of the television. "It put you straight in the crosshairs of the Circle of Thirteen. It almost got you arrested. In fact, you might *still* get arrested at some point. You're getting blamed for the chaos they created. Maybe that was by design," Sierra said.

Jenna stopped pacing at stared at the two of them. "But who? And why?"

A sudden thought occurred to Denver. "We're forgetting something. This isn't the first time in recent memory that someone else has used magic in public around you." Denver flashed back to the fight outside of the café. Now that he knew that Jenna was a witch, it was more obvious that what had happened had been a very subtle fight between two people with magic powers. They hadn't done anything flashy or overtly magical, but he'd seen Jenna punch the air, and the other woman twenty feet away had stumbled backward. The other woman was probably also a witch. Something tickled the back of his mind. "Wait a minute. Play the video again."

Jenna's eyes narrowed. "Why? We've seen it a million times. There's nothing there."

Denver sat back down on the couch, but at the edge of the cushion as if the extra six inches it brought him closer to the TV screen would help him see better. "Humor me."

With a shrug, Jenna hit play on the video once more. This time, however, Denver wasn't looking at Jenna or at the gorilla enclosure. His eyes scanned the screen frantically. Suddenly he yelled, "Stop!"

Jenna paused the video just as the on-screen version of herself was conjuring the wall of water into place.

And there, just on the edge of the footage, was a partial view of a small woman with mousy-brown hair. She was turned away from the camera lens, so it was impossible to make out her face, but it might have been the same woman from the café. He stood up and tapped his finger over the woman on the screen. "Does she look familiar to you?" He didn't want to get too excited in case his brain was making connections that didn't really exist.

Jenna squinted at the screen, then gasped slightly. "Maybe? It could be the woman from outside Cinder & Spice. But who is she?"

They watched the video a few more times, but much to their annoyance, the woman never turned to look at the camera. There wasn't definitive proof that they were the same person, but once again, it stretched the definition of coincidence if it wasn't.

"Can you take this to the Circle?" Sierra asked. "They would know all the witches in the area. They would have to know who this woman is."

Jenna was already shaking her head. "The Circle would never believe me. There's not enough to go on. Not only can you not see her face, you can't even tell if she's doing magic or not. She's mostly off camera. The only reason we think this woman might be involved is because of the fight outside the café."

"Then let's focus on the incident at Cinder & Spice. Can you guys remember who else was around? We could ask around town to see if any of those folks recognized her." Sierra suggested.

A brilliant—though possibly illegal—idea occurred to Denver. "Wouldn't it be handy if we happened to be friends with a police officer who could ask around for security camera footage?"

Chapter Twenty-Three

J ENNA WIPED HER SWEATY palms on her jeans as subtly as possible as she approached Cinder & Spice the following day. She'd agreed to meet Denver and Holden for lunch, but that wasn't the problem. She didn't know Holden well, but he'd seemed nice enough in the few interactions she'd had with him.

No, her jumpiness was twofold. First, she was deliberately walking into Brigit's home turf, which was something she'd been studiously avoiding for a while now. Second, she was meeting with another ordinary with the express purpose of talking about her magic. It wasn't much comfort that Holden already knew. According to Denver, Holden had been the one who figured out what she and her friends were in the first place. She was already in trouble with the Circle. It's not like telling one more person could make her situation worse. The zoo incident pretty much took the cake at this point.

She paused outside the door and took a calming breath. She could do this. It would be fine.

Except when she pushed open the door, the first person she saw was Brigit. Her beautiful ex-friend stood next to a booth, laughing about something. Brigit reached out and touched the person's arm in a casual and familiar way. She took a slight step to the side, and it was only then that Jenna realized who she was talking to and touching so comfortably.

Denver.

Jenna stopped in her tracks just inside the door. Unfortunately, someone else had been following her, so when she stopped abruptly, the other woman ran smack into Jenna's back. "Oh, I'm so sorry," Jenna said, giving the woman an apologetic smile. The other woman waved her off and headed to the counter.

At the sound of Jenna's voice, both Brigit and Denver turned toward the door. Denver smiled, but Brigit's fingers wrapped more tightly around his biceps. Her eyes narrowed and she smirked. Jenna watched from afar as Brigit's finger traced up and down Denver's arm for a moment before she sent him a honey-sweet smile and headed back to her kitchen.

That probably didn't mean anything. It was perfectly normal for a woman to trace a male friend's biceps, *right*? Denver had given Jenna every impression that he was with her, not Brigit, so there was no reason to think otherwise. Swallowing down a slight ball of unease, she headed to the booth, where she only now realized Holden was also sitting.

"Jenna, nice to see you," Holden said as she sat down across from them.

"Likewise," she responded, running her hands over her jeans one more time under the table.

Before Jenna or Denver could bring up their request, Holden started talking. "I think I can guess why you've asked me here."

Confusion raced through her. Had Denver already mentioned the surveillance video to him? Jenna glanced at Denver, who looked just as puzzled as she felt. "You can?"

Holden was already nodding. "I've been waiting for you to come talk to me about your parents' death. I honestly expected you to ask me about it a while ago, but I didn't want to rush you. I know it can be hard to contemplate coming face-to-face with the person who caused the death of someone important to you, but I'm here to help you through that whenever you're ready."

Denver froze, a panicked look on his face. "That's not why we're here," he rushed out.

Jenna was glad he said something, because she wasn't sure she could have said anything if she'd wanted to. As much as she missed her parents, she hadn't given much thought to the drunk driver who had killed them. She'd had a sense of rage and impotent anger but hadn't directed that rage at anyone in particular. Just the world, which had taken her parents far before their time.

But now that Holden had brought it up, it seemed like a grave oversight on her part that she hadn't asked more questions about what had happened and who was responsible. Was she ready for those answers? It sounded like Holden had information for her, probably even the name of the person responsible. Would it make her feel better or worse to know who she had to blame for the incredible loss she'd suffered?

"There's no rush, Jenna," Denver said. He reached his arm across the table to brush her arm lightly. He sent a meaningful look in Holden's direction—who looked mildly chastised—then focused his attention back on her. "I know that was sort of sprung on you and not why we came here today."

Right, the witch. The Circle. The potential surveillance footage. Holden had planted a seed in her mind, and now she wanted to know more about her parents' death, but right now she had bigger issues at hand. Her parents died a few months ago. Information on the person responsible could wait a bit longer. Dealing with her impending arrest couldn't.

She nodded at Denver, and he removed his hand. She missed its warmth immediately. Jenna wasn't quite sure where to start, so she just dove right in. "Denver and I have been talking, and apparently you had some suspicions about me, Sierra, Aura, and Brigit. About what we are, or really what we could do."

Holden's eyebrows shot up, and he glanced from Jenna to Denver in surprise. "Wow, okay. Not what I thought we were here to talk about at all. But to answer your question, yes. I've always known there was something up with the four of you."

Before Jenna could continue, a server came to take their order. The waitstaff always seemed to have the worst timing—like they were doing it on purpose. They ordered their lunch, and when the server finally left, Jenna picked up the story once more. "Right, so I'm not sure what Denver has already told you, but the four of us are witches." She practically whispered the last word.

Holden barely flinched. "That tracks."

"You've seen the video from the zoo?" she asked. When Holden nodded, she continued. "The existence of that video got me into a bit of hot water. I'm not supposed to use my magic in public."

"Got you in trouble with who, the magical police?" Holden asked with a slight laugh.

Jenna didn't join him, and neither did Denver. "Sort of." She quickly explained about the Circle of Thirteen, glancing around the café several times to make sure she wasn't overheard.

Holden whistled. "I had no idea that was a thing."

Denver barked out a quick laugh. "I think that's sort of the idea."

Holden nodded in agreement. "Fair point. But now you're here talking to me. So how do you think I can help? I'm not sure how good my badge is going to be against a witch."

Denver picked up the story and explained the altercation with the other witch outside Cinder & Spice.

"I hadn't heard about that one, but I guess I'm not surprised. If no one called the police station, then we wouldn't know what went down. I'm sorry if that's not what you wanted to hear."

Jenna looked at Denver in desperation. She knew what they were asking Holden to do wasn't exactly on the up-and-up. He had no reason to do it for her, but maybe if Denver asked, he'd at least consider it.

Denver didn't disappoint. "Do you think that any of the local businesses in the area would have security camera footage that might have caught the incident?"

"It's possible. I don't need a warrant if a business is willing to hand it over," Holden said. As soon as the statement was out of his mouth, the door to the kitchen swung open, and Brigit walked out, balancing a tray full of food.

The three of them watched as Brigit approached their table.

Jenna's stomach sank. If her future was relying on Brigit's kindness and sense of duty to her friends, then Jenna was screwed. She couldn't exactly tell Holden that though, especially not with Brigit standing right beside her.

"A Reuben sandwich for Denver, a turkey club for our detective in the corner, which leaves the chef's salad for the Rock Cove princess," Brigit said as she placed their food in front of them. Honestly, she'd called Jenna worse, even if it was a dig at her family's lengthy lineage and history of magic.

Brigit lingered, resting her hand on Denver's shoulder and giving Jenna a pointed look. Denver glanced between the two of them, no doubt sensing the tension, but he clearly didn't want to wade into the middle of their relationship.

Holden had no such hesitation. Either he couldn't sense the tension, or he ignored it, because he turned on a megawatt smile and gave all his attention to Brigit. "I've been hearing some stories that there was a bit of a dustup outside your shop a week or two ago." He picked up a french fry and munched on it.

Brigit's eyes narrowed, and she glanced at Denver and Jenna quickly before focusing back on Holden. It was clear she didn't know what he wanted from her. She hadn't called the incident in to the police station, but was that going to get her in trouble? Jenna could practically see her weighing her options before Brigit responded carefully. "Someone may have mentioned it to me in passing. I didn't see what happened myself."

Holden smiled again, and it struck Jenna exactly how attractive he was. Not as gorgeous as Denver, obviously, but when Holden batted his lashes, his brown eyes were unfairly enticing. "And if an interested party wanted to find out more about what happened, any chance your cameras out front would have caught that disagreement?"

Brigit cocked her head and rested her fist on her hip. "It's possible. Are you asking in an official capacity?"

Holden shrugged good-naturedly. "Just a concerned citizen who happens to care about the safety of our local residents." He turned his smile on Brigit.

She eyed him with suspicion. "Sure. I always make it a point to help Rock Cove's finest."

Jenna wanted to scoff at Brigit's attempt to play nice—especially since Jenna knew that she had a history of stabbing people in the back—but held it in. Brigit was willing to do what they needed. Jenna needed to be thankful for that.

The three of them tucked into their lunch, happily chatting about things that had nothing to do with magic. As they finished up, the door to the kitchen opened once more, and Brigit came out. She walked to their table and dropped two things on the glossy wooden surface. The lunch bill and a flash drive.

Another huge smile spread across Holden's face. "Much appreciated."

Brigit nodded at Denver and Holden. "You're welcome." She glared at Jenna, then strode away like there was a fire in the kitchen that needed her immediate attention.

"Now what?" Jenna asked as she picked up the small storage device.

"Leave it to me," Holden said with his hand out.

Jenna reluctantly placed the drive in his hands, knowing that her entire future could be riding on the contents of that small device.

Chapter Twenty-Four

D ENVER KNEW THE ROLES—HOLDEN was the cop, and he was just a boat captain. But there was no way he was placing Jenna's future entirely in someone else's hands. Not even Holden's. Denver needed to be part of this, even if they had never officially defined their relationship. He wanted her, and she obviously wanted him. That was enough for now.

Denver paid the bill for lunch despite Jenna and Holden's protests. Too bad. Holden had done them a huge favor, and Jenna needed to be spoiled. She'd had a rough few months with the death of her parents, and now facing arrest by the Circle. The least he could do for her was pick up the tab for lunch.

As soon as they were done eating, and after one more reluctant glance at the USB drive, Jenna headed home. It was clear that Holden was expecting Denver to follow suit, but there was no way. He needed to know what the surveillance footage showed. He was going wherever that flash drive went.

Holden headed out of the café, and Denver followed hot on his heels. Holden glanced in his direction and rolled his eyes. "Can I help you?" he asked sarcastically.

"Nope, but I think I might be able to help you," Denver replied. "I know exactly what we're looking for."

Holden crossed his arms and raised his eyebrows. "Do you honestly think it will be all that difficult to find a fight between two witches on a few hours' worth of video footage? Especially when I know when it happened and who was involved?"

Well, when he put it that way, no. But he couldn't let Holden cut him out of this. "Maybe not, but I can point out the woman we suspect in the zoo footage. She wasn't obvious the first dozen times we watched it." It was a stretch, Denver had to admit.

Luckily, Holden either bought it or caved to their friendship. "Fine, come on. I can do this easier back at the station."

Denver followed Holden to the police station, pulling his battered old truck into the lot next to Holden's much nicer black SUV. Holden wasn't on duty, but no one blinked an eye when they entered the building and made their way to his desk.

Holden plugged the USB drive into his laptop and opened the footage that Brigit had copied for them. The footage covered the entire day, so Holden dragged the time-stamped slider bar to around lunchtime.

"There," Denver said as he saw himself come on camera and tie Rosie to the fence before going inside. Holden skipped carefully through the part when Jenna met Rosie and they sat down for lunch. "This is it."

Holden hit play as Jenna was getting up from the table to say goodbye. They watched her bend down and give Rosie scritches, then turn to leave. Just as she was about to head out, a pair of legs showed up at the top of the screen. The rest of the woman's body was frustratingly just out of frame.

The video version of Jenna started making calculated hand gestures, ones Denver now associated with her casting magic. "Damn it. You can't see the other woman's face." Denver growled in frustration.

"Chill out. It's not over yet," Holden said, eyes glued to his laptop screen.

The fight had been short, and Denver watched in increasing desperation as Jenna cast her last spell. She punched out with her arm, and the other woman stumbled sideways just far enough that she was fully visible to the camera for a split second. Holden punched the pause button and zoomed in on the woman's face. "Gotcha."

Relief flooded through Denver all the way to his fingertips. Finally, they had proof that there was another witch in the area—not Jenna, Sierra, Aura, or Brigit—and they even knew what she looked like.

"Now what?" Holden asked as he hit print on his laptop, and the laser printer next to his desk started whirring. "We know what this other witch"—he glanced around quickly then corrected himself—"woman looks like. I might even be able to track her down through facial recognition, though that's a long shot. What do we do with that information? I somehow doubt it's a good idea for you or me to go after her on our own. At least not without Jenna's help. Or even one of the others."

Denver was already shaking his head. "I think Jenna should stay as far away as possible. We're trying to prove that she's innocent in all of this, and that this woman is to blame." He gestured to the picture as he grabbed it off the printer. "I don't want to confuse the matter by having Jenna go after her and make herself look even more guilty."

Holden crossed his arms and leaned back in his chair, making it creak slightly. "Then what do you suggest, oh wise one? It's not like we have any other leads."

"Maybe she's been elsewhere around town? I mean, if she broke into Jenna's house and she's been around Cinder & Spice, maybe there's a chance she's been to other shops that might have cameras?" It was a long shot, and the look Holden gave him showed how likely they were to find that needle in the haystack. "Or maybe one of the other officers noticed her?"

Holden rolled his eyes. "The police in this town have better things to do than follow one unknown woman around town. You do realize we're in the middle of tourist season, right? This one woman wouldn't stand out in the crowds of people looking for the *real New England experience*." Holden used air quotes to emphasize his point.

"I know it's not likely, but maybe just try anyway?" Denver realized he was grasping at straws, and it was a sign of their long-standing friendship that Holden didn't immediately laugh in his face.

"You owe me for this," Holden whispered under his breath to Denver. "Hey Marty," he called over his shoulder at the middle-aged and slightly pudgy man sitting at the desk next to his. He had the look of someone who used to be in shape, but the desk life caught up to him.

Marty pulled his gaze off whatever he'd been staring at on his monitor. "What's up, Kay?" he asked.

Holden rolled his chair over to the other man's desk. "Just a quick question. Have you ever seen this woman around town before?" Holden handed him the printed photo.

Marty grabbed the image and held it closer to his face. Instead of the immediate rejection Denver was prepared for, he was surprised when Marty said, "Yeah, sure. She's been hanging around town for a few weeks now. I've seen her all over. She isn't exactly hard on the eyes, if you catch my drift."

Holden sat up straighter and gave Denver an incredulous look. "You're telling me that this woman," he tapped the page, "has been hanging around Rock Cove for at least a few weeks?"

Marty took one more look at the image on the page before handing it back to Holden. "Yeah, why? She do something wrong?"

Holden didn't bother answering the question but countered with another one of his own. "Anywhere in particular you've seen her hanging out? Anything she seems to be interested in?"

Marty sat back in his chair and grabbed his mug of coffee, taking a slow sip. He appeared to be considering his answer carefully. "I mean, I've seen her from one end of town to the other, but if I had to pick one spot, I'd say I've seen her the most near the flower shop."

"The Petal Patch?" Denver could no longer stay silent. This witch from out of town was hanging around Sierra's shop in addition to Cinder & Spice? That couldn't be good.

"Yeah, that's the one. Well, obviously. It's the only flower shop in town." Marty took another sip of coffee before setting his mug down. "She do something I need to be aware of?" His mustache started twitching.

Holden shook his head. "She's just a person of interest I wouldn't mind having a conversation with, that's all. No need to go after her or anything, but would you mind giving me a call if you happen to see her again?"

"Sure thing, Kay. Whatever you need."

"Thanks, man." Holden rolled his chair back to his own desk, and Marty went back to ignoring them.

"You up for another walk?" Denver asked.

Holden nodded once. "I could use some air." He yanked the USB drive out of his laptop, tucked it in his pocket, and stood.

Denver followed his friend out of the station but didn't say a word until they were well out of earshot. "This can't be a coincidence. This woman is spotted outside of Sierra's flower shop and Brigit's café and gets into a fight with Jenna? The only one she's missing is Aura, and that doesn't mean she hasn't tried going after her too."

Sierra's shop was only a few blocks away, so it didn't take them long to get there. Rock Cove wasn't a big city, so everything was relatively close together.

The flowering vines growing up the exterior of the building always seemed so cheerful to him. He'd vaguely wondered in passing how she'd managed to get them to be as lush and full as they were, but he'd never thought too deeply about it. Now that he knew she was also an earth witch, her shop made a lot more sense.

The old-fashioned bell that hung from the door tinkled merrily as they entered the bright pink building. The inside of the Petal Patch was just as riotously in bloom as the outside, and the smell was amazing. Just this side of overwhelming, but pleasant and relaxing at the same time.

At the sound of the bell, Sierra came bustling through the curtain that separated the back of her shop from the front. Her face broke into a smile when she recognized them. "What can I do for you fine gentleman today?" she asked with a wink.

Holden opened his mouth to speak—probably to pull his *I'm just a friendly cop asking questions* routine—but Denver cut him off. "Sierra, we've got some updates. You remember that woman we were talking about from the zoo and the café? Well, she's been hanging around your shop too."

The smile immediately slid off Sierra's face. "Oh?"

Holden gave Denver a glare, but he didn't care. "She's already in the loop. No reason to hide anything from her," Denver said.

Holden rolled his eyes but didn't contradict him. "We were wondering if you happened to have any surveillance footage showing the outside street view of your store. If we get lucky, we might catch a glimpse of her and see what she's been up to."

Sierra was already nodding. "Of course. Whatever you need." She led them into the rear of her shop and showed them to her small office. She pulled up the security camera feeds and said, "Knock yourselves out. If this woman is targeting Jenna, then I want her caught."

Denver opened his mouth to tell Sierra that the other witch might be after her, too, but Holden subtly shook his head. Right. Maybe it was better to hold that information back until they had proof. No reason to freak her out unnecessarily.

Holden sat in her desk chair and immediately began searching through the footage. Since Sierra's shop sat on a corner, she had several cameras pointing in different directions. That was great from a coverage perspective, but bad in the sense that it was twice as much footage to go through.

"You might as well pull up another chair. I have a feeling we're going to be at this for a while," Holden said.

He wasn't wrong. Even though Marty had said that he'd seen the other witch outside of Sierra's shop several times, they had no idea what days or times that might have been. "Maybe we should try the days leading up to the fight outside Cinder and Spice? Maybe this chick was casing both places, and Jenna just happened to show up when she was there?" It was a stretch, but since they had nothing else to go on, Holden shrugged and pulled up the day before the fight. They watched the footage on fast forward, the people scurrying around like rats. It took them the better part of an hour to get through that day's footage.

Nothing.

Undaunted, Holden pulled up the prior day and did the same thing.

Denver's eyes were starting to dry out and blur, but he couldn't afford to take his gaze away from the monitors. He was worried that if he blinked, he would miss something.

Sierra came to check on them and offered them bottles of water and a bag of cookies she had stashed in her desk. She asked how it was going, but Holden's wordless grunt told her everything she needed to know. The bell on her front door tinkled again, and she left them to see to her customer.

It was halfway through the third day's footage that Denver said, "Stop. Right there." Holden hit pause, and Denver tapped the screen. The woman they were looking for had just wandered into the frame. "Play it from there at regular speed." The woman was eating an ice cream cone and looking like she was enjoying a day out on the town as a tourist, glancing in each of the shop windows. She meandered over to a bench across the street from the Petal Patch and sat down. She glanced around like she was people watching, but her eyes kept coming back to the bright pink building across the street. She wasn't there by accident. She was watching for something.

When it seemed she was in it for the long haul, Holden hit fast forward again. The woman stayed exactly where she was for almost an hour. She eventually pulled out a book and pretended to read, but it was clear that she spent more time staring at the shop than the pages in front of her.

Eventually, a black car pulled up in front of her and stopped. The woman casually stretched and tucked her book into her purse before crossing to the car and getting in the passenger's seat.

"Can you get a plate number or anything on that car?" Denver asked. The camera wasn't at the right angle, though, so he wasn't expecting anything.

Holden gave him a glare. "Why didn't I think of that? Oh wait, I did. You can't see it."

"Right, sorry." The car pulled away from the curb and then stopped at the stop sign at the corner before turning onto the next street. They followed the car's progress as it went right in front of the second camera. "Holy shit." Denver reached over and smashed the button down to pause the footage, earning him a glare from Holden. "I recognize the guy behind the wheel."

Chapter Twenty-Five

THE FOLLOWING DAY WAS so nice that Jenna decided to take her laptop to the park and work while getting some fresh air and sunshine. The park wasn't far from downtown, and it was just high enough on a hill that it sat above the town's buildings and got a fresh breeze off the water. She parked her car in the small lot and then hiked the short distance to the picnic tables before spreading out and diving into her research.

"Well, if it isn't princess troublemaker," a snide voice jolted Jenna out of her work a short time later. She'd been so focused on the numbers and spreadsheets in front of her that she hadn't felt or heard Brigit come up behind her.

Jenna closed her eyes and took a moment to gather her thoughts. She thought about packing up her stuff and heading home but decided against it. She wasn't letting Brigit chase her out of a public park. Jenna wasn't ceding any more ground to her. She opened her eyes and slowly turned on the bench to confront Brigit.

Brigit wasn't alone. Flanking her were Aura and Roderick.

Perfect. Three of the people she least wanted to see in the world.

"Troublemaker?" Roderick asked, one eyebrow going up. "I seem to have missed something. What on earth could our sweet Jenna have done to get herself into trouble?"

Jenna strained to hear any sarcasm in his voice, but his surprise seemed genuine. "It's nothing." Jenna wasn't about to tell her former mentor about the fight outside the café, and she *definitely* wasn't going to mention the incident at the zoo or that she attacked Mabel.

Unfortunately, Brigit had no such reluctance. "The queen bee here had a bit of a run-in with another witch outside my shop. Right out in public and everything." Aura looked a bit surprised by the news, which meant it was possible that Brigit hadn't immediately run to tell her everything, but Brigit's sickeningly sweet smile was all for show. The hint of mean in her eyes convinced Jenna that she was happy to be ratting Jenna out to Roderick.

Roderick crossed his well-muscled arms and looked down his nose at Jenna. "Really? You know that's against the code. What if the Circle finds out?"

Jenna tried to school her features and not react. "I didn't exactly have a choice since she attacked me, not the other way around, but it ended before anyone figured out what was going on. There's no reason for the Circle to find out about it." Unless someone who had it out for Jenna told them, which was a new, terrifying prospect. Would Brigit go that far with her hatred?

Roderick turned to Brigit and sent her a proud smile. "I'm glad you didn't involve yourself in that mess. I wouldn't want you to draw any unwanted attention to yourself or your abilities."

Wow. Point taken, Roderick. He cared if Brigit was exposed to the Circle, but it barely bothered him to learn that Jenna might now be in their crosshairs. *Noted.*

"Jenna is doing that enough for all of us. She's already involved two ordinaries in witch business." Brigit sneered.

"Jenna! I know you've disregarded some of my teachings in the past, but this is unacceptable," Roderick barked at her.

Jenna dropped her gaze. No matter how much distance, physical or metaphorical, she put between herself and Roderick, it still stung when he chastised her.

"Who was the other witch?" Aura asked, drawing everyone's attention.

Jenna glanced in Aura's direction. Finally, a good question. "I don't know. I didn't recognize her," Jenna said.

"That's how the ordinaries got involved." Brigit rolled her eyes. "Jenna enlisted Holden—our resident detective—to help figure it out. I turned over the surveillance footage from outside my store in case it was useful." Brigit practically preened as she waited for Roderick's stamp of approval.

He didn't oblige. "You have security cameras that caught the fight with the second witch?" His eyes narrowed. "And you turned that footage over to a member of the non-magical community?"

Jenna enjoyed the wounded look on Brigit's face a little too much. It was definitely atypical for Roderick to rebuke Brigit and her pinched expression reflected that.

"Only sort of. You can barely see the woman. She didn't really come in range of the cameras," Brigit hastily answered, but it didn't seem to lessen Roderick's irritation.

Jenna had wondered if Brigit had seen the footage, and the answer was clearly yes. Jenna had been dying to find out what the video showed and was disappointed to learn it wasn't useful.

"You should have come straight to me with this. Both of you," Roderick said, sending a pointed glance Jenna's direction. "I know I'm no longer officially your mentor, but I can still help you. It's a shame that we can't identify her. If we have a rogue witch running around, someone should get her under control. We don't want her to risk exposing the magical community to the rest of the world. I can speak to the Circle and fill them in on the situation. Maybe they can locate her."

"Well, maybe Holden and Denver can figure out something from the footage, even if it's not the identity of the witch," Jenna said.

"Oh, right. Denver. Not sure why he's helping with the investigation. I adore the man, but I'm not sure how his skill set really lends itself to police issues. Or magic, for that matter. Not that he's not a doll to help you out. In fact, I was just telling him that first thing this morning. Isn't he such a sweetie?"

Jenna's pulse started pounding in her ears. "You saw Denver first thing this morning?" Jenna had texted Denver last night and asked if he wanted to come over, but he'd said he was busy with something and couldn't come by. Now she had to wonder what—or who—he'd been busy with.

Brigit's smile was predatory. "Oh yeah. The sun rises so early this time of year." Aura sent Brigit a narrow-eyed look but didn't say anything.

Jenna's stomach sank. The sun rose around 5 a.m. If Brigit had seen Denver at sunrise, how many possible explanations could there be? Denver had given every indication that he was interested in Jenna, but they'd never had any sort of talk about their relationship status. They'd never agreed to be exclusive, nor had they ever talked about labels.

They'd only been together romantically for a week or so. Was it possible that Denver was also seeing Brigit? Jenna knew that Brigit wasn't opposed. They'd slept together in high school after all. Was it possible that Brigit and Denver had been seeing each other—or at least sleeping together—for more than a decade? Were they in a real relationship, and Denver was cheating on Brigit? Or was it more of a friends-with-benefits situation?

"You're seeing this Denver person?" Roderick asked with interest. "And he's involved in looking for the rogue witch?" He seemed to be chewing on that information.

Jenna hoped that Brigit hadn't just painted a target on Denver's back. Lying jerk or not. Not that he'd ever actually *lied* to her. Jenna had never even asked him if he was seeing someone else. So technically, it wasn't a lie if he was.

"A lady doesn't kiss and tell." Brigit winked at Jenna.

Jenna wanted to be sick. She slammed the lid of her laptop closed harder than she probably should have. She shoved it in her bag and flung the strap over her shoulder. She took a step closer to Brigit, her power crackling under her skin, ready to be released at the slightest command.

A quick jolt of fear crossed Brigit's face before it was quickly masked.

"I have no idea what went wrong between us or what you think I did to you, but I hope you enjoy being a bitch, Brigit. You're really good at it." Jenna stalked toward her car. She thought she heard Aura calling her name, but Jenna didn't stick around long enough to confirm. She needed to get out of there. Now.

Jenna did what she always did when she and Brigit got into a fight. She sought out Sierra. She knew it wasn't really fair to always put Sierra in the middle of whatever was going on with her and Brigit, but she didn't have anyone else to talk to about it. Jenna briefly thought about finding

Denver and trying to talk to him about it, but since he was part of the source of her current angst, she couldn't bring herself to do that.

She was torn about what Brigit had said. Denver had never told Jenna that he wanted exclusivity. Without having had that conversation, it wasn't fair of her to be mad if he was also dating someone else. Just because Jenna couldn't comprehend the idea of seeing more than one person at a time didn't mean that other people agreed with her.

But why did it have to be Brigit of all people? Objectively, she was extremely attractive. That was obvious to anyone who could see her, even if they weren't attracted to women. Cinder & Spice appeared to be doing brisk business anytime Jenna happened to step inside, so Brigit was also a savvy businesswoman and a good cook. It was really her personality that was the issue. Not that she was as much of a bitch to anyone else as she was to Jenna.

Jenna was parked outside the Petal Patch before she'd even registered driving there. She threw the car into park and climbed out. The bell over the door jangled cheerfully, belying Jenna's sour mood. The usual cloud of sweet floral scents greeted her. It was often enough to lift Jenna's mood, but not today.

Sierra had just finished ringing up a customer buying an enormous bouquet of sunflowers, tulips, daisies, and snapdragons that practically buried the woman as she attempted to carry it out of the shop. Jenna held the door open for her, then tugged it closed behind her.

"Good morning, Jenna. I'm happy you stopped by, but shouldn't you be working?" Sierra asked as she brushed a few stray flower petals off her counter and into a compost bin.

She absolutely should be working, and it annoyed Jenna that she'd let Brigit get so far under her skin that she needed to vent before she could go back to concentrating on her job. She was reluctant to dump her crap in Sierra's lap. She hesitated long enough that Sierra started talking again.

"Did you find anything on the footage from the café?" Sierra grabbed a bunch of loose flowers from her counter and started trimming the ends of the stems and gathering them together into a beautiful bouquet.

Thankful for the conversation starter, Jenna wandered around the shop as she watched Sierra work. "No. Well, I don't know. I haven't seen it."

Which was another thing that bothered her. This was her life, and *she* had been the one to get into the fight with the other witch. If anyone deserved to see that footage, it was her. But instead, Holden had taken it back to the police station with him, and if she wasn't mistaken, she'd seen Denver heading in that direction with him. Holden and Denver knew what was on the footage, but Jenna didn't? She was the powerful witch, and it was her future on the line. She should be kept in the loop.

Jenna filled Sierra in on what had happened at the café and the surveillance footage. "Even Brigit has seen it, and I haven't." She hadn't meant for her comment to sound quite as bitter as it had, but too late now.

Sierra paused what she was doing, a pink rose clutched in her hand. "How do you know that Brigit has seen it? And what's the big deal if she has? It is her security camera after all. Holden and Denver came to my shop and looked at my security camera footage too. Are you going to be mad at me for trying to help you too?" Sierra cocked her eyebrow and pinned Jenna in place with what could only be described as a mom glare.

Jenna knew that she was being irrational. Brigit had every right to watch her own security camera footage. It was her attitude that got to Jenna. "I just ran into her, Aura, and Roderick in the park. She took the opportunity to taunt me again. It makes me feel like we're eighteen all over again. I have no idea what she has against me. Honestly, one day we were best of friends, and the next she was treating me like I was the gum on the bottom of her shoe."

Sierra's face pinched, and she went back to carefully building her bouquet. "I don't know what happened between you either. She's still the same person she always was to me. Though I recognize that she treats you differently and not a little unfairly." Sierra finished her floral arrangement, tied a ribbon around it, and set it in a vase before starting on the next one.

"She also threw me under the bus with Roderick. What was I supposed to do?" As much as she tried to keep her tone even, even Jenna could hear the bitter twist of her words when she mentioned Roderick's name.

"Ah, now I get it," Sierra said as she added a daffodil to her current mixture. "You've never really liked Roderick. Even back when he was training us."

Jenna crossed her arms and leaned against the glass-fronted refrigerator where Sierra kept her ready-made bouquets. She wanted to deny what Sierra was saying, but she couldn't. It was well known among the four of them that Jenna didn't like Roderick and only worked with him because she had to. The Circle had assigned him as their mentor. It wasn't like there was a way to request that the Circle change their collective minds about it. "You can't tell me that after the Trials you had a *good* experience with Roderick. Plus, he's always favored Brigit and Aura over the two of us."

Sierra finished another bouquet, placed it in a vase, and took both arrangements to the fridge, where Jenna was standing. Jenna grabbed the door for her, and Sierra placed them carefully inside. "I don't think that's true. Roderick was just doing his job as our mentor. It was his responsibility to give each of us what we needed to grow as witches. That's what he did for each of us, including the two of us."

"Oh yeah?" Jenna told Sierra what he'd said in the park. "He fawned all over Brigit for not getting her pretty hands dirty when the other witch attacked me and Denver."

Sierra closed the fridge door and looked Jenna straight in the eye. "I think your relationship with Brigit is clouding your judgment. You could have gotten in trouble. In fact, you *did* get in trouble. The Circle is after you now, Jenna. This is serious."

Jenna threw her hands up in exasperation. "I *know* it's serious. I was the one Mabel tried to arrest, remember? I'm very aware of how serious this situation is. You're all making it sound like I had a choice in the matter. I didn't. That bitch attacked me. I was just defending myself and Denver."

"I'm sure Roderick is just looking out for you. He wouldn't want anything bad to happen to you or any of us."

Jenna had had it. "I'm sure that's it." She was sure of no such thing. Jenna needed to get out of there before she said or did something she couldn't take back. "I'll talk to you later." She stalked out of the flower shop.

Chapter Twenty-Six

I DENTIFYING THE WITCH WHO had attacked Jenna—or rather identifying one of her known associates—was only sort of helpful. The real question was what Denver and Holden were supposed to do with that information.

Denver had spent the night restlessly tossing and turning trying to come up with ideas. He eventually gave up around 5 a.m. and grabbed a cup of coffee and some breakfast at Cinder & Spice. He didn't need to be out on the water, so he took advantage of it to do a little relaxing and thinking.

Holden wouldn't be at work until a much more reasonable hour in the day, so Denver killed the time alternating between reading a spy novel and thinking about Jenna. It hadn't been all that long since they'd gotten together, but he was ready for more. He didn't want to push her, though, since she'd been so reluctant to get involved with him in the first place. Best to take it slow and steady and let her come to him when she was ready for more.

No matter how much he wanted her, he wanted to protect her more. She was so sweet, and so smart, and a badass witch to boot. What wasn't to love? Well, not *love*, just you know, love. It was far too soon to be thinking about love with a capital *L*.

Or was it?

He enjoyed spending time with her. Her quiet but secretly super powerful persona tied him in knots. Not to mention that she was stunning and they had amazing physical chemistry.

He wondered what her parents would have thought about him dating their daughter. He'd like to think they would have been okay with it. Russ and Brooke had always been supportive of him and had practically treated him like their own son. Hopefully, that would have extended to them being on board with him dating their daughter. It was too bad they weren't around to ask. He would have nervously—but happily—talked to her father and asked his thoughts. Russ's opinions meant a lot to him. Denver didn't want to think about what he would have done if Russ hadn't been supportive of him dating Jenna. Part of him thought he would have backed off out of respect for the man. The rest of him thought he would have done it anyway because Jenna was that amazing.

Eight o'clock finally rolled around, and Holden opened the door right on schedule. Denver took the opportunity to watch his friend without him realizing it. Holden glanced behind the counter hopefully, and his face fell just slightly presumably because a certain redhead wasn't the one behind the register. Nevertheless, he gave the cashier a smile and ordered coffee and a chocolate chip muffin to go.

Denver had no idea what was preventing Holden from pursuing Brigit. It was obvious to everyone except Brigit that he was mooning after her and desperate to be with her. For some reason, he held himself back. Holden had never been willing to explain why that was, so Denver just assumed he had his own reasons for it. That didn't stop him from trying to nudge his friend into action anyway.

"You know," Denver said casually, amused when Holden practically jumped sideways at the sound of his voice. "If you picked up the phone and called her—or hell, even texted her—she might actually be around when you stop by." Denver casually sipped his third cup of coffee of the morning. He probably should have stopped at two, given how much he was twitching from all the caffeine, but too late now.

Holden regained his composure and sent a haughty look Denver's direction. "I don't know what you're talking about." The barista called Holden's name, and he stepped up to the counter to grab his drink and muffin.

Denver smirked. "Sure, you don't."

Holden headed for the door, and Denver followed right behind him. "Do you have a reason for jump scaring me this morning? Or was that in and of itself the reason you're here following me around like a puppy?" He stopped next to the door of his black SUV and set his coffee cup on the roof of the vehicle just long enough to open the door.

"Oh, right. I think I have a lead." In all his enjoyment of messing with Holden, Denver had forgotten the reason he was stalking him in the first place.

"I thought we already identified the guy behind the wheel. Did you figure something out about the woman?" Holden leaned inside his car long enough to put his coffee and muffin in his cupholder, then turned to face Denver.

"No, sadly. Still no idea who she is. But I may have something better. When we talked yesterday, we had no idea what to do with the information we had, right? The two of us shouldn't be going up against witches on our own. We also agreed Jenna shouldn't be the one to go after them either."

Holden nodded his head reluctantly. He hadn't been fully onboard with Denver's beliefs that they should sit tight. Holden wanted to believe that his badge could stop bad guys in their tracks, which sadly wasn't the case.

Denver smirked. "I think I know where we can find another witch."

That piqued Holden's interest. "Get in." He gestured to the passenger's side of his SUV. They both climbed in, and after a quick stop at the police station, they headed back out. They drove out of Rock Cove and toward Boston. Twenty minutes later, he stopped at a large Victorian house in one of Boston's many suburbs. "This place?" Holden asked skeptically.

Denver had to admit that the house-turned-law-firm was not where he'd expect to find a powerful witch, but he was confident in what he had seen. This had to be it. He shrugged and climbed out of the car.

The front door of the converted Victorian was deep walnut and inlaid with decorative glass panels. Denver pushed the door open and stepped onto plush carpet so thick his steps didn't make any noise as they walked to the reception desk. The crisp-looking woman behind the desk appeared to be in her mid-twenties and was dressed in a trim pale-gray suit. Behind her head, the elegant wood-paneled wall had a metal sign saying, "Berringer, Cox, and Associates."

"Can I help you, gentlemen? Do you have an appointment?" The young woman asked, a mask of politeness.

Holden immediately turned on his charm and sent her a wide and toothy smile. "You know, you just might be able to help us, but I didn't catch your name."

The woman blushed slightly and leaned forward across her desk. "I'm Ellie Dodds. How can I help direct you this morning?"

Holden leaned against the desk like he was about to get comfortable and stay for a while. "Well, Ms. Dodds, I'm Holden Kay, and this here's Denver Wallace." Denver nodded when Holden pointed in his direction. "Unfortunately, we don't have an appointment, but we were hoping you could get us in to see Mr. Cox." Holden crossed his arms, which just so happened to flex his muscles in the process.

Ellie's eyes were immediately drawn to Holden's biceps. She quickly glanced at his face as if she realized she was doing something she shouldn't be. "We don't normally have walk-in hours, but let me check his schedule." She clicked away at her keyboard, her perfectly manicured nails making a gentle tapping sound against the low keys. She was already shaking her head. "I'm sorry, Mr. Kay, but Mr. Cox is totally booked this morning. I can make you an appointment for early next week?" she asked hopefully as her eyes raked over his arms and chest once more.

Denver practically rolled his eyes at how much she was ogling Holden, but since it might just get them what they needed, he didn't say anything.

"Unfortunately, next week isn't really going to work for me." Holden reached into his pocket, pulled out his leather wallet, flipped it open, and showed her his badge. "I'm afraid what I need to speak with him about just can't wait."

They were taking a risk doing what they were doing. If Denver was right, the man they were trying to get in to see was not only a lawyer who knew the law and his rights, but also a powerful witch. This plan could easily backfire. Hopefully, they weren't biting off more than they could chew.

Ellie's face immediately cooled as she looked at the shiny badge Holden was holding out in front of her. "Let me go see if Mr. Cox is available." She stood from her fancy leather desk chair, brushed her perfectly pressed skirt down her legs, and left them standing in the lobby while she went further into the house, presumably to Cox's office.

Denver was certain that the phone on her desk, which had more buttons than he'd ever seen in his life, had a way to call back to Cox's office. She probably just didn't want to let them listen in when she told the man there was a police officer there to see him.

Ellie returned moments later. "It appears Mr. Cox's next appointment is running late, and he can see you now." She turned and gestured for them to follow her down the hallway. She opened the heavy office door at the end of the hall and stepped back to usher them inside.

"Thank you so much," Holden said, still piling on the charm. This time, Ellie seemed unaffected. Amazing what a badge would do to some harmless flirting.

Holden entered the office first, with Denver right behind him. Holden took in the large man sitting behind a massive desk, then glanced at Denver.

Denver nodded. Derrek Cox was exactly the man they were looking for.

"What can I do for you, gentlemen?" Derrek said as he stood and shook each of their hands. "Ellie said you needed to speak to me?" He gestured to the two guest chairs that faced his imposing desk.

Denver and Holden sat. As much as Denver wanted to jump in and start asking questions and making accusations, he knew that Holden was the one with the experience. He also had the badge, even if he was out of his jurisdiction.

"It has come to my attention that you were in Rock Cove just over a week ago." Holden paused for effect.

Derrek glanced from Holden to Denver and back, cool as a cucumber. "I don't see how my alleged presence in Rock Cove is of any concern of yours."

Holden leaned forward, putting his forearms on his thighs like he was going to reveal a secret. "See, my associate here saw you driving recklessly down one of our roads behind the wheel of a black Mercedes-Maybach. Almost plowed into him, in fact. Good thing he managed to catch your license plate, or we may never have been able to track you down."

Derrek took his eyes off Holden and gave Denver a closer look before easily dismissing him and focusing on who he viewed to be the bigger threat. "Is he trying to press charges? You know as well as I do that this isn't how that sort of thing works."

Holden leaned back in his chair, casually crossing one leg over the other and draping one of his arms over the back. "Not exactly. We have a different reason for being here."

Derrek let out an exasperated huff. "And what exactly is that reason? I don't have all day. My client should be here in the next few minutes."

Holden glanced at Denver who took over the conversation from there. "We're looking for a witch."

Derrek tried very hard to mask his shock, but he flinched just enough to give himself away. He clenched his jaw so hard his pulse was visible from across the room, banging away in his neck.

"You see," Denver continued, "we're trying to get a hold of a member of the Circle of Thirteen, and, given that you were seen chauffeuring one of them around Rock Cove, we figured you were a good place to start."

Derrek stood, shoving his chair back hard enough to hit the wall behind him. "I don't know what the two of you are talking about. Do you hear how ridiculous you sound? Witches? The Circle of Thirteen?

It sounds like something out of a children's book." He tugged his suit jacket down and buttoned it up. "Now, if you'll excuse me."

It was a clear dismissal, but Denver didn't let himself get deterred. This was their one lead, and they couldn't blow it. "Is that what you're going with? Denial and gaslighting? These aren't the witches you're looking for?" He waved his hand like Obi-Wan Kenobi for effect. "Not even when I happen to have these in my possession?" Denver opened his phone and pulled up a photo of the nullifier cuffs. Derrek didn't need to know that *in his possession* really meant *tucked safely in a spelled box at Jenna's house.*

Derrek stiffened once more. If the man got any more rigid, he'd probably keel over. "Look, I don't know who you two think you are or what you intended by coming here today, but you are out of your depth. Remove yourselves from this situation, and my office, and I'll consider not telling the Circle about this little interaction." He sneered at them like he was making a good point.

Denver took great joy in bursting his bubble. "Oh, but that doesn't really work for us. We *want* you to tell them about us stopping by. And while you're at it, give them this." He reached into his pocket and retrieved the USB drive containing the footage and placed it on Derrek's desk. "Watch it. You may see a familiar face on there." With that, Denver left the office. Holden gave a cheeky nod in Derrek's direction before following.

Chapter Twenty-Seven

J ENNA PUSHED OPEN THE door of the squat brick building that housed the Rock Cove police station. She'd waited several days for either Denver or Holden to tell her what they'd seen—or not seen—on the surveillance footage, but she was tired of waiting. Since she was currently angry at Denver for being involved with Brigit, she skipped over him and went straight to the source.

She'd never been inside a police station before. It was on the small side, which made sense considering the entire police force was less than fifteen people, including the police chief. The building was basically one open room with an office in the back corner for the chief. There were a few doors that led off to either side, but for the most part, it was just a sea of desks corralled behind a low half-wall. At one end of the entryway was a desk with a very young-looking officer sitting behind it. Since it was the only desk on this side of the wall, she walked up and cleared her throat.

"Excuse me," she said. "I'm looking for Holden Kay."

The officer glanced around, but he didn't see Holden at any of the desks either. "I can see if he's around. Who should I say is asking for him?"

"My name is Jenna Hastings." She tucked her hair behind her ear to get it out of her face.

The officer blanched slightly before his expression turned into one of sympathy. "I see. Yes, I'll let him know immediately that you're here to see him."

The young officer got up and badged himself through the low wall. He wound through the sea of desks and disappeared into an unmarked door along the back wall. Seconds later Holden came out, crossed the floor, and stopped near her.

"I wasn't expecting you to show up. I assume Denver told you?" Holden opened the half-door and let her through. He turned around and led Jenna the direction he'd come from.

There was something to tell, and Denver hadn't told her? Her earlier anger at him only intensified. Her power crackled under her skin, but she choked it back hard. Now was not the time nor the place to lose control. She was better than this. She could deal with Denver another time. "Um," she didn't know what to say. Should she admit that Denver hadn't told her anything? Or would that make Holden less inclined to share whatever he knew? Had they identified the witch outside the café?

"He's through here. He's been asking to speak to you for a while," Holden said as he badged her through the door he'd just emerged from. "Honestly, I didn't think you'd want to see him, but far be it from me to tell you what to do either way. Hopefully, talking to him will give you some closure."

Jenna was utterly confused. Holden kept saying "he," so he wasn't referring to the rogue witch. Who on earth was he talking about then?

She didn't have to wait long to find out. Holden had brought her to the cellblocks. The first two cells were empty, but the last one at the back had a single bed containing a scrawny-looking man with graying-brown hair and the sickly look of someone who didn't have enough meat on their bones.

"Nelson, wake up," Holden called as he approached the cell. "Jenna Hastings is here to see you."

The man—Nelson—instantly sat up and stared at her. She watched as he slowly got to his feet, something slightly off about the way he moved and acted. She couldn't quite put her finger on what was wrong with him. He just looked *off*.

"I'll leave you two to talk, but I'll be right outside that door whenever you're ready." Holden gestured to the door they'd entered from and then left her alone with the stranger.

Jenna had no clue where to start or what she was supposed to say. "Nelson, is it?" she asked.

The twitchy man stepped closer to the bars at the front of his cell and leaned on them, staring at her hungrily. "Ken Nelson," he said, and waited for her to react.

Except Jenna had no idea who this man was. She'd never seen him before in her life, and she'd never even heard the name Ken Nelson before that moment. "I heard you wanted to speak to me." Which was technically true. Holden had told her that two minutes ago.

Ken stuck his arms through the bars and sagged against them like he could no longer support his own weight. "Yeah, I suppose I did. I know there's nothing I can say that will ever make up for what I did to you, but I just wanted to tell you that I never meant to do it. I wasn't myself that night, I swear to you."

Jenna was tired of being in the dark and was rapidly losing her patience. "Mr. Nelson, I don't know what you're talking about. Tell me what you mean, or I'm leaving."

Ken flinched back, eyes narrowing in suspicion. It was like he was trying to get a read on her, but she wasn't sure what he was looking for. "You don't know who I am?" He swallowed thickly. "Or what I did?"

"No. Obviously." She crossed her arms, the fingers on one hand tapping her opposite elbow in irritation.

"Oh, wow. I wasn't expecting you not to know," Ken said as he backed away from the bars and started pacing in agitation. "How is it possible that you don't know? If it was me, I would have immediately been asking questions."

A sinking sensation started in her throat and traveled all the way to her toes. Her mind flashed back to what Holden had said in Cinder & Spice the other day. With all the worry about the rogue witch she'd completely forgotten about the rest of the conversation. Jenna was suddenly certain she knew who Ken Nelson was, but she needed to hear it from him.

"Let's pretend like I've never heard your name before in my life. Now tell me who you are." Jenna clenched her jaw as she braced for the invisible blow.

"I'm the one that killed your parents."

The whisper was so quiet that Jenna barely heard the words from where she was standing ten feet away. Even though she'd started to suspect, his confession slammed into her. She stumbled backward and hit the wall, her arm blindly reaching for something to support her and stop her from crumbling to the ground.

Ken began agitatedly pacing around his cell, his hands yanking on his graying hair and muttering under his breath.

But Jenna couldn't focus on what he was saying. Logically, she'd known that a drunk driver had killed her parents, but at the time of the incident and the following funeral, she hadn't wanted to know the details. She'd specifically told Holden that she didn't want to know anything, and she'd left it there.

For months.

Her parents' killer was standing in front of her and sending her awkward sideways glances. Her parents had been two of the nicest people to ever live. They'd been generous and kind, loving and gracious. Her dad had even acted like a surrogate father to Denver, and this man had taken them from the world.

She couldn't be here right now.

She pushed away from the wall and stumbled toward the exit.

"Wait!" Ken called after her. "I didn't mean to do it. I swear."

She spared him one last glance over her shoulder. "It doesn't matter if you didn't mean to kill them. The fact of the matter is, you did."

"I wasn't myself. It was almost like something grabbed hold of me. Like it made me get behind the wheel that night. As drunk as I was, I still knew well enough not to drive home."

Jenna rolled her eyes. "Yeah, right. No drunk person has ever gotten behind the wheel when they shouldn't have. Goodbye, Mr. Nelson. I hope you rot in hell."

"You have to believe me! That little bitch at the bar. Maybe she slipped something in my drink."

"Nice try." As she turned to leave again, she saw something out of the corner of her eye. Turning to face Ken more fully she squinted, and it happened again. A gray wispy cloud swirled around Ken's head for less than a second, leaving his face even paler and more sunken than before.

She slowly returned to Ken's cell door. He'd started begging and pleading for her to listen to him, but she tuned it out. She didn't care what *he* had to say. She cared what his energy had to say.

Jenna closed her eyes and muttered a quick spell under her breath quietly enough that Ken wouldn't be able to hear it above his ranting. When she opened them again, she gasped.

Ken's energy signature was a sickly yellow. It didn't look particularly appealing or comforting, but that wasn't the issue. The problem was that swirling amid the yellow was a gray energy that shouldn't be there. It wasn't coming from him, yet somehow it was fully entwined with his own. It was unmistakably a witch's energy.

Holy shit. Ken was right. Someone had put a whammy on him, but it hadn't been in the form of a date rape drug. A witch had cast a spell on him, and the remnants of it were still clinging to him months later.

"Tell me more about the bitch at the bar," Jenna demanded, cutting off Ken's ramblings.

Ken looked shocked that she was engaging with him at all, but he answered her question readily enough. "She was on the skinny side, honestly. Not a lot of meat on her bones. A few inches shorter than you, with light brown hair and very pale skin. Looked on the young side. Seemed like maybe she wasn't quite old enough to be in the bar, but I'm not the police, you know? Not my usual type, but I woulda hit that, if you catch my drift."

Without a photo or video it was impossible to know for sure, but Jenna was just about as positive as she could be that the witch who had spelled Ken Nelson was the same witch that had attacked her outside the café. And based on the energy signature she could feel radiating off him, she was also the same witch who had broken into her house.

Her parents had been killed months ago, which meant that Ken had been spelled even before that. What on earth was the witch's end goal? Three interactions with the same rogue witch—even if one was through the proxy of Ken Nelson—were not a coincidence. This woman was after her, and she needed to figure out why.

But first, she needed to help Ken. As much as she resented the man in front of her for killing her parents, it was at least as much the witch's fault as it was his. Maybe even more so. She had an obligation to help him even if she didn't want to.

She started circling her hands and swishing them back and forth in front of her. She gathered her magic to her, preparing to cast her own spell.

"Hey now, what exactly are you doing?" Ken said nervously as he backed away from the bars. Fortunately for her—and unfortunately for him—his cell was small. He couldn't go very far.

She felt her water magic rise to the surface and fill her with energy. She quietly muttered her spell, and then with a pushing motion, she urged her energy to surround Ken. Then she carefully swirled her blue energy—invisible to ordinaries—around him and, with a gentle tugging motion, began untangling the gray energy from his own. With one final yank from Jenna, the gray energy left Ken's. Jenna swirled her own magic around it to fully contain it, then slowly drew it across the room to where she was standing. With one more concentrated shove she crushed the gray swirls beneath her more powerful cocoon of magic. It fizzled out and she released her energy with a sigh.

Ken was staring at her like she was an alien life form. "You doing some sorta zen yoga shit?"

Jenna ignored his question. "How do you feel?"

"What do you mean, how do I feel? You're the one doing bizarre meditation exercises." He might have been deflecting, but he was still pressed against the far wall of his cell. He knew she'd done something to him, even if he had no idea what it was.

"Mr. Nelson, please, for my sake. Tell me how you feel."

He seemed to stop and think about it. His eyes narrowed, and he rolled his shoulders like he'd just woken up from a nap. "Actually ... I feel good. Better than I've felt in months." He stared at his hands like he'd never seen them before, but Jenna knew what had happened. She'd removed the magical monkey that had been on his back since that night at the bar. Her job here was finished. He looked at her again, eyes narrowing. "What did you do to me?"

"Mr. Nelson, I can't save you from whatever fate awaits you with the justice system, but I was able to do that for you."

"Well, I'll be damned. I have no idea what you did but be sure to thank my son the next time you see him. I'm assuming it was Denver that convinced you to finally come see me?"

All the good energy Jenna had after helping Ken with his magical hanger-on vanished in a puff of smoke. "Denver is your son?" She wanted to puke. If Denver was Ken's son, then he obviously knew what Ken had done, and he'd deliberately kept it from her. Not only was Denver a cheat, but he was also a liar. He'd kept one of the most important pieces of information about her parents' death from her.

"I thought you knew that. Holden mentioned you were close."

"I need to leave. I hope I never see you again."

Ken Nelson had ruined her life not once, but twice. Not only had he killed her parents, but he'd just proved without a doubt that Denver was someone she never should have gotten involved with. If she'd listened to her instincts at the beginning, she never would have let herself care about him or sleep with him. She'd known it was a bad idea, and she'd let his gorgeous face and his—obviously fake—kindness lure her in. She was done with him.

He and Brigit deserved one another.

Chapter Twenty-Eight

Denver pulled into the police station parking lot and got out of the car. He was hoping that Holden had an update from their witchy lawyer, though he wasn't really counting on it. He was also planning to take his friend out to lunch as a thank you for helping Jenna. He'd gone above and beyond considering that not only was the lawyer's office out of his jurisdiction, but ambushing a potentially pissed-off witch was a bit above his pay grade.

He reached out his hand to open the door, but it was shoved open from the inside, forcing him to jump out of the way. Jenna emerged, and she looked mad enough to spit nails.

"Hey, Jenna."

Jenna stopped abruptly and spun to face him. "That's all you have to say to me? Hey?" She flung her loose hair over her shoulder. Her blue eyes iced over and pinned him in place.

He took a half step back, uncertain what was going on. She was furious about something, but he had no idea what he'd done. He racked his brain trying to figure out what he could have missed, but he was coming up blank. "Is something wrong?" he asked tentatively. He assumed there was, but he didn't want to try to guess what it might be.

"How could you have known all this time and not told me?"

Denver didn't need to ask her to explain. It suddenly clicked that Jenna was here, at the police station. Where his father was. The man who'd killed her parents.

"Oh shit," he whispered.

"No kidding," Jenna said as she spun in a circle, flinging her arms out at her sides. He didn't know what she was doing, but the pressure he felt building meant she was probably doing something with her magic. That couldn't be good. The leaves on the trees started to whip frantically through the air, responding to whatever spell she was casting.

Denver reached out and grabbed Jenna's upper arm, tugging her away from the front of the building and off to the side behind a clump of trees.

"Get your hands off me," she practically shouted.

He glanced around to make sure no one else overheard their conversation. "Jenna, I get that you're pissed at me, but look where you are. You can't do magic in public. What if someone sees?"

"Honestly, what does it even matter anymore? The Circle is already after me. I might as well be guilty of the crime they're trying to punish me for."

Despite her angry words, the pressure against his skin eased, and the leaves started to calm. They were still blowing around harder than they probably should be, but she was no longer at risk of creating a storm.

"You don't mean that. No part of you wants to put yourself in the custody of the Circle." He desperately wanted to hug her against his body and keep her safe, but there was no way Jenna would welcome his touch. Not at the moment, at any rate.

"At least the Circle never lied to me or cheated on me. They've been very clear from the start what they wanted from me. Honest and transparent about the fact that they want me in shackles for my supposed crime. That's more than I can say for you." The wind started to pick up again, and fat raindrops started falling from the darkening sky.

"All right, yes. I did lie to you, but only by omission." Her eyes narrowed as she stared at him. "And yes, I realize how that sounds when I say it. I truly am sorry that I didn't tell you."

"Your father killed my parents." She practically spat the words in his direction.

"The man in that jail cell is not my father. He may share 50 percent of my DNA, but that does not make him a father. It makes him a sperm donor. He didn't raise me, and we're not involved in each other's lives." Denver could feel sweat pouring off him, both from the warmth of the June day and from the dread that she wouldn't believe him. "Truthfully, I knew from the moment I saw you in the cemetery that Ken had killed Russ and Brooke. I didn't want to tell you that because I wanted a chance to get to know you again and didn't want you to associate me with him."

Not one ounce of understanding crossed her face. It was like talking to a brick wall. He wanted her to hear him and understand what he was telling her, but she wasn't in a receptive mood. Maybe this called for a different strategy. "How about this? I'll leave you alone for now, and you can be as pissed as you want to that I kept this from you. But I'll come over tomorrow night and hopefully by then we can sit down calmly, and I'll apologize again."

Jenna spun around and stormed away from him. She hadn't gone far before she turned around and gave him a withering stare. "Why would I want to spend time with a man who cheated on me?"

Denver felt like he'd been sucker punched. "Cheated on you?" He had no idea what she was talking about. Denver wasn't seeing anyone else. He hadn't even been on a date with another woman since before he'd seen Jenna at the funeral.

All of a sudden the righteous anger seemed like it was sucked right out of Jenna. Her shoulders slumped and the gathering wind completely died. She took a shuddery breath before she spoke at a much more reasonable level. "You and I have never discussed our relationship or where we stand. I get that, I really do. But when I'm with someone, I'm only with *them*."

"Me too. You're all I need, Jenna." He couldn't figure out where any of this was coming from.

"I know you were with Brigit. Don't bother denying it, she told me herself," she said, her voice wobbly.

Brigit? He wasn't seeing Brigit. She had to know that. "What are you talking about? The only time I've seen Brigit recently was at the café." He shoved his hand through his hair trying to figure out exactly when everything had gone sideways.

But it was like Jenna didn't even hear what he was saying.

A sadness crept into her eyes that he would give anything to kiss away. "I can't even be surprised really. You two were together all the way back in high school even though she knew I had a crush on you. I wasn't good enough for you then and apparently, I'm not good enough for you now."

Denver's feet were practically rooted to the ground as he watched her walk away. He wanted to run after her and convince her that she was wrong, but he didn't know how. She wasn't going to hear anything he said right now. No matter how truthful.

But why did she think he'd been with Brigit? He'd never been interested in Brigit. Not in high school and not now.

A memory flashed to the front of his mind of the first time he'd seen Jenna and Sierra together in the Copper Lantern. At Holden's insistence, he'd gotten up the nerve to go talk to Jenna. Before he'd even crossed the floor, Brigit had waylaid him, and by the time he'd gotten away from her, Jenna had left.

Damn it.

She was pissed at him for multiple reasons, but this one, at least, wasn't his fault. But he knew whose fault it was. "Fucking Brigit."

"Talking to yourself?" Holden's voice startled Denver enough that he jumped.

"Jesus, man. What are you doing out here?" Denver glanced around frantically, not even sure what he was looking for.

Holden just cocked his eyebrows. "I happen to work here. You're the one who doesn't belong at the police station."

Right. He'd come to see Holden and take him out for food. Running into Jenna had completely derailed his plans though. "I just bumped into Jenna leaving the station."

Holden rocked back on his heels and crossed his arms. "Ah, I get it. And Jenna just spoke to Ken."

"She talked to him? Oh great, no wonder she's pissed. No telling what Ken told her." Denver began pacing in a circle, trying to work off his agitation. A sickening thought occurred to him. "Did you bring her here? You knew I hadn't told her who Ken was or what he'd done. Dick move, man."

Holden's eyes narrowed. "I'm going to pretend like my best friend didn't just accuse me of sabotaging his relationship. As much as I believe that Jenna deserved to know the truth—and that you should have been the one to tell her—I would never go behind your back. Even though Ken has been asking to see her for days."

Denver changed the direction of his pacing so he wouldn't get dizzy. "If you didn't call her, then why was she here?"

Holden cocked his head. "You know what? I have no idea. I assumed when she showed up that you had finally told her about Ken. I took her back to the jail to see him."

This was all his fault. He should have told Jenna everything, right from the start. Deep down he knew that, but he hadn't wanted her to think badly of him. But where had that gotten him? She probably thought worse of him now that he'd gotten involved with her and betrayed her trust than she ever would have had he told her the truth right away.

He had to find a way to make this up to her. He had no idea what he could do that would atone for his lie of omission, but he had to think of something. Maybe if he talked to Sierra, she would have an idea of how to get through to Jenna. At the very least, she had flowers, and those were never a bad place to start.

A thought occurred to him, and he froze mid-circle. It wasn't Sierra he needed to talk to. It was Brigit.

"Got to go, Holden. I'll catch you later." Without a backward glance, Denver bolted to his beat-up truck and flung himself behind the wheel.

It only took a few minutes to reach Cinder & Spice—and most of that had been waiting for a stoplight to turn green. He slammed his truck into park and stalked inside the cozy restaurant. Thankfully it was between the morning rush and the lunch surge, so most of the tables were empty except for a booth in the back where a young couple was cozied up over a shared croissant. *Perfect*. Less of an audience.

He stomped to the front counter. The pleasant smell of coffee filtered into his lungs, but it didn't do anything to settle his rage.

"How can I help you today?" Corrine, the cheerful server, asked from behind the register.

"I need to talk to Brigit. Now."

Corrine jumped at the bark in his voice, but to her credit, she stood her ground. "I'm sorry, but Brigit is in the middle of something. Can I be of assistance?"

Now that was a well-trained customer service person. Feeling a bit bad for Corrine—she wasn't the source of his anger—he softened his tone. "I'm sorry, but no. I need to speak to Brigit as soon as possible. If you could just tell her that Denver needs to talk to her, I'm sure she'll speak to me."

Corrine gave him a dubious look, but with a shrug, she left her post behind the sparkling white counter and headed through the swinging door back to the kitchen. Brigit emerged a moment later, her wine-colored apron smudged with flour. She must have been in the middle of baking something. Her ginger waves were bundled up beneath a baseball cap—the same red as the apron—that should clash with the color of her hair and yet somehow looked good anyway.

"Outside." He herded her out of the back of the restaurant through the emergency exit. Behind the café was an alley, if you could call it that. It was a small road that separated the back of the historic building from the edge of the water beyond. There was a fence made of iron posts with thick ropes draping between them that prevented people from falling into the water. He stopped next to an overflowing dumpster and spun to face her.

"What can I do for you, Denver? I was in the middle of prepping my dough for tomorrow morning." She was hovering in the doorway like she might escape back inside with the slightest provocation.

He tipped his head at the open doorway. "Are you sure you want other people to hear what I have to say to you?" He tucked his hands in the pockets of his shorts, then immediately pulled them back out, still too agitated to stand still.

She gave him a bland look. "Since I have no idea what you want to say to me, I think I'll take my chances."

If that's how she wanted to play it, fine. "I just ran into Jenna. It seems she has this bizarre idea that you and I are sleeping together. Now where do you think she got that impression?" Denver didn't bother to lower his voice, but as soon as he'd said Jenna's name, Brigit had slammed the door shut behind her, cutting them off from the patrons inside.

"That's what I thought." The smell of garbage wafted into his nostrils, a much less pleasant odor than the brewing coffee inside.

Brigit took a few steps toward him, wiping her palms on her apron. "I'm not sure where she got that idea." Her voice quavered just enough to reveal her statement for the lie he knew it to be.

"Bzzt. Try again," Denver said.

"Okay, fine. I may have run into Jenna in the park the other day and implied that." Her hands twisted together in front of her.

Denver balled his fist, turned around, and aimed for the dumpster. Thankfully, he thought better of it before making contact and dropped his hand back by his side. He didn't need to add a broken hand to a pissed-off girlfriend. If that's what Jenna even was. He'd been pretty sure they were on the same page, but now that Brigit had stirred stuff up, he had no idea where he and Jenna stood.

He dragged his fingers through his hair and spun back around to confront Brigit. "Look, I have no idea what happened between the two of you in high school, but you need to either sort that shit out or leave Jenna alone. I have no idea how something that happened more than ten years ago could still be that big of a deal."

Brigit reeled back like he'd slapped her. "No, you don't know what happened between us back then. You have no idea what she did to me. So maybe it's none of your business and you should just back the hell off."

Denver could feel the rising pressure radiating off Brigit that he'd so recently experienced coming at him from Jenna. Now that he knew what to look for, it was obvious that Brigit's power was surging, but he had no idea what she was capable of.

He glanced at her hands, which were currently balled in fists and planted on her hips. He held his hand up, palms out, in front of him. "I have no idea what sort of elemental whammy you're about to toss my direction, but if there's any sense left in you, you need to reel that back in. We're outside. Anyone could walk by." As if to prove his point, a young boy raced around the corner of the building chasing a runaway ball.

Brigit's jaw dropped open, and the surging energy plummeted. "She told you about me?" she whispered.

Denver shrugged. "Holden's the one that figured it out. Jenna only confirmed it when I confronted her about it after the video of her using her powers wound up on YouTube."

"What?!" Brigit practically screeched. Color flooded her cheeks. "Jenna would never do that. Miss Goody-two-shoes wouldn't put one of her perfect hairs out of place if she could help it."

As angry as she seemed to be at Jenna, Brigit's reaction filled Denver was a tiny trickle of hope. She couldn't possibly be that upset about the situation if there wasn't at least a little bit of residual caring and love between the former friends.

"Yeah, well, it wasn't exactly her fault. Now she's in trouble with the Circle—"

Brigit cut him off before he could finish his thought. "You know about the Circle? Oh, we're so fucked." She clenched her hand, conjured up a tiny ball of flame, and threw it at the water where it immediately sizzled out.

Denver took heart in the fact that Brigit said *we're* fucked, so she wasn't as unemotional and uncaring as she tried to make herself out to be.

"Me knowing about the Circle is small potatoes at this point. Jenna—you know, the woman you used to spend all day every day with when you were growing up—is in deep trouble. I'm trying to help her out, but the last thing she needs right now is you coming out swinging with lies about me and you. And while we're at it," he paused his rant to glare at her, "why does she think we were together in high school? You and I both know that's not true."

Brigit's shoulders slumped and her face fell. "I may have let her believe that we slept together at the senior party our last year in school. You had already graduated by then, but you came back for the party so you could hang out with your friends."

All the puzzle pieces started snapping into place. Jenna had confessed that she'd had a crush on Denver in high school. She'd also revealed that she'd fought with Brigit because she'd slept with someone Jenna had wanted to be with. That person was obviously him. Brigit had been disrupting their potential relationship for more than a decade.

He wanted to strangle her.

"Here's what's going to happen. I'm going to leave and figure out how to do some groveling of my own, but you're going to go find Jenna and tell her the truth. She doesn't deserve whatever war you've been waging on her all this time. If you can't bring yourself to be her friend, then at least stop actively making her life worse."

Chapter Twenty-Nine

T HE SMALL LAKE WAS flat and placid, reflecting the cloudless sky of early dawn. A fish rose to the top of the water and nibbled on something before darting beneath the surface once more. The gentle breeze brought the scents of summer heat and flowers. The setting was idyllic.

Jenna hated it.

Well, not really. This lake was as much a part of her as her magical powers were. She couldn't wish ill on something that was so intrinsically tied to one of the deepest parts of herself. She could, however, be extremely bitter that her maybe-boyfriend had not only been lying to her for months about his own father's role in the death of her parents but was also sleeping with one of her mortal enemies.

Her power rose beneath her skin, an itching sensation racing across her like it was trying—and so far, failing—to find its way out. She'd had this exact feeling before and it hadn't ended well. Her power needed an outlet, and until she released it, the buzzing beneath her skin wouldn't go away.

Luckily, she had something she needed help with. She stood on the sturdy wooden dock that jutted out into the water, stretched her arms wide, and began to chant.

> *"Water rise and heed my cry,*
> *Open for me, oh precious sky."*

The sky above instantly changed from bright azure to gray and then slid toward deep charcoal.

> *"Rain may fall, and waves will crash,*
> *Rivers rise and puddles splash."*

The heavens opened up and rain poured down, instantly soaking her clothes.

> *"Typhoons will blow and geysers burst,*
> *None shall slake this endless thirst."*

The lake water started to churn and swirl, a spiraling column of water rising from the depths, rapidly gathering speed and size. Dozens of cascading towers of water sprang up from the lake like fountains, violently splashing back into place. The roar of the storm practically drowned out her shouted words.

> *"My powers rise and ebb and flow,*
> *Help disburse this endless woe."*

The surging energy flowed from her core, down her limbs, out her fingers, and into the environment around her. She channeled her excess intensity into the spell, bending the water and the weather to her whims.

Eventually the power ebbed, and she slowly released the hold she had on the elements. The funnel of water was the first to go, slowly dissipating and turning into a puff of wind. The geysers were next to vanish, with one last eruption spewing water into the air before they sank beneath the surface of the lake. The rain was the last to leave, slowly turning from a monsoon to a shower, to a sprinkle, then a mist. The sky returned to its cerulean perfection, and the lake once again started gently lapping at its banks.

Jenna collapsed to her knees on the dock. All the excess magic had withdrawn from her body. Yet the pain remained. The spell may have released her pent-up magical energy, but it had done nothing for her brooding thoughts.

She knew that magic wouldn't fix a broken heart, but it was worth a shot, right? She had so much power—more power than one of the members of the Circle of Thirteen. It seemed like she should be able to use her power to her advantage to help ease her pain. Too bad that wasn't how magic worked.

"Denver wasn't kidding. You really are pissed."

Jenna jumped to her feet, hands in front of her. She suddenly wished she hadn't expelled quite that much magic when she might need it to defend herself.

Brigit stood less than twenty feet from her, looking like a pissed-off drowned rat. She summoned a ball of fire in her open palm and began waving it near her clothing to dry it. Jenna couldn't even imagine what she looked like. Good thing the water didn't bother her.

"What the hell do you want?" Jenna said, not lowering her hands for a moment. She didn't really believe that Brigit would attack her, but she wasn't taking any chances either. Since Jenna hadn't been around her much, she had no idea how much of a magical punch Brigit packed these days.

Jenna waved her hand in a complicated pattern and pulled the water from her own clothes. The water formed a small ball in the center of her palm before she turned her hand upside down and dumped it on the grass.

"Show-off," Brigit muttered. She continued to dry her clothes one limb at a time.

Once she was confident that Brigit wasn't intending to lob a fireball at her head, Jenna dropped her defensive stance and crossed her arms. "I do *so* enjoy your constant insults. But seriously, why are you here?"

Brigit closed her palm and extinguished the ball of fire letting her arms fall limply by her side. "Denver came to see me."

The last thing she wanted to do right then was talk about Denver with the woman who had stolen him away from her. *Again*. She stormed down the dock and marched past Brigit. "I'm not talking to you about Denver." Her long strides ate up the ground from the lake to the clearing with the stone circle in it. She could hear Brigit chasing after her but didn't turn to look at her.

"I think we need to talk about it," Brigit called after her.

"Why? What's there to talk about? For the second time in my life, you swooped in and stole the man I wanted. Silly me for thinking the situation had changed. It's even the same guy. You'd think I would have learned my lesson back in high school."

"Jenna, wait!"

"No thanks, I'm heading home. You should do the same." Jenna kept striding across the clearing, the path to her house in sight.

Something hot slammed into her shoulder and she froze. Brigit had thrown a fireball at her back, though thankfully it hadn't burned her. Jenna spun around and made a slashing motion with her arm. She pulled moisture from the air and formed a watery blade, then sliced it across Brigit's chest and ripped the shirt she was wearing. Since Jenna had no intention of killing Brigit, there was no blood, but they both knew she could draw it.

"I don't get it. You've won. He's yours. Isn't that what you wanted? Did you just come here to gloat?" Jenna said as she swirled her hand, and a column of water surrounded Brigit, pinning her in place.

"Just let me explain." Brigit struggled against the wall of water now surrounding her. When it didn't give, she clenched her fists and fire raced from her palms, up her arms, down her torso, and to her feet. With a shove of magical energy, the flames expanded outward, and the water barrier Jenna had conjured exploded into mist. Brigit's clothes were a bit charred, but at least she wasn't standing there naked. She looked pissed.

Jenna raised her hands again, but Brigit got there first. She moved her arm in a huge vertical sweeping motion, and a wall of flames erupted halfway between them.

Jenna threw a few balls of water at it, but they instantly evaporated. Brigit was standing between her and the lake, so Jenna could probably pull water from there and hit her from behind, but what was the point? This fight wasn't solving anything.

"I'm done here." Jenna spun around and walked away.

"I've never slept with Denver." Brigit didn't yell the words, but she might as well have.

For the second time in as many minutes, Jenna froze in place. She didn't really believe the words, but if there was any chance they were true …

She slowly turned around but didn't come any closer to the flaming wall. Brigit, on the other hand, walked right through it. The perks of being fireproof.

"Explain."

Brigit sighed and dropped the wall of flames. "Denver is nice and all and he's superhot, but he and I aren't together. We never were."

Jenna advanced toward her former friend. "Then why would you tell me otherwise? Is your whole mission in life to torture me?" Jenna had gone over it again and again in her mind. Twelve years later, she still had no idea what had come between them. Maybe she was about to find out.

"You showed back up on Rock Cove out of the blue. I'd thought you were gone for good, and my mind had gotten used to that. Then your parents died, and you were suddenly back. I didn't know what to do with that, so I instantly reverted to the way I acted senior year. I saw an opportunity to dig the needle in, and I took it." Brigit tucked her hands in the pockets of the tiny shorts she was wearing and shrugged.

That was the crappiest explanation Jenna had ever heard, but it still only explained half the problem. "Explain to me what happened senior year of high school, because I've been over it hundreds of times, and I still don't know what went wrong. One day you were one of my best friends, and the next it was like you were my mortal enemy."

Brigit huffed. "The fact that you don't know what you did wrong is part of the problem. After everything we went through training together with Roderick. All the blood, sweat, and tears, and you couldn't be bothered to put your friends first for a change. No, everything always has to be about you." Tears started falling down Brigit's cheeks, but she furiously wiped them away. "We all lost something during the Trials. Maybe it's time you ask yourself what your actions cost the rest of us."

Jenna flinched like she'd been slapped. "I have no idea what you're talking about. What about the Trials?"

"The final Trial! You cost me everything!" Brigit practically yelled. "You know what? Never mind. You clearly don't care." Brigit turned her back on Jenna and headed out of the clearing. She paused at the edge of the trees but didn't look back. Her voice was quiet, almost defeated when she said, "You really should forgive Denver. None of this was his fault. He's a really good guy, and I'm sorry if I screwed things up for you two."

"Whether I forgive Denver or not isn't up to you. Believe it or not, the entire world doesn't revolve around you. I can have more than one reason to be mad at him."

Even while she was saying the words, Jenna felt the lie in them. Yes, it was true that Denver had lied to her, at least by omission. He should have told her that his father was responsible for her parents' death. But Denver wasn't his dad. Denver wasn't responsible for what Ken had done. Actually, given that Ken had been put under a spell by the same witch that was currently tormenting Jenna, it wasn't even entirely Ken's fault her parents had died.

She had no idea what to do with that. Her anger at Denver slowly dissipated. She'd screwed up with him—twice—and it was up to her to figure out how to make things right. Thankfully, there was still one person she could safely be pissed at.

"Fine, you've delivered your message. Now, I suggest you get off my land before I force you off." She swirled her wrist, and a wave of magical energy jumped to obey her whims. She sent a slight pulse of it in Brigit's direction, so she knew she meant business.

Brigit slumped, her shoulders caving toward her chest. "I'm going."

Jenna stood in the grove with the stone circle long after Brigit had disappeared into the trees. She breathed deeply and let equilibrium return to her magical stores. Now if only her relationship with Denver could be fixed as easily as she returned the balance to her magic.

Just as the calm began to settle over her, the shrill sound of her cellphone split the air and immediately jacked her blood pressure back up. Only one person in her contacts list had that ringtone, her boss.

She fished the phone out of her pocket and swiped to answer it. "Hi, Trevor. Now's not really a good—"

He cut her off abruptly. "Jenna, get to the aquarium as soon as possible. We've gotten reports of an injured right whale. It's entangled in fishing line. We need to mount a rescue immediately."

Jenna's stomach dropped to her toes. She immediately switched to business mode, her personal issues losing all importance. The top two causes of death for right whales were vessel strikes and entanglement in fishing gear. The right whale population was too small already. Every life was precious and key to preserving the species.

"Have they been able to identify who it is yet?" There were several hundred right whales in the Atlantic Ocean, but somehow, she knew what Trevor's answer would be before he even said the words. She could already picture her and her calf that was still too young to take care of itself.

"Jenna I'm sorry, but it's Diamond."

Chapter Thirty

D ENVER EMERGED FROM THE Petal Patch clutching a bouquet of what was supposedly Jenna's favorite flowers. He had no idea what any of them were, so he was trusting Sierra not to lead him astray. He'd tried to subtly pump her for information about how he should go about making things up to Jenna, but she hadn't had a ton of advice for him. "Give her some space" wasn't exactly what he wanted to hear.

He wanted to fix things now.

His cellphone vibrated, and his heart skipped a beat when he saw Jenna's name on the screen. Maybe she didn't need as much time as Sierra thought.

He swiped to answer. "Hey, Jenna. I was hoping you would call. Are you at home? I'd like to swing by and talk to you." He stuck his nose in the flowers and took a whiff. The sweet scent reminded him of Jenna's living room, and he could picture her decorating her whole house with flowers not only to support her friend's business, but because she liked them.

"There's no time for that. We need to get to the aquarium ASAP. There's an injured whale in the bay and we're mounting a rescue mission."

Her no-nonsense tone immediately wiped the smile off his face. "I'll be at your house in ten minutes, and we can carpool. No reason to drive separately." He hit the red button to hang up before Jenna had time to argue with him. He climbed behind the wheel and put the flowers on the passenger seat. He glanced over his shoulder quickly, then peeled out of his parking spot and headed to her house on the edge of town.

Jenna was waiting in the driveway with a bag full of gear and a tense expression. She tossed her bag in the back of his truck, then yanked open the door. She paused when she noticed the flowers on the seat.

"I bought them for you. Even if this day isn't going exactly as planned, I figured you might still enjoy them." He held his breath slightly as she slowly reached for the flowers and climbed into the seat. He threw the truck in reverse. As he glanced over his shoulder and navigated down her driveway, he saw her lean in and take a small sniff of the bouquet. He smothered his smile in his shoulder as he looked for oncoming traffic.

They drove in silence for several minutes, the air between them tense. Denver desperately wanted to cut through the strain, but he didn't know where to begin. He hadn't had time to prepare his apology speech.

"Thank you," Jenna finally broke the silence that was suffocating him. "These are lovely."

Finally, a safe topic. "Sierra said they were your favorite. She certainly has a knack with flowers."

Jenna smiled as she set the flowers gently on her lap and petted a few of the petals with her finger. "The perks of being an earth witch. Plants respond naturally to her, even when she's not actively using her powers. Everything seems to bloom a little bit brighter when she's around."

"Jenna, I'm sorry—" Denver started to bumble his way through an apology, but Jenna cut him off.

"Have you ever been on a whale rescue before?" Her tone had moved from soft to businesslike.

Apparently, she still wasn't ready to talk about it. Fine. One thing at a time. "No, I haven't. What do I need to know?" If she wanted to limit their discussions to work, he could do that. He was a professional too.

"From the information Trevor was able to find out, it appears that Diamond got caught in fishing line. It's wrapped around her and impeding her movement."

Denver's hands clenched on the wheel as soon as he heard Diamond's name. He was relatively new to the world of right whales, but he already had a soft spot in his heart for that one. After Jenna had mentioned there was a whale registry database where you could look up photos of all the known right whales, he'd spent a happy few hours digging into it, immersing himself in the subject Jenna was so passionate about. Diamond was one of the few right whales he could identify on sight by her markings alone.

"Fishing line? Can't she just snap the line?"

Jenna was already shaking her head. "It's not fishing line like from a fishing pole. It's the rope that runs from underwater commercial crab and lobster pots to the buoy on the surface. If whales swim through the area, they can unknowingly get tangled in the ropes and get stuck."

The visual of a majestic creature like a whale tied up in ropes and man-made dangers was sickening. "Got it. Yeah, they were just testing out some new equipment to prevent that when I was getting out of the lobster business. But how do we help Diamond?"

That was exactly the right question to ask. Jenna nodded once. "Trevor is getting a few folks together who will meet us there. We'll head out on the *Sea Bliss* and bring the Zodiac. Once we find Diamond, we'll have to play it by ear. If she's relatively calm, we'll approach her in the Zodiac and try to cut off some of the rope with grappling hooks and hooked knives. If she's too agitated, we may have to plant a tracking device on her and monitor her to see if she settles down and try again later."

Tension seeped into Denver as he pictured what they were about to do. Going anywhere near an injured whale was dangerous, possibly life-threatening. It was also the right thing to do.

They spent the rest of the drive in silence, each buried in their own thoughts and plans. When they pulled into the parking lot of the aquarium, there were two people waiting for them. The first was Trevor, their boss. The second was a fit-looking, middle-aged man whom he didn't recognize, but based on the way that Jenna perked up, she seemed to know who he was.

"Richard," she said as she hopped out of the truck. "What are you doing here?" she asked as she approached the other man and hugged him.

Jealousy immediately bubbled to the surface. Denver had no idea who this Richard person was to Jenna. He was probably at least fifteen years older than she was, but that didn't mean much. He was fit and good-looking. His complexion was a healthy sort of tan—the kind you got from having a job that kept you out in the sun all day—and even his small wrinkles made him look experienced and distinguished rather than old.

Was Richard one of Jenna's exes?

"I was in the neighborhood, talking to a few of your colleagues here at the aquarium about mutual areas of research when I heard about the distress call. Put me to work, boss." Richard winked at Jenna, and her return smile had acid churning in Denver's stomach.

As much as Denver knew this was not the time to get into whatever was going on between him and Jenna—not to mention something he wanted to bring up in front of his boss—it took a herculean effort to smash down his feelings and do his job.

"Is this everyone?" Jenna asked Trevor.

Trevor nodded. "Everyone else is out on another of our boats tracking a group of sand tiger sharks in Boston Harbor. They're going to try to meet us there."

Right, that was Denver's cue. "Let's load up. We can shove off in less than ten minutes." Turning his back on Jenna and her maybe-ex-boyfriend, Denver strode to the boat and prepared for departure while Jenna and the scientists loaded up their gear.

They headed for the last known location where someone had spotted Diamond. Not for the first time, Denver wished that his boat could travel as fast as a car. After speeding down the highway fueled by tension and adrenaline, the slower progress across the waves of the harbor, and then out to the bay, felt agonizing. He just hoped they could find Diamond once they got there. Who knew what could have happened to her since she'd last been spotted.

"There!" Jenna shouted. Denver slammed the boat into low gear to slow it down. His eyes raked the water in front of him, trying to spot the distinctive V-shaped blow of the whale.

A powerful plume of mist shooting into the air told him that Jenna was right. They'd found her. A second, much smaller plume told him that she wasn't alone. Diamond's calf, Siren, was right next to her.

Denver's stomach dropped like a stone. If Diamond was entangled, did that mean Siren was too? It was too horrifying to think about.

He threw the boat into idle, cut the engine, and went out onto the deck to see what he could do to help. Jenna and Richard were efficiently readying the smaller rubber-bottomed Zodiac boat to launch. Trevor was readying a grappling gun with a rope attached to it.

"More rope? Doesn't that defeat the purpose here?" Denver asked as he watched his boss's efficient movements.

"You'd think so, but actually no. We use this"—he gestured to the grappling gun—"to catch the rope she's trailing behind her. Once we do that, we attach a series of buoys to it to create drag. It'll slow her down and tire her out, then we can attempt to approach her in the rubber dinghy."

Movement in the water drew Denver's eye, and he turned just in time to see Diamond breach the surface. The distinct diamond-shaped white patch on her head was unmistakable. Unfortunately, so was the bright red rope that was wrapped around her middle and her tail. It looked like it had tightened around her, digging into her skin, and causing her to bleed.

Trevor took aim at the mass of rope that Diamond was pulling behind her. The gun went off with a bang, followed by the whirring sound of an unwinding rope. It hit the water with a splash. Trevor yanked on the end of the rope to make sure it was well and truly caught in the fishing line attached to the whale. He smoothly and efficiently started attaching floating buoys to the line and tossing them overboard one by one.

Jenna and Richard had finished whatever they were doing with the rigid inflatable boat and came to stand next to Denver and Trevor at the railing.

"Nothing to do but wait," Richard said as he stared out over the gently lapping waves.

"It's hard to imagine that I watched that little baby being born," Jenna said softly as she watched Siren breach the surface near her mother. "This needs to work out. I can't stand the thought of that little one being an orphan. She wouldn't survive."

Hours went by as they watched the mother and calf. The sun crested overhead, beating down with the heat of a cloudless sky. Diamond's movements were getting slower, and the floats prevented her from diving too deep.

"It's probably about as safe as it's ever going to get," Jenna said as she headed to the stern of the *Sea Bliss*. She hit the button to lower the gate. "Help me get this boat in the water."

The four of them hefted and shoved the inflatable boat off the back of the *Sea Bliss* and into the water. Trevor braced the raft while Jenna hopped onto it. Richard started to follow her, but Denver reached out to stop him. "I'm the pilot here. I'll drive the boat." He hopped on behind Jenna and took up a position at the rear of the boat near the motor.

Honestly, it was a dumb move for him to make. Of the four of them, he was by far the least experienced with whale rescue missions. And he was also by far the most experienced pilot, which meant his responsibility was to stay with the *Sea Bliss*. He needed to be available to pilot the boat back home.

None of that made any difference. If Jenna was putting herself in harm's way, he was going with her. Plus, anything he could do to prevent Jenna and her maybe-ex from spending time together was a bonus in his mind.

Richard raised his eyebrows but didn't say anything. Trevor shoved the Zodiac away from the larger boat without a word.

Jenna armed herself with a long pole that had a hooked blade on the end of it. She turned to face him as he navigated the smaller craft closer to Diamond. "You have an incredibly difficult job here. You need to get me close enough to her that I can slice through the rope without injuring her. But you're also driving a weapon. Vessel strikes from motor blades are one of the top causes of injuries. Remember, it's not just Diamond out there. Siren is swimming around too, and probably won't like it that we're getting close to Mom. And, no matter how tired she may be, Diamond weighs around seventy tons. She's still capable of a tremendous amount of damage, so stay sharp."

Denver's hand clamped around the rudder. His stomach was in knots, but he was determined to do this. He wasn't immune to fear, but he tamped it down. Saving Diamond was more important.

Denver carefully navigated their small craft between Siren and her mother. He slowed their speed as he approached her middle, trying to coast closer to the giant mammal. Like lightning, Jenna reached out with her sharp pole and slid it under the rope wrapped near Diamond's fins. With a tug and a slice, it came free. Diamond thrashed slightly, clearly uncomfortable, so Denver steered the boat safely away from her.

He pulled around in a circle, once again approaching her from behind where she would be less likely to spot them. He pulled the small craft as close as he could get to her tail while staying out of her way. Jenna went to work on the rope with her pole, slicing through line after line. Unfortunately, the last one was so tight that Jenna couldn't easily get her pole around it.

"I'm going to slice through the trailing line to release her from the buoys. We may have to just leave that last one in place. I can't get to it."

Both Denver and Jenna were soaking wet from the spray of the boat and the splash of the water Diamond was sending their way with her tail. Jenna looked exhausted but determined, and Denver was following her lead.

Jenna reached out one more time and sawed on the rope Diamond was pulling behind her. With a final tug, the rope cut, and Diamond was free.

She clearly knew it too. She flipped her fins and flicked her tail to dive for the first time in hours. Unfortunately, the flukes of her tail hit the side of their small boat and lifted one edge as she dove into the depths.

The small boat wasn't designed to tip backward. Jenna came tumbling across the vessel toward him. She rolled into him as the boat capsized. The pole Jenna was still clutching in her hands smacked into Denver's temple as they plunged into the chilly Atlantic Ocean, the dark water instantly surrounding them.

Chapter Thirty-One

J ENNA'S HEAD BROKE THE surface of the water, and she gasped in a deep gulp of air. Blood rushed in her ears and blocked out almost every other sound. She was rattled, but as far as she could tell, unharmed.

She treaded water as she frantically looked around, trying to get her bearings. The Zodiac was turtled—floating upside down—about a dozen feet from her. The *Sea Bliss* was a few hundred feet away, and she could see Trevor and Richard scrambling on deck, but she couldn't make out what they were shouting at her.

Denver was nowhere to be found. Instant panic set in as she looked in every direction and waited for him to surface.

He didn't.

A flash of memory came back to her, and she saw—as if in slow motion—the pole smash into Denver's temple seconds before they'd toppled overboard.

If he were unconscious, he could be floating face down in the water, seconds away from drowning. She spun in a circle, but still didn't see him anywhere. That could only mean one thing.

He was sinking.

She dove beneath the gently lapping waves and opened her eyes in the burning salt water, hoping to catch a glimpse of him. The water was so churned up that she couldn't see more than a handful of feet in front of her in any direction.

She kicked to the surface and sucked in another deep breath. She had to find him. She'd only just come around to realizing that most of the reasons she'd been mad at Denver hadn't actually been his fault, and the stuff that was his fault was ultimately forgivable. Almost anyone would have done the same.

But Jenna hadn't had a chance to tell him that. She'd thought about coming clean on the drive to Boston, but they'd had other things on their minds. She'd told herself that there had been enough going on with the impending whale rescue that their own personal drama could wait. She wouldn't be able to stand it if she lost him now, and she'd never gotten to tell him that she loved him.

Because she did. There was no doubt in her mind that she loved Denver. She wouldn't have gotten quite as mad or worked up about either the Brigit situation or the Ken problem if she hadn't already fully invested herself in making things work with Denver.

She wasn't about to let that go now. If her weak human eyes couldn't find the love of her life, she knew one way that could.

Jenna took a deep, calming breath and spread her arms wide, letting her legs do the work to keep her afloat. She closed her eyes and concentrated on her magical center harder than she ever had in her life.

She was a water witch. The ocean was her *bitch*.

She gathered as much power as she could, her veins practically buzzing with it. She released it in a large pulse, sending waves of water in every direction. The Zodiac—which had drifted closer to her—bobbed up and down with the crests of the waves. She could sense the fish below her scattering, not sure what to make of her wave of power.

There, a dozen or so feet below the surface and sinking, was exactly what she was looking for. She didn't even have to see him. Her power told her everything she needed to know.

"Jenna, hang in there! We're coming!" The words went right in one ear and out the other. She didn't even know who had yelled. It wasn't her she was worried about. Didn't they know that Denver was dying?

She had to save him.

Jenna once again gathered up her power, but this time, instead of pushing it away from her, she *pulled*. She focused all her attention and energy on that one human-shaped anomaly below the waves and tugged him toward her like there was a rope connecting them. All she had to do was keep pulling.

She could feel her magical stores starting to drain with the amount of power she was using, but she couldn't let them drop. This wasn't over yet.

Seconds later, Denver's gorgeous face crested the surface. Blood welled up from the cut at his temple and ran down his cheek. Her heart skipped a beat as she realized how pale his skin already was. He almost assuredly had water in his lungs, and he was going to die if she didn't save him.

"Jenna, grab on!" Trevor yelled from somewhere behind her.

An orange and white lifesaver ring plopped into the water next to her. Jenna wrapped one arm tightly under Denver's arms and grabbed the flotation device with the other.

Trevor and Richard were both on the deck of the *Sea Bliss* pulling on the rope attached to the lifesaver. Within seconds, she bumped up against the stern of the boat. Richard reached for her, but she said, "No, Denver first."

Richard and Trevor each wrapped an arm under Denver's armpits and tugged him aboard, laying him flat on the metal deck. They were instantly back to pull her out of the chilly water. She flopped on the hard surface and heaved out a few breaths. She was safe.

But Denver still wasn't.

Trevor reached for Denver's neck and felt for a pulse. He must not have found one, because he placed his hands—one on top of the other—on Denver's chest and started doing chest compressions. He bent over and blew two deep breaths into Denver's mouth.

Jenna watched Denver's chest rise as Trevor forced air into his lungs. Unlike in the movies, Denver didn't immediately respond and cough the water out of his lungs.

Her muscles were exhausted and starting to cramp. It didn't matter. She tucked the pain out of her mind as she crawled her way to Denver's side. She heaved herself to her knees next to him.

"Don't you die on me, Denver. I won't allow it." She started gathering what was left of her power, which stirred reluctantly beneath her skin. "I love you. Do you hear me? You can't leave me. I need you to stay."

Trevor shot her a narrow-eyed glance but never stopped doing CPR.

Her power finally rose to the surface. The next time Trevor leaned over to blow in Denver's mouth, she stopped him.

"What are you doing?" Trevor asked, but she didn't bother responding.

She placed her hand gently about an inch above Denver's mouth and stretched her powers into his body. She sensed the water in his lungs and pulled on it, carefully maneuvering it up his trachea and out of his mouth. Not bothering with finesse, she let the water stream out of Denver and splash on the deck next to him.

"What the hell?" Richard asked, but Jenna ignored him.

Now was not the time for explanations. Since Trevor was also staring at her like she was a bit of an alien, she took over the chest compressions herself. "Come on, Denver. Come back to me." She leaned over and breathed for him. Once. Twice. Then back to the compressions.

Denver took a small breath. Then a second. Then let out a racking cough. Trevor recovered enough to roll Denver to his side in case there was more water he needed to cough out, but Jenna already knew she'd gotten it all.

She collapsed sideways like a puppet whose strings were cut, all energy gone. Somewhere in the back of her mind she realized that both she and Denver had been in the Atlantic Ocean for several long minutes. Even though it was June, the water itself was probably still in the upper fifties, which meant that they needed to get out of their clothes and warm up before it started to affect their muscles.

Almost of its own accord, her hand groped sideways until she felt Denver's beneath hers, and she squeezed. She vaguely processed that Richard was wrapping her in a mylar thermal blanket while Trevor did the same to Denver. She was forced to drop Denver's hand when Richard and Trevor carried them inside the boat's cabin.

She didn't even care when they stripped her naked and shoved her into a pair of sweats and thick wool socks. It felt wonderful not to be in the cold, damp clothes anymore, but she was so exhausted she could barely move.

There was noise and chaos around her, and she felt the vibrations beneath her that meant someone had started the boat. All she cared about was that she and Denver were both safe and sound and currently cuddled on the cushioned bench in the cabin while someone else piloted them back to safety. Jenna zoned in and out as Richard and Trevor took turns keeping her and Denver awake and forcing warm liquids down them.

"Jenna," Denver's voice was raspy and hoarse from the salt water he'd inhaled.

"Shh. Don't try to talk yet. Just rest." She leaned her head on Denver's shoulder and put her arm around his waist. The simple touch reassured her that he was alive, if a bit worse for wear, and that they had time to sort through whatever was going on between them. No need to deal with anything now. Now was the time for rest and recuperation.

However, by the time they were almost back to the dock, Jenna's mind had cleared enough to start asking questions. "What about the Zodiac?" The boat wasn't the most pressing of their current concerns, but they weren't cheap either. It would be an unfortunate loss for the aquarium.

Trevor's glanced at her as Richard piloted the boat. "First, your lives are far more important than any dinghy. Second, the other aquarium boat—the one with the shark research team—showed up and agreed to tow it to shore. The Zodiac is fine. Now we just need to make sure you two are." He paused, then gave her a significant look. "And then later you're going to tell me what the hell that was back there, right?"

Her stomach sank as she remembered that she'd used her magic in front of Richard and Trevor without even thinking twice. She'd reacted instinctively with no regard for the consequences. And if it meant saving Denver's life, she would do it all over again.

An ambulance was waiting for them as they disembarked. The EMTs looked her over and declared she was mostly recovered, but decided Denver was worth a trip to the hospital to get checked out, just in case.

He turned to her, vulnerability in his eyes. "You're coming with me, right?" The EMTs put an oxygen mask over Denver's mouth and told him to inhale deeply.

"Always." Jenna hopped in the back of the ambulance and grabbed Denver's hand. The EMTs didn't seem overly concerned, so she chose to believe everything was fine.

Now that they were back on dry land and Denver was getting the care he needed, Jenna's mind started to crash. She no longer had the numbness of muscle impairment dulling her senses, and she also didn't have the panic of worrying if Denver was going to be all right. Her body started shaking uncontrollably, despite her best efforts to hide it from Denver.

"It's the shock. You're going to be fine," the EMT said as she handed her yet another silvery emergency blanket. She wrapped it around her shoulders and hunched forward until her forehead rested on Denver's arm, which lay on the stretcher. He couldn't talk because of the oxygen mask, but she felt his hand in her hair, and it helped soothe her system.

They survived.

She knew that doing whale rescues was dangerous. It was part of the job. You didn't go up against a seventy-ton creature without a healthy dose of respect and awareness. But she'd never had anyone fall overboard before, least of all someone she loved. It had been terrifying.

But they were safe. She had made sure they were safe. Her powers had saved Denver's life. Yes, she'd done magic in front of ordinaries—*again*—but given the same situation, she would do it again in a heartbeat. Nothing was more important than saving the man that she loved.

"I can't believe I almost lost you." Jenna lifted her face to meet Denver's eyes. He started to reach for his oxygen mask, and she stopped him.

"I already knew that I owed you an enormous apology for how I treated you the other day. Brigit came and explained herself—well, as much as she ever does anyway—and it made me realize that I already knew the truth. I know you aren't sleeping with her. And even if you two had been an item back in high school,"—she had to stop him from removing his mask again—"and I know now that you weren't, but even if you had been, that was more than ten years ago. The past is the past. The present is what's important."

Denver squeezed her hand but didn't try to talk this time. She had to finish. To say everything she needed to. "And I forgive you for the situation with your dad. It took me a while to realize why you hid that information from me, but I got there eventually. You're not your father, and even he might not have been fully responsible for his actions. Our friend from the café and the zoo got to him first."

At that, Denver sat up and ripped off his mask. "What?" His voice was still raspier than usual, but it was good to hear it nevertheless. The irritated EMT grabbed the mask and put it back over Denver's mouth and gently shoved him back until he was lying down again.

Jenna glanced at the EMT, frustrated that she couldn't speak as plainly as she would have liked. "Yeah, I think she found him in the bar that night. Either way, it's no longer a concern. I took care of him." She tried to make him understand through eye contact alone that she'd removed the spell the other witch had placed on his father. "But either way, under the influence or not, Ken is his own person. He's not you, and you aren't him. You're not responsible for the sins of your father. I just wanted you to know that so that you could trust me when I tell you that none of it matters anymore. Brigit and Ken, they're not what matters. We're what matters. I love you."

Denver ripped the mask off his face once more. "I love you too. So much."

The EMT let out an irritated huff. "Look, folks, I appreciate that you're having a touching moment here, but he's not just wearing that mask to play dress up. His body needs the oxygen, so if you could save your romantic reunion for after?" The woman lifted her eyebrow and stared them down, but the side of her mouth twitched. Jenna had a suspicion she was a secret romantic.

Jenna smiled at her. "I've said all the important bits for now. The rest can wait."

Chapter Thirty-Two

D ENVER WAS WRECKED. OF course, nearly drowning would do that to a person. It was going to take a while to fully process that one.

The cut on his temple needed a few stitches, and the ER doctors took an x-ray of his chest to make sure he didn't have anything remaining in his lungs. When the scan came back clean, they gave him the all clear to leave with firm instructions to come back immediately if his breathing worsened or if he noticed signs of an infection.

"You're a lucky man," the doctor said as he signed the discharge paperwork.

Denver didn't think luck had anything to do with it. He'd bet money that Jenna had used her magic to save him, but since they'd been surrounded by medical professionals nonstop since getting off the boat, he hadn't had a chance to ask her about it.

"You ready to get out of here?" Jenna asked as he changed from the hospital gown back into the sweats they'd shoved him into on the boat.

"More than ready."

Since they were at the hospital and his truck was at the aquarium, they had to grab a ride share back to the parking lot. When they got there, he handed his keys over to Jenna without her having to ask. He was probably fine to drive, but there was no reason to push it.

She stuck the key in the ignition but didn't turn it on. She turned in the driver's seat and looked at him. They were finally alone for the first time in hours. "Let me," she said as she placed her hand on his chest. He felt it start to warm, and then a soothing sensation raced through his body from where her hand rested. He instantly felt better. He wasn't fully recovered, but whatever she had done had drastically helped.

"What was that?" he asked when she removed her hand, taking the comforting warmth with her. He grabbed her hand before she retreated and placed it back over his heart and squeezed it.

"A healing spell. I would have done it sooner, but I couldn't explain to the EMTs why you *didn't* need to go to the hospital after nearly drowning. Plus, it's always good to have the experts weigh in. I'm good at a lot of things—including basic healing—but I'm not all-powerful. Modern medicine still has its place in the world."

"Can you explain what happened back there on the water? I remember the boat starting to tip over and then nothing but black until I came to on the deck of the *Sea Bliss*." He wasn't sure he really wanted to hear about his almost death, but he needed to know. Her hand curled into a fist beneath his, and for a moment, he thought she wasn't going to answer.

"As the boat was tipping, the pole of the hook hit you in the temple right before we both fell into the water. I came back up, but you didn't. You were unconscious and sinking fast. I used my powers to bring you back to the surface, and then Richard and Trevor pulled us on board the *Sea Bliss*. You weren't breathing." She choked out a small sob, and he pulled her against him, or as close as he could from across the front seats of his truck. "Trevor started CPR, but I knew it wasn't going to be enough. I could feel the life seeping out of you, so I used my powers to pull the water out of your lungs."

Denver kissed the top of her head and held her close. He'd suspected he had her to thank for his life, and he'd been right. "You used magic in front of ordinaries."

She pulled away from him and looked him dead in the eye, even though hers were still watery. "And I would do it again in a heartbeat, even if I now have to figure out what to tell Trevor about what I did. You're mine, Denver Wallace. I love you, and I'll do anything in my power to protect you."

"Jenna. My beautiful Jenna." Denver leaned forward and captured her lips in a gentle kiss. "I know I don't have magical gifts like you do, but you're mine to protect all the same. And I don't care if you and Richard dated in the past."

"What?" She looked stunned. "Richard and I never dated. Where on earth did you get that idea?"

Denver let out a chagrined huff. "Jealousy, I guess. But it doesn't matter, because you're still mine. Whatever I have is yours. I love you."

She looked like she was going to protest again, so he pulled her into a searing kiss instead. Denver's hand dove into Jenna's long locks and gripped the back of her head, holding her mouth against him. They kissed as if their very lives depended on it, and after today, it almost felt like they did.

Jenna made a noise of frustration as she tried to move closer to him and was stopped by the center console of the truck.

Denver gentled their kisses, finally giving her one last peck on the lips. "There's plenty of time for that later. Right now, I just want to be home."

"If by home you mean my house, then I absolutely agree. There's no way I'm letting you out of my sight any time soon. Will Rosie be okay by herself?"

Denver smiled and then leaned over and gave her one last quick kiss. "That sounds perfect, and Rosie will be fine. I asked my neighbor to check on her."

Unfortunately, the healing spell hadn't fixed his exhaustion. The day had started early and felt like it had lasted for weeks. The pressing darkness outside the car windows must have lulled him to sleep because the next thing he knew, they were pulling into Jenna's driveway.

They climbed out of the car and started up the path to her front door. Denver wanted nothing more than to snuggle up to Jenna on the couch and veg out for a while. There was so much he wanted to tell her and share with her now that they were back on even ground again. "Oh, I can't believe I forgot to tell you what Holden and I learned from the surveillance footage. We know more about the other witch, specifically who she was collaborating with."

Jenna stopped abruptly in the middle of the front walkway, held her hand up to silence him, and cocked her head like she was listening for something. Denver couldn't hear anything, but then again, he didn't have superpowers either. Maybe she could hear something he couldn't.

"There's something wrong with my wards," she whispered. "It's like someone tried to force their way through them."

He felt the increasing hum of her power as she gathered it. She lifted her hands in front of her like she was leaning against a wall and closed her eyes. Denver felt a wave of magic wash over him.

"Nothing. No one managed to get through, but someone was here. The magic feels like the witch from the café—who also placed a spell on Ken if that wasn't obvious from what I said in the ambulance. The magic has the same gray color and sense of *wrong* that I felt intertwined with his aura back at the jail. That bitch better not have damaged anything."

"You can just call me Danika." The sneering voice came out of the darkness near the side of the house.

"Jenna watch out!" A sudden and suffocating pressure wrapped around Denver's throat and cut off his air supply. He was abruptly yanked off his feet and dragged across the ground until he was dropped unceremoniously next to Danika's feet. She relaxed the pressure on his throat enough that he could take a gasping breath, but not enough for him to talk.

"Enough of that," Danika said.

"What do you want?" Jenna asked, her arms out in front of her, ready to wield.

"I want to know what's so special about you. What the big deal is about the Elementa. From everything I can tell, you're nothing to write home about." Danika kicked him in the ribs, forcing an oomph of air out of his already restricted airway. "You can't even keep your little boy toy safe."

"Whatever this is between us, Denver isn't a part of it. Let him go."

Danika just laughed. "Not a part of it? Oh, but he is. You made him a part of it. You took him to the zoo, and you're the reason he's been looking all over town and poking his nose where it doesn't belong. *You're* the reason he's in danger."

Jenna's devastated look said it all—Danika's barb had struck true. He wanted to shout that it wasn't true. Danika was the reason he was in danger, not Jenna. But it didn't matter. No sound would come.

Jenna rolled her neck and squared her shoulders. Denver could see the wheels turning in her mind as she figured out how best to deal with Danika.

Denver felt a slight tug as his body slowly slid across the grass.

Jenna didn't so much as look in his direction, but it was clear she was trying to get him away from Danika. "You want to know what's so special about me and my friends? Not only are we each individually powerful in our own right, but together, we're the strongest coven in the country. When we combine our power, we're capable of truly breathtaking magic."

With a hard yank of power, Danika pulled Denver back to her side, not even bothering to be subtle like Jenna. "Coven? I'm not sure what delusion you're living under, Ms. High-and-Mighty, but your friends have deserted you. You're all alone, or at least you will be as soon as I dispatch your boyfriend here." Danika swished her hand in a circle. The space in front of her was empty one moment and then suddenly held a blade that glinted in the light of the full moon. With the flick of her fingers, the blade flew directly at Denver's throat.

Chapter Thirty-Three

Jenna's power lashed out almost without her having to guide it. She pulled moisture from the very air they were breathing and slammed a shield of water in front of Denver before Danika's blade got anywhere near his skin.

Negotiation time was over. No more Ms. Nice Witch. No one threatened the people Jenna considered hers. And Denver was—without a doubt—hers.

Danika's magical blade slammed into the wall of water with an audible clang. Jenna wrapped the wall of water around the blade, cocooning it in a watery prison. Jenna clenched her fist, and the water froze solid, trapping the magic blade inside, sending the whole thing crashing to the ground.

Danika's growl of frustration sent a thrill through Jenna's entire being, but there was no time to waste. She used her magic to grab Denver and forcibly pull him across her front yard and shove him behind her wards. There, he would be safe from whatever Danika decided to throw at them next.

An arc of gray magic reached for Denver, attempting to pull him back, but it slammed into the protective barrier. The energy scattered, slowly covering the wards as if looking for a way in.

Jenna used Danika's distraction and reached for the water that flowed freely in the decorative fountain on her front porch. The fountain drew its water from her house's well, and through that Jenna could access whatever water flowed beneath the surface of the earth. She called the water across the yard toward her, formed it into the shape of a club, and slammed it into Danika's shoulder, knocking her sideways and stopping her assault on the wards.

Without warning, something smacked into her from behind and knocked her to her knees. Danika's gray smoke swirled around her, a magical tornado with Jenna in the eye of the storm. The wall of wind closed in around her, pulling the breath from her lungs.

"Jenna!" Denver screamed, then immediately started coughing. Whatever Danika had done to his throat had clearly done some damage. Jenna could just barely see him trying to get to his feet.

"Denver, stay where you are!" She needed to take this fight away from Denver before he got the dumb idea to join in. He needed to be safe. She couldn't bear the thought of anyone hurting Denver because of her.

Jenna placed one hand on the grass and held the other out in front of her. She pulled water directly through the earth—which wasn't nearly as easy as pulling it straight from the source—and slammed it outward, disrupting the gray swirl that had been trapping her. She launched to her feet and sprinted toward Danika.

The smaller woman braced like she was expecting to be tackled, but Jenna charged right past her, letting loose a tendril of her magic as she raced by, just enough to keep Danika's attention. As Jenna hoped, her lure worked. She raced into the woods, Danika close behind.

"Running away already?" Danika taunted.

Jenna didn't bother responding, instead pushing all her energy into running as fast as she could into the trees. A pulse of gray magic shot past her ear, and she flinched sideways. She sent a wave of magic over her shoulder, not really trying to hit the other woman so much as keep her occupied. She just needed to get there. With a final burst of speed, Jenna shot out of the trees and into the clearing that held the stone circle.

Danika somehow realized what Jenna intended, because she sent a wall of gray magic to block Jenna's access to the stone.

It didn't matter though. This was her place, her magical center, her world. Jenna turned to face Danika and lifted both arms, palms facing up. She could feel the centuries' worth of magical history fill her.

She swirled her hands, and water from the nearby lake responded instantly. It rose at her command, formed into a ten-foot-tall stallion, and charged across the ground toward Danika.

Danika's eyes widened, and the wall of gray magic behind Jenna vanished. Danika twisted her fingers in a complicated pattern. A rope shot across the clearing, wrapped around the stallion's legs, and forced it to stumble. It tripped and hit the ground, splashing into a huge puddle.

Jenna didn't let that stop her. Her magic instantly reached for the puddle and reformed it into a towering, swirling column of water. She sent the tower barreling in Danika's direction. The wind in the clearing picked up, responding to Jenna's magic. The trees started swaying and leaves whipped through the air. Small branches and stones came next as the churning power of the vortex rose.

"Using my own trick against me? Weak." Danika sliced down and out with her hands and the vortex poofed into mist. With a sweep of her arms, she picked up all the debris left behind by the column of water and sent it flying toward Jenna.

The remaining mist formed into a solid wall in front of Jenna. The sticks and rocks smashed into it and fell uselessly on the ground. She took a small step backward, and her heel hit something solid.

The stone circle.

Without hesitation, Jenna stepped onto the sacred stone and instantly felt relief as her rapidly depleting energy stores began to refill. The magic of her ancestors filled her until she could no longer contain the power. It exploded out of her in a pulsing wave that wouldn't cease. The magic blew Danika off her feet and slammed her to the ground. The younger witch feebly waved her hand, and a tiny wisp of gray emerged, but Jenna made a slashing motion and pinned Danika's hand to the ground.

"Are you starting to get it yet?" Jenna said. "It doesn't matter how much power you *think* you have, I will always have more. And you weren't wrong earlier. I am currently alone. Imagine how much more power I would have if the rest of my coven were here with me?"

Danika let out a pained groan. "You'll never know again." She coughed and gasped for breath. "I've been watching your so-called coven for the last several months. Let me just say, they don't seem particularly fond of you."

Jenna couldn't let her see how much of a direct hit that was. As much as she would have loved to have her coven back to the way things used to be, it was unlikely. She had no reason to doubt Sierra's loyalty, but she wouldn't have been much help in a magical fight. Plus, Jenna had barely spoken to Aura and Brigit since she'd been back to town, and even when she did, every interaction was one laced with anger and resentment.

"And to answer your question, no. I still don't understand why he favors you. He seems to think the sun rises and sets with you, and from what I can tell, you're no better than any other witch out there."

He? "What are you talking about?" The question slipped out before Jenna could stop it. This was obviously much bigger than just a grudge from some random witch she'd never met.

Danika let out a weak laugh but didn't try to wield again. "You don't know, do you? Of course you don't. You're not meant to."

"*Who* are you talking about?" Jenna's voice rose.

"The Architect."

Jenna flashed back to her parents' attic on the day of the funeral. Just as she'd been getting ready to leave her mother's sacred space, she'd stumbled across a piece of paper tucked into her mother's book of shadows. "The Prophecy," she whispered.

For the life of her she couldn't remember the exact wording of it, but she was dead certain it had mentioned both her coven and the Architect. "Who or what is the Architect?"

"You know better than to listen to the lies of others," a droll voice said from behind Jenna. "Besides, that story isn't even worth listening to." Roderick waved his hand and Danika grabbed her throat. It was clear that she could still breathe, but he appeared to have taken her ability to speak. "Don't worry. It's a temporary spell. I'm sure someone will want to interrogate her later."

"What on earth are you doing here?" Jenna dropped her hands and relaxed her battle-ready stance, though only slightly. She glanced warily from where Roderick was standing near the tree line to where Danika lay on the ground, grasping ineffectually at her throat.

He crossed his arms and leaned against the tree next to him. He nodded in Danika's direction. "I've been following this one around town.

She's been stirring up quite the hornet's nest, it seems. She *is* the one you got into a fight with outside of Brigit's café, right?"

Wait, Roderick had actually done what he'd said he would do in the park and looked into the witch that attacked her? It almost didn't compute. Yes, he'd been her mentor as much as the other three, but she'd always thought he'd favored Brigit and Aura over her. Even Sierra had a better relationship with Roderick than Jenna did.

"Yes, she is." It came out more like a question than a statement.

Roderick just nodded. "I've been looking into her. She clearly has some shady associates, including whoever this Architect person is—if there really is such a person." He glanced around the clearing and seemed to notice all the destruction caused by the fight. "Have you had any other encounters with her? Apart from today, obviously. If we're going to go to the Circle of Thirteen, we should have all our facts straight first."

Danika's eyes widened, and she sent a panicked look from Roderick to Jenna.

"The Circle? Have you already spoken to them?" She could hear her pulse pounding in her ears, uncertain what answer she was hoping for. If he'd already spoken to them, it would show he'd kept his word that he would try to intervene on her behalf. It would also mean he knew about them attempting to arrest her.

Roderick rolled his eyes and pushed away from the tree. "Of course. Where else would we go to report a misbehaving witch? They are our government and our police force, as you well know."

Of course, the code. "You're right. We should probably report her to the Circle."

Roderick crossed the clearing and stopped between where Jenna stood on the stone circle and where Danika was sprawled on the ground. "Was she also responsible for the incident at the zoo?" He asked casually as if they were talking about nothing more interesting than the weather. He was examining Danika's sprawled form like she was a bug under a microscope.

Jenna swallowed thickly. He did know. Of course he knew. "The zoo?" She tried feebly to deflect the question.

Roderick just rolled his eyes again and then continued to stare at the witch pinned to the ground. "Jenna, do you honestly think something like this could happen to one of my charges and I wouldn't find out? I care about all my girls equally. Though, I do wish you would have mentioned it to me in the park. I shouldn't have had to find it out on my own. What is the purpose of a mentor if not to guide our charges through situations where they are clearly out of their depth?"

She wanted to protest that she didn't need his help. She was a strong, independent woman and a bad ass witch with more power than even she had realized. But the Circle scared her. Yes, she'd managed to overpower one of the witches. She may have been able to best Mabel Hexley, but it didn't mean that she stood a chance against the entirety of the Circle.

Before she'd consciously even decided to speak, the truth poured out of her. "Yes, our friend Danika here was the instigator of the zoo incident, or at least as far as I can tell. And yes, she was the one that attacked me outside of the café. However, the Circle seems to think it's all my fault. They saw the video of the zoo incident on YouTube, and well … It's pretty obvious it's me using magic."

Roderick didn't even react to her story, except to raise one eyebrow. "Yes, well, going viral on the internet is not exactly keeping a low profile. The *code*, Jenna."

Jenna's shoulders slumped. "I had no idea someone was filming it when it happened. The glass broke and the gorilla was going to escape. I did what I needed to do to protect all those innocent people, but …" she trailed off before she finally admitted the worst part. "It definitely looks like I'm the one who caused the whole thing in the first place." She hated to admit it. She knew that she hadn't been the one to break the glass. And yes, there was a shadowy figure that *might* be Danika off to the side of the frame, but Jenna had to admit that if she were one of the members of the Circle, she would doubt Jenna's story too.

Roderick pulled his phone out of his pocket and swiped the screen for several moments. The familiar audio of the chaos at the zoo was surprisingly loud in the silence of the clearing. The audio cut off, and silence stretched between them. Finally, Roderick sighed. "I see your point. The video is quite damning, isn't it?"

Jenna could only nod. As hard as she and Denver and Holden had worked over the last several days to prove that she was innocent, it was going to be extremely hard to prove it beyond the shadow of a doubt.

Roderick spun to face her, his expression lighting up with inspiration. "I may have an idea, though I will admit, it's one you're not going to like." He paused, waiting for her reaction.

Jenna glanced from Danika—who was still unable to speak—to the phone in Roderick's hand, which was paused for maximum effect to show Jenna wielding her magic in the form of that damned wall of water, and said, "What is it?"

Roderick took a small step closer but didn't go so far as to join her on the stone circle. "What you need is a show of faith. Something that lets the Circle know that you aren't a threat and you intend to abide by their rules. That your magic is under control and you don't intend to wield it in public again. You don't, right?" He glared in her direction.

Jenna thought back to the moment in the ocean when she realized that Denver was sinking and the only way to save him was to use her magic. And then—fast-forwarded a few minutes—when she'd used her magic in front of both Trevor and Richard to pull the water from Denver's lungs. She'd broken the code so many times in recent weeks she was almost starting to lose count.

Jenna hadn't been the cause of the incident at the zoo, but she'd done magic in plain sight of ordinaries. The same thing happened at the café and on the boat after rescuing Denver. The worst part is that given those same circumstances, she would do the same thing over again.

Did she deserve to be locked in nullifying cuffs for the rest of her life? No, she didn't think that punishment fit the crime—if you could call it that—but maybe the Circle wasn't wrong either. She had gotten too comfortable using her magic regardless of the consequences. Perhaps it needed to stop.

"What did you have in mind?" The question came out as barely a whisper.

"Your talisman."

Jenna immediately rejected the thought. Her talisman helped her wield her gifts. It wasn't the source of them, but it was a conduit. Giving up her talisman was like giving up access to part of her very soul. "No. Not possible."

Roderick smiled sympathetically. "I understand. It won't be comfortable to part from it, but think about it. If you give your talisman to me, I can in turn present it to the Circle on your behalf. You wouldn't be giving up your powers, just muting them for a while. Allowing the Circle time to review the evidence we provide that will clearly show that she"—Roderick jammed his finger in Danika's direction, much to the other woman's distress—"is to blame for all of it. Once they truly believe you aren't guilty, I'm sure they'll give you your talisman back. It's not within the code for the Circle to bind the powers of the innocent."

Jenna considered Roderick's offer. Her conscious mind immediately hated it but maybe that was the point? She was a powerful witch. She knew that, and blowing Mabel off the front porch had only driven that home even harder. Jenna knew she wasn't guilty, but the Circle had other ideas. What harm could it do to mute her powers for a while as a show of good faith? It wasn't like she'd be powerless. More like power-lite.

Roderick waited mutely for her decision. It was the hardest thing she'd had to do in her entire life, but Jenna reached up and unclasped her necklace. She cupped it briefly in her hands, profoundly wishing that they would be reunited quickly, and then stretched her arm in Roderick's direction. "You'll see they get this promptly?" she asked as she reluctantly released the charm into Roderick's outstretched hand.

"Of course," he said with a bob of his head. "And I'll take care of this little problem as well." He waved his hand and Danika staggered to her feet and followed behind him like a zombie. "I'll see you soon, Jenna. Wait for me."

Chapter Thirty-Four

D ENVER WATCHED IN IMPOTENT anger and fear as Jenna dashed into the woods with Danika hot on her heels. Logically he knew there was nothing he could do about it. He had no power of his own. Besides, Jenna didn't need his help.

That didn't mean he wouldn't offer it to her.

He sat up slowly. She'd told him very clearly to stay behind her protective wards but fuck that. If there were any chance he could help her, he would. He just needed to figure out how to do it without becoming a liability. Getting taken hostage, however temporarily, hadn't exactly helped the situation. He had no intention of being Jenna's weak point.

His mind flashed back to the magic nullifying cuffs that the Circle member had tried to put on Jenna. If he could grab those and get them to her, maybe she could use them on Danika instead. The problem was that he'd watched her put them in a box and spell it closed. There was no way he could get it open without her. But maybe if he brought her the box, she could open it herself.

Denver climbed to his feet, not letting the pain of getting dragged and tossed around the yard get to him. He could feel the pain later. Now was the time to move.

He ran into the house and dashed all the way to the third-floor attic where he'd seen Jenna hide the cuffs. The decorative wooden box was sitting on one of the many bookshelves, its rich mahogany inscribed with dozens of runes. A jolt of what felt like electricity zapped him as he grabbed the surprisingly heavy box and ran back outside.

There was only one place she would have gone. He raced into the trees, doing everything he could not to trip in the dark. He'd only been to the stone circle once, but he was confident he could find it again, even in the dim moonlight. If not, the sounds of the fight should tell him where the action was.

Except there were no sounds. The forest was eerily quiet. Unnaturally quiet. Was Jenna hurt? Or God forbid, was she dead? Denver burst out of the trees into the clearing and frantically looked around.

Jenna was alone, standing on the stone circle with a moonbeam shining directly on her like she was the chosen one. Danika was nowhere to be found.

"What happened? I brought the cuffs, but it looks like you don't need them." Denver carefully searched the area again just to make sure he wasn't walking into a trap and then slowly made his way to where Jenna was standing, frozen in place. "Jenna?" he prompted when she didn't respond.

Jenna turned and looked at him, devastation clear in every line of her face. "Denver?" she asked, her voice coming out as a whisper.

"I'm here baby." He placed the wooden box on the ground near the circle and then opened his arms. Jenna walked into them, and he tugged her as close as he could possibly get to his body, trying to support her if that's what she needed. "Where's Danika?"

She sniffled into his neck. "Gone."

"Did you ..." He didn't know how to politely ask what he wanted to know, so he just blurted it out. "Did you kill her?"

She shook her head but still wouldn't look him in the eye. "No, I didn't kill her. She was alive when she left the clearing."

He let out a sigh of relief. He hadn't really believed she was capable of killing someone, but he had no other explanation for her anguish. "Whatever it is, baby, we'll get through this. You're still a bad ass witch, and we've got all the evidence we need to talk to the Circle and clear your name. Everything is going to be fine."

She finally lifted her head, her icy blue eyes wet with her tears. "That's just it. I'm not a bad ass witch anymore."

Denver froze. "She took your powers?" Was that even possible? He was so new to this whole magical world that he had no idea what witches could do to one another.

"Not exactly." She sniffed. "I gave them up. Or at least I dulled them." She burrowed her way back into the crook of his neck, so he hugged her tightly once more.

The shock of her confession stunned him momentarily. Why on earth would she have voluntarily given up her powers? It didn't make much sense. He didn't want to set her off, but he needed more information. "Can you explain what happened?"

With a deep sigh, she pulled away from him, then promptly sank down and sat on the stone circle. "It seemed to make the most sense. We have the footage from both incidents, but neither of them is really damning or clear that it was Danika. Me giving up some of my power is my way of showing a good faith effort to cooperate with the Circle while we work through this mess."

Denver sat next to her and put his arm around her shoulders. "That doesn't really sound like you. I thought we had a solid plan. Holden and I even found more video footage that would help. I thought you wanted to fight this."

"I did, but now ..." she reached up and twined her fingers through his where they lay against her shoulder.

"What changed?" If this was really what she thought was best, he would stand behind her, one hundred percent. But he sensed doubt.

"I mean, it was Roderick's idea, but I'm the one who agreed. I gave him my talisman."

"That's extremely unfortunate news."

Denver's head whipped around as he watched an ancient-looking woman walk into the clearing flanked on one side by Derrek Cox, the lawyer-witch, and on the other by a trim-looking Asian man who appeared to be in his mid-fifties. Denver could only assume given Derrek's presence, that the other two must be members of the Circle of Thirteen.

Jenna shot to her feet once more, her hands immediately going out in front of her like she was bracing for a fight. "What are you doing here, Mabel?" Jenna asked.

Ah, so this was Mabel Hexley, the witch that terrified both Jenna and Sierra. Things just got more dangerous. Denver stood and made his way to Jenna's side.

"Coming to find you," Mabel responded.

"That was fast. Did Roderick already find you?" Jenna's stance relaxed slightly, but her eyes bounced from one witch to the other.

Mabel carefully picked her way across the debris-covered grass, her beady eyes taking in the wreckage of the clearing with nothing more than raised eyebrows. "Roderick McCann? Is that who you're asking about?"

"Obviously. I only know one Roderick."

Denver could feel the impatience rolling off Jenna in palpable waves. He placed his hand on her lower back. He appreciated her anger and frustration, but now was not the time to goad the Circle members, especially if Jenna was operating at less than her full magical strength.

"And tell me," Mabel continued as she eyed Denver up and down before summarily dismissing him. "Why do you think that Roderick would be coming to find us?"

Confusion raced across Jenna's face. "Because he told me he was going to. He said that if I gave him my talisman, he would bring it to the Circle as a sign of good faith that I was willing to cooperate with your investigation into the other witch—whose name is Danika, by the way. No idea about her last name. She wasn't exactly polite enough to share before she attacked me again."

Mabel and the Asian man shared a knowing glance before he spoke. "It would be very unwise of Roderick to come to us for any reason, and I imagine he knows that. Especially considering he's the one we're investigating. I'm Kai Shen, by the way. It's nice to make your acquaintance."

"No. What? No." Jenna's arms fell to her sides as she slumped. "Why would you be investigating Roderick? He's been our mentor since we were sixteen."

Silence fell, and Denver cleared his throat. "That's what I was trying to tell you when we got home, before Danika attacked us. Holden and I found some additional footage from outside Sierra's shop. Danika has been working with Roderick. Holden and I tracked down Derrek and gave him the footage so he could give it to the Circle and hopefully clear your name."

Jenna rounded on him, her eyes flashing with anger. "And you didn't think to *tell* me?"

Denver wished for nothing more than that, but it was too late now. He ran his finger along the collar of his shirt like it was suddenly choking him. "Well, it took us a little while to find anything, and by the time we did, you weren't speaking to me." He hadn't wanted to bring up the Brigit-shaped elephant in the room, but she obviously knew exactly what he meant.

Her shoulders drooped again, and her eyes shuttered. "So not only is the man I've known since I was sixteen one of the bad guys, but I willingly gave him my talisman, which makes it even harder for me to fight him if he comes back."

"It looks that way." Kai frowned. "The Circle will be tracking him of course, so if we do come across your talisman in the process, we'll be sure it's returned to you promptly."

Jenna nodded slightly. "Thank you for that. Do we have any idea why he wanted it? The necklace is tied to my power, so it shouldn't work for anyone else, right?"

Mabel pursed her lips. "In theory, yes."

"In theory?" Jenna's voice rose as fire came back into her eyes. This is the Jenna he was used to seeing, and Denver was grateful for her return.

Mabel clenched her hands in front of her. "Roderick was your mentor, which means he's helped guide your magic from the beginning. While it shouldn't be possible for him to tap into the conduit your talisman provides, there's also no telling what he may have learned or what he did to you over the years while you worked with him."

Jenna crossed her arms and stared down the Circle members. "That means it's not just me who's in danger. The rest of my coven is too."

Kai grimaced. "It is possible, yes. Are you aware of the Prophecy?"

Jenna's eyes went wide. "You know about the Prophecy? I found a copy mixed in with my mother's belongings after she died. I've read it once or twice, but that's about all. I don't really know what it means."

Mabel and Kai exchanged another knowing glance before Kai spoke. "If you've read it, then you know it speaks about an Architect raising the Harbinger."

"Yes," she said impatiently, "But what exactly *is* the Harbinger?"

"A soulless creature bent on destruction. If the Architect were to successfully raise it, the Harbinger would destroy anything in its path. It wants nothing but power and destruction," Mabel said.

"Then what can I do? How do we stop it?" Jenna asked.

Kai and Mabel shared another significant look. "There's only one power on earth that can stop it. The Elementa," Mabel said.

"You mean us. My coven." Jenna's voice was flat, almost toneless.

"Yes. Exactly," Kai replied. "I realize that's a lot of pressure on you and your friends."

A slightly hysterical laugh bubbled out of Jenna, making Denver's fists clench impotently at his side. He wished he could help her with this, but this was her fight. He would support her in any way he could, but it was her responsibility. She didn't disappoint him.

"It's going to take the four of us—who haven't practiced magic together in twelve years—to defeat some sort of big bad evil creature bent on destroying the world." Jenna's jaw firmed. "I guess I have my work cut out for me. Time to get the band back together again."

Kai sent her a proud looking smile. "We'll leave you to it."

Mabel gave her a nod of acknowledgement but added, "Don't think we won't be talking about this at some point." She waggled her wrinkly finger between Jenna and Denver. "He's an ordinary. There are rules."

"Understood," Jenna said.

The three of them turned to leave the clearing but Denver couldn't let them go, at least not yet. "Hey, Derrek?" Denver asked tentatively as he brought his hand to his neck and squeezed the base of his skull. He waited for the large man to acknowledge him before he continued. "Ken Nelson—my ... father—he's in the Rock Cove jail right now for vehicular manslaughter. Turns out that Danika hit him with some sort of magical whammy to make him do it."

"What's your point?" Derrek asked.

"It might do him some good if he had a lawyer that understood all of ... this." Denver waved his finger around to indicate the magic all around them.

Derrek seemed to contemplate it before he gave a curt nod. "I'll see what I can do."

Denver let out a whoosh of air. He'd honestly had no idea how much he cared about his father's fate until that moment. While he still had no desire to be involved in Ken's life, no one deserved to be held accountable for someone else's actions.

The Circle members each gave Jenna a final nod before they turned around and left the clearing, vanishing back into the trees as quietly as they'd arrived.

"So, what now?" Denver asked.

She gave him a grim smile in return. "Now I save my sisters."

He turned to face her and grabbed one of her hands in each of his. "No. Now *we* save your sisters. I love you, Jenna Hastings. I know I'm not some über powerful being, but I'm not going anywhere. No evil witch is going to scare me off. You're stuck with me now."

Her head bowed slightly. "Even if I'm not an über powerful being either?"

Denver let go of one of her hands and tipped her chin up so she met his gaze. "I never loved you because you were a witch. You're an amazing person, with or without your powers, and I can't wait to spend the rest of my life with you."

A tremulous smile appeared on Jenna's face. "Well, that's good news. Because I don't plan on letting you go. I love you, Denver. I know my life might be a bit chaotic right now, but we'll muddle through it."

"We'll conquer it together."

Epilogue

T HE WAREHOUSE WAS DARK and smelled like rotting plants. Roderick ignored it all. He didn't even bother telling Danika to follow him inside, because he knew she would. He was the only one that could remove the silencing spell he'd put on her, after all.

But not yet. She needed to learn her place. She'd *once again* gone against his orders and had attacked Jenna directly. But this time, it worked in their favor.

Roderick pulled the talisman and its silver chain out of his pocket. It hummed with latent energy, but he knew from experience he couldn't access it. At least not directly. He traced the intricate knot design with his blunt finger. It called to him.

This was the secret. He was certain of it.

Danika waved her hand in front of his face, clearly trying to get his attention. *Fine.* He waved his hand and released the spell he'd placed on her in the clearing.

"Would you really have done it?" She glared at him and crossed her arms.

What was she blathering on about now? "Done what?" Roderick's eyes dropped back to the talisman.

"Turned me over to the Circle of Thirteen!" Danika yelled. "I thought we were in this together, and yet not half an hour ago you were telling that bitch you were going to turn me over."

He waved a hand dismissively. "Of course not." Not unless it benefited him anyway. She didn't need to know that though.

She stared at him suspiciously. "Why should I believe you?"

The petulance in her voice caught his attention. Perhaps it was time to do a little placating. Danika still might be of use. "My dear, I'm the one that found you huddled in that dank alley, remember? I took you in, and I've spent years cultivating your magic into something we can both be proud of. When we needed to lure Jenna back to Rock Cove, you were the one that forced that drunk to get behind the wheel and kill Jenna Hasting's parents. And after I came up with the plot to ambush Jenna at the zoo and leak the footage on the internet, you executed it brilliantly. I couldn't have done it without you. Why would I turn you in this close to our goal?"

The wrinkles in her forehead smoothed out. "You're not mad at me?"

He tsked his tongue. "I didn't say that. If you want to assist me with this task, you're going to have to learn your place. But not tonight. Tonight, we can celebrate. One down. Three to go. After the challenge that Jenna posed, Sierra Dalton should be a pushover. Now fetch me a glass of wine."

A smile lit up her narrow face. "Yes, Architect."

Thank you from Elizabeth

If you made it this far, THANK YOU for reading *Siren's Song*. I hope you enjoyed reading this book as much as I enjoyed writing it, and I hope you'll stick around to find out what happens to Sierra, Aura, and Brigit in future books.

Reviews and ratings are the life blood of independent authors. If you liked *Siren's Song*, I hope you'll consider leaving a review.

If you want to be the first to hear announcements and updates about future books, please consider joining my newsletter. As an added bonus, you'll get exclusive content only available to subscribers.

https://www.elizabethsalo.com/newsletter

Acknowledgements

This book would not have been possible without a host of people who believed in me and made it happen. Among those I should thank are my editor Chris from CK Editorial Services and my cover designer GraphicSoulArt. I also want to thank the constant support of my write-in buddies Elizabeth Meyette, Brynn Paulin, and Stephanie Michels and my beta readers Dayna, Terra, and Amy. And last, but certainly not least, Phillip, who not only bothered to answer the unsolicited email from an unknown author who wanted to talk about whale research, but took the time to meet with me and answer my endless questions. Phillip was a trove of information about whales and any mistakes or inconsistencies are my own.

Also by Elizabeth

The Amazons of Themyscira Series

Amazon in Exile

Amazon in Darkness

Amazon in Hiding

About the Author

Elizabeth Salo is a Michigan native who loves magic, myths, and mayhem. She writes paranormal romance, romantic suspense, and urban fantasy books and is a sucker for a strong female lead. She firmly believes she should have been born with superpowers, but since she wasn't, she'll have to make do with writing about people who do.

She currently lives in Michigan with her family and more fur babies (and feathered babies, and scaly babies...) than is probably wise.

http://www.elizabethsalo.com/

www.ingramcontent.com/pod-product-compliance
Lightning Source LLC
Chambersburg PA
CBHW021041310726
48969CB00006B/1750